MALDOROR

Les Chants de Maldoror

MALDOROR

(Les Chants de Maldoror)

BY LAUTRÉAMONT

translated by Guy Wernham

together with a translation of Lautréamont's

Poésies

NEW DIRECTIONS

SIXTH PRINTING

A Note on Lautréamont

ALTHOUGH *Les Chants de Maldoror* has won acceptance as a classic of French literature—there have been at least three new editions with different Paris publishers since the War—little information has been unearthed by scholars about its author, Isidore Ducasse, who took the mellifluous pen-name of Comte de Lautréamont. The best summary of the verifiable facts is, I believe, in the introduction by Maurice Saillet to the *Livre de Poche* edition of the *Oeuvres* published in 1963. I have drawn heavily on Saillet in correcting the foreword to *Maldoror* which I wrote in 1943 when New Directions first published the Guy Wernham translation.

Ducasse's birth and death certificates have been found, and the texts of six short letters written between 1868 and 1870, the year of his death. Copies of the first printings of *Maldoror* (1868-9) and *Poésies* (1870) survive, but no manuscripts or other literary papers. There are some verbal accounts transmitted from schoolmates and others who knew him casually . . . but apart from these—almost nothing—we have the mystery

[*v*]

of an unconventional young man who died early (at 24) and who was not, apparently, accounted of much importance while he lived.

The name of Lautréamont begins to appear in French letters only toward the turn of the century; at that time a second edition of *Maldoror*, published by Genonceaux in 1890, caught the attention of such writers as Huysmans, Léon Bloy, Maeterlinck, Jarry, Fargue, Larbaud, and Remy de Gourmont. Real fame came only much later when the Surrealists and Dadaists hailed *Maldoror* as a masterpiece and canonized Lautréamont as an ancestor of Surrealism. The Surrealists attempted to create a personality and a biography for their hero, but it seems to be largely fictitious; the identification with a Ducasse who was a radical orator done away with by the secret police of Napoleon III has been disproved.

Isidore Lucien Ducasse was born April 4, 1846, in Montevideo, Uruguay, where his father, François Ducasse, was first a clerk and later Chancellor in the French Consulate. François Ducasse had emigrated from a small town near Tarbes, just north of the Pyrenees, and married a girl from the same region, Jacquette Célestine Davezac, who died, some think by suicide, eighteen months after the birth of Isidore. Nothing is known of the poet's boyhood in Uruguay beyond the reference to its civil wars at the end of the first canto of *Maldoror*. François Ducasse may have had business outside the Consulate for he seems to have been well off in later life. In 1859 he returned to Tarbes on a visit, taking Isidore with him. He left the boy there, presumably in the care of relatives, who placed him from 1859 to 1862 at the *lycée* of Tarbes, and then from 1863 to 1865 at the *Lycée Imperial* in nearby Pau.

Lautréamont

Thanks to the research of François Alicot, who tracked down a surviving schoolmate, Paul Lespès, we do have a picture of Lautréamont in adolescence. Lespès remembers "a tall, thin young fellow, a bit round-shouldered, pale, with hair falling over his forehead and a sharp, high voice." His appearance was "not attractive" and he had a "distant manner" of "haughty gravity." Isidore's health was frail; he was plagued with migraine headaches. "Most of the time he was rather sad and silent, as if turned in on himself."

Lespès recalls that Ducasse was a fair student but hated Latin verse and showed little interest in mathematics, although later, in *Maldoror*, he would write:

> O austere mathematics! I have not forgotten you since your learned teachings, sweeter than honey, distilled themselves through my heart like refreshing waves.

"He liked Racine and Corneille and above all Sophocles' *Oedipus Rex* . . . particularly the scene in which Oedipus, knowing the truth at last and having torn out his eyes, cries in pain and curses his fate. He felt that Jocasta, to complete the tragic horror, should have killed herself on the stage." Lespès reports that the "excesses (*outrances*) of thought and style" in Ducasse's compositions so dismayed the professor of rhetoric that on one occasion he punished the boy by keeping him in after school.

Ducasse left the *lycée* at Pau in 1865. There is no trace of his taking entrance examinations or attending any university. In fact, the record is blank until 1868, when we know he was living in Paris. Saillet deduces that he may have returned to Montevideo, spending as much as two years there with his father. He may also have spent some time in Bordeaux and made literary contacts there, since later he was to enter the first canto of *Maldoror* in a poetry contest conducted by Evariste Carrance, a Bordelais editor.

The publisher Genonceaux reported that Ducasse "came to Paris intending to study at the Polytechnique or the School of Mines," but no enrollment records have been traced at either institution. From the letters to his father's Paris banker, Darasse, it seems clear that the elder Ducasse provided a regular allowance, sufficient to enable Isidore to live in comfortable lodgings (Saillet infers this from their street addresses), and, from time to time, extra amounts to finance the printing of his work.

The first canto of *Maldoror* was published in August, 1868, privately printed by Balitout, Questroy et Cie, and with no author's name on the title page. A few months later, Ducasse arranged with Albert Lacroix of the Librairie Internationale, Boulevard Montmartre, for the publication of the complete work, making a deposit of 400 francs. Lacroix has left us this description of the author: "He was a tall young man, dark-complexioned, clean-shaven, nervous, but orderly (*rangé*) and hardworking. He wrote only at night, seated at his piano. He would declaim his sentences as he forged them, punctuating his harangues (*prosopopées*) with chords on the piano." It is in this edition that the pseudonym Lautréamont first appears, based, no doubt, on Eugène Sue's historical novel, *Latréaumont*.

Lacroix sent the manuscript to his partner, a printer in Brussels named Verboeckhoven, and in the summer of '69 the author received twenty copies. Then someone got cold feet; none of the books were put on sale. "When it was printed," Ducasse wrote Darasse, "he refused to bring it out because life is painted in colors too bitter and he is afraid of the attorney general." Despite the author's remonstrances, the sheets lay in the printer's shop (at least he did not destroy them!) until 1879 when the business changed hands and the new owner finally released the book. There was no immediate critical response, but it must have had enough circulation to induce Genonceaux to reissue it in Paris in 1890. And not long thereafter Remy de Gourmont began the chorus of praise which was to follow when he wrote that *Maldoror* was "a magnificent, almost inexplicable stroke of genius, which will remain unique."

Was it only his discouragement with publishers which led Lautréamont to try, rather ineffectually, to change the direction of his work? In February of 1870 he tells Lacroix that he will soon be sending him a new manuscript, a group of poems in entirely different vein, and in March he writes to Darasse: "I have now completely changed my method . . . from now on I will sing only of HOPE, FAITH, CALM, HAPPINESS, and DUTY." These are not, however, precisely the sentiments which figure in the little book of *Poésies* that appeared in April, not with Lacroix but from the Librairie Gabrie, Passage Verdeau.

This final volume, which is not verse at all but aphoristic prose (Lautréamont called it *"prosaïques morceaux"* in the dedication), is sometimes labeled the preface for a collection of poems that were never written. Saillet, however, believes that this is not the case; he thinks that Ducasse abandoned the project he had sketched to Lacroix of poems which would "correct" the spirit of Lamartine, Hugo, Musset, etc., in favor of a completely different conception.

The dedication to *Poésies* speaks of further installments to follow, but if more were written, they have never come to light. A death certificate tells us that Isidore Lucien Ducasse, "bachelor, no further information," died in his lodgings at 7 rue du Faubourg-Montmartre early on the morning of November 24, 1870. His body was interred the next day in the *cimetière du Nord*; about twenty years later, the City of Paris condemned the site for housing and the remains of those buried there were deposited in the Pantin Ossuary.

The critical literature on Lautréamont is now extensive; an excellent bibliography of it will be found in the revised edition of the *Oeuvres* published by José Corti, Paris, 1961. That edition also contains the valuable essays on Lautréamont by Genonceaux, Gourmont, Jaloux, Breton, Soupault, Gracq, Caillois, and Blanchot. Read in sequence, these essays are fascinating literary history, the record of how a reputation is made and changes. But the Corti edition should be supplemented with Maurice Saillet's *"Notes pour une vie d'Isidore Ducasse et de ses écrits"* in the *Livre de Poche* paperback. Saillet, a thorough scholar, has researched every possible source of information, published and unpublished, on Lautréamont, including those in Uruguay, and I find his synthesis judicious and convincing. A copy of the superb Skira edition of *Maldoror* with illustrations by Salvador Dali may be seen in the library of the Museum of Modern Art, New York.

J. LAUGHLIN

June, 1965

MALDOROR

(LES CHANTS DE MALDOROR)

1

MAY it please Heaven that the reader, emboldened
and become of a sudden momentarily ferocious
like what he is reading, may trace in safety his
pathway through the desolate morass of these
gloomy and poisonous pages. For unless he is able to
bring to his reading a rigorous logic and a spiritual
tension equal at least to his distrust, the deadly
emanations of this book will imbibe his soul as
sugar absorbs water.

It would not be well that all men should read
the pages that are to follow; a few only may savor
their bitter fruit without danger. So, timid soul,
before penetrating further into such uncharted
lands, set your feet the other way. Listen well to
what I tell you: set your feet the other way like
the eyes of a son who lowers his gaze respectfully
before the august countenance of his mother; or
rather, like a wedge of flying, cold-trembling
cranes which in the winter time, with much medi-
tation, fly powerfully through the silence, full sail,

towards a predetermined point in the horizon from which of a sudden springs a strange, strong wind, advance-guard of the tempest. The oldest crane, solitary pilot, shakes her head like a reasoning person on seeing this and raises a clatter with her beak and is uneasy (as I would be in her place), while her old bald neck whose falling feathers have measured three generations of cranes undulates in irritation as she gives warning of the approaching storm. After having gazed calmly about her on all sides with her wise old eyes, this first crane (for it is she who has the privilege of displaying her tailfeathers before her less intelligent companions) utters the warning cry of a sorrowing sentinel and to repel the enemy which threatens them all alike deftly puts about the point of the geometric figure (perhaps it is a triangle, but one cannot see the third side formed in space by these curious birds of passage) either to port or starboard like a skilfull captain; and maneuvering with wings that seem no larger than those of a sparrow, she shapes, since she is not stupid, another course, safer and more philosophical.

Reader, it is perchance hatred that you would have me invoke at the beginning of this work! How do you know that you would not snuff it up, lapped around with limitless sensations of pleasure,

[*2*]

as much as you want of it, snuff it up through your wide, thin, prideful nostrils, turning up your stomach like a shark in the fine dark air as if you understood the importance of the action no less than the importance of your legitimate appetite as you inhale the ruddy emanations? I assure you the savor will rejoice those two malformed holes in your hideous snout, O monster, if beforehand you breathe in three thousand times the accursed consciousness of the Eternal! Your nostrils, which will be enormously dilated with ineffable content, with motionless ecstacy, will demand nothing better of space, no sweeter perfume, no finer incense: for they will be sated with a complete happiness like unto the angels which peacefully and magnificently inhabit the pleasant heavens.

In a few lines I shall establish how Maldoror was virtuous during his first years, virtuous and happy. Later he became aware that he was born evil. Strange fatality! He concealed his character as best he could for many years; but in the end, because such concentration was unnatural to him, every day the blood would mount to his head until the strain reached a point where he could no longer bear to live such a life and he gave himself over resolutely to a career of evil . . . sweet atmosphere! Who could have realized that whenever he embraced a young child with rosy cheeks he longed to slice off those cheeks with a razor, and he would have done it many times had he not been restrained by the thought of Justice with her long funereal procession of punishments. He was no liar, he acknowledged the truth and admitted that he was cruel. Humans, did you hear? He dares to repeat it with this trembling pen! Hence it is a force more powerful than the will. A curse! Could a stone resist the law of gravity? Impossible. Impossible that evil should form an alliance with good. I have stated this before.

There are those who write to gain the applause of men by inventing noble sentiments of the heart, which indeed they may even possess. As for me I use my genius to depict the delights of cruelty! No passing joys these, nor are they false, but they were born with Man and will die with him. May not genius ally itself with cruelty in the secret resolutions of Providence? Or, because one is cruel, may one not possess genius? The proof of this you will find in my utterances: all you have to do is listen to me if you will.

Excuse me: it seemed to me that my hair was standing up on my scalp, but it is nothing, for I can easily smooth it down again with my hand.

He who is singing now does not claim that his songs are new. On the contrary, he is proud in the knowledge that all the lofty and wicked thoughts of his hero reside within all men.

❦

All my life I have seen narrow-shouldered man, without exception, perform innumerable stupid actions, brutalize his fellows and poison minds by every conceivable means. The motivation of such behavior he calls, 'Glory.' Seeing these things I have desired to laugh with the others, but this strange imitation was impossible for me. I have taken a pocket-knife and severed the flesh at the spot where the lips come together. For a moment I thought to have accomplished my end. I looked into a mirror and inspected the mouth I had deliberately butchered. It was a mistake! The blood falling copiously from the two wounds made it impossible to distinguish whether this was really the laughter of other men. But after several minutes of comparison I could see clearly that my smile in no way resembled human laughter: in other words, I was not laughing.

I have seen men, men of hideous aspect with terrible eyes set deep in their skulls, transcend the hardness of rock, the rigidity of cast steel, the cruelty of sharks, the insolence of youth, the insensate rage of criminals, the treachery of hypocrites, the most outlandish clowns, the force of character of priests, the most introverted beings, and creatures colder than earth or heaven.

[5]

The moralist wearies of seeking their hearts and of bringing down upon them the implacable wrath from on high.

I have seen them all together, now with a powerful fist raised towards heaven like that of a child already defying its mother, probably inspired by some sprite from hell, their eyes filled with a remorse at once burning and hateful, in glacial silence, daring not to unleash the mighty and evil meditations that they harbor in their breasts, so pregnant are they with injustice and horror, saddening with compassion the God of mercy.

And I have seen them at every moment of the day from infancy to old age, while scattering about them the most unbelievable insensate curses against everything breathing, against themselves and against Providence, prostitute women and children and dishonor those parts of the body consecrated to modesty.

Then the oceans rise up and drag down the ships into their depths; hurricanes and earthquakes destroy buildings; plagues and divers sicknesses decimate the praying families. But men are not aware of all this. I have seen them also blushing and paling with shame for their conduct on earth: this rarely.

Tempests, sisters of hurricanes; blue firmament, whose beauty I do not admit; hypocritical sea, image of my heart; mysterious-bosomed earth; dwellers upon other planets; vast universe; God, who created it all magnificently, it is you whom I invoke: show me a good man! But let your grace increase tenfold my natural strength, for at the sight of such a monster I might die of astonishment. One dies for less.

One should let one's fingernails grow for fifteen days. O, how sweet it is to snatch some child brutally from his bed, a child who has nothing as yet upon his upper lip, and, wide-eyed, to make a pretence of passing your hand smoothly over his brow, brushing back his beautiful hair! Then, suddenly, when he is least expecting it, to plunge your long nails deep into his soft breast in such a manner as not to destroy life; for should he die you could not later enjoy his sufferings. Then you drink the blood, passing your tongue over the wounds; and during this time, which should last as long as eternity lasts, the child weeps. There is nothing so delicious as his blood, extracted in the manner I have described, and still warm, unless it be his tears, bitter as salt.

Man, have you ever tasted your own blood when by accident you have cut your finger? How good it is, for it is tasteless! Moreover, do you recollect how on a certain day amid your sorrowful meditations you raised your cupped hand to your sickly tear-wet face, and then how inevitably your mouth sucked up the tears from that goblet that trembled like the teeth of a schoolboy as he glances at him who was born to oppress him? How good they were, for they taste of vinegar! One might call them the tears of the greatest lover among women, but the child's tears are more pleasant to the palate. The child will not deceive you, knowing nothing yet of evil. The greatest lover among women would betray you sooner or later . . . I divine this by analogy since I am ignorant of what friendship and love are (it is probable that I shall never accept them, at least from the human race).

Well, then: since your own blood and your own tears do not disgust you, be nourished with confidence upon the blood and the tears of the child. Bind his eyes while you are rending his palpitating flesh; and having listened for hours to his sublime outcries which resemble the piercing shrieks torn from the throats of the dying wounded on a battlefield, rush away from him like an avalanche; then return in haste and pretend to be coming to his assistance. You will unbind his hands with their swollen nerves and veins, then restore sight to his wild eyes, and you will again begin to lap up his tears and his blood. How real a thing, then, is repentance! The divine spark that dwells within us and shows itself so rarely appears: too late! How your heart overflows with joy that you are able to console the innocent whom someone has hurt!

"Child, who have suffered such cruel pain: who could have perpetrated such a crime upon you, a crime for which I can find no name! Wretched infant, how you must have suffered! And if your mother knew of it she would be no nearer to death (so greatly dreaded by the guilty) than I am at this moment. Alas! What is good and what is evil? Are they one and the same thing, by which we savagely bear witness to our impotence and our passion to attain the infinite, even by the most insensate means? Or are they two different things? Yes . . . they had better be one and the same, for if they are not what will become of me on the Day of Judgment?

Child, forgive me! It is he who now contemplates your noble and sacred countenance who broke your bones and tore the flesh that hangs from your body. Was it a delirium of my ailing reason? Was it a secret instinct, unrelated to judgment, like that of an eagle rending its prey, that forced me to commit this crime? And yet I too suffered as much as did my victim! Child, forgive me! Once I am rid of this transitory life I want us to be joined together through eternity, to form one inseparable being, my mouth pressed forever upon your mouth. Even in this wise my punishment will not be complete. You shall rend my flesh unceasingly with teeth and nails. I shall deck my body with scented garlands for this expiatory holocaust, and we shall suffer together, you from rending me and I from being torn . . . my mouth pressed forever upon your mouth. O child, O golden-haired, gentle-eyed child, will you do as I counsel you now? In spite of yourself I want you to do it, and you will soothe my conscience."

Having spoken thus you will at once have done injury to a human being and be loved by that same being: this is the greatest happiness the mind can conceive.

Later you can take the child to a hospital, for the cripple will be unable to earn his livelihood. They will call you a good man and wreaths of laurel and medals of gold will hide your naked feet. O you whose name I will not inscribe upon this page which is dedicated to the sanctity of crime, I know that your pardon will be as all-embracing as the universe. But I: I still exist!

I have made a pact with prostitution in order to sow disorder among families. I remember the night that preceded this dangerous alliance. I saw before me a tomb. I heard a glowworm, large as a house, saying to me:

"I will be your light. Read the inscription. It is not from me whence comes this supreme command."

A vast bloodred radiance at the appearance of which my jaws chattered and my arms fell powerless to my sides, spread out through the air to the horizon. I leaned against a ruined wall, for I felt myself falling, and I read:

"Here lies a child who died consumptive. You know why. Pray not for him."

Many men perhaps would not have had my
courage. Meanwhile a naked and beautiful woman
came and lay down at my feet. Sad-faced, I said to
her:

"You may arise."

I offered her the hand with which a fratricide
disembowels his sister. The glowworm said to me:

"You: take a stone and kill her."

"Why?" I asked.

"Beware," he said to me, "you are the weaker
for I am the stronger. This woman is called
Prostitution."

Tears rushed to my eyes, rage to my heart, and
I felt an unknown power born within me. I seized
a great rock and after a struggle raised it barely to
the level of my breast. I balanced it upon my shoul-
der. I climbed to the summit of a mountain: thence,
I crushed the glowworm. Its head was forced into
the earth to the height of a man; the stone bounded
into the air as high as six churches and fell into a
lake the waters of which momentarily sank, whirl-
ing, hollowing into an immense inverted cone.
Then the confusion subsided, the bloody glare was
no more.

"Alas, alas!" shrieked the naked and beautiful
woman, "what have you done?"

"I prefer you to him," I replied, "because I
pity the unfortunate. It is not your fault that eter-
nal justice created you."

"Some day," she said, "men will render me jus-
tice. I will say no more. Let me go and conceal my

infinite sorrow at the bottom of the sea. Only you, and the loathsome monsters that haunt those murky depths, do not despise me. You are good. Farewell, you who have loved me!"

And I:

"Farewell, again farewell! I shall love you always. From today I abandon virtue!"

It is for this reason, O peoples of the earth, that when you shall hear the winter wind sighing over the sea and along its shores, or across the great cities which long ago were decked in mourning for me, or through the icy polar regions, you shall say:

"That is not the spirit of God passing. It is only the bitter sigh of Prostitution mingled with the solemn groans of the Montevidean."

Children, it is I who tell you this. And so, full of pity, fall upon your knees; and let mankind, more numerous than lice, offer up long prayers.

By moonlight in lonely places near the sea when you are plunged in bitter reflections you see that everything assumes a yellowish appearance, vague, fantastic. The tree-shadows, now swift now slow, chase hither and yon as they flatten themselves against the earth. Long ago when I was borne upon the wings of youth this seemed strange to me and made me dream; now I am used to it. The wind murmurs its langorous strain through the leaves and the owl intones his sad complaint while the hair of those who hear stands on end.

Then infuriated dogs snap their chains and escape from distant farms; they rush through the countryside, here, there and everywhere, in the grip of madness. Suddenly they stop, turn their fiery eyes in all directions, savagely uneasy, and, as elephants in the desert before dying cast one last glance towards heaven, desperately lifting their trunks, their ears hanging limp, so the dogs' ears droop and they raise their heads: their necks swell horribly and one by one they commence to howl, like a child crying from hunger, or a cat wounded in the stomach up on the roof, or a woman about to be delivered of a child, or a plague victim dying in the hospital, or a young girl singing a divine melody.

The dogs howl at the northern stars, at the eastern stars, at the southern stars, at the western stars; at the moon; at the mountains which at a distance resemble giant rocks reclining in the shadows; at the keen air they breathe in deep lungfuls, burning and reddening their nostrils; at the silence of the night; at an owl, whose slanting flight brushes the dogs' muzzles as it wings swiftly on its way carrying a rat or a frog in its beak, living food, sweet morsel for the fledglings; at the hares that vanish in the wink of an eye; at the robber who is galloping away on his horse after his crime has been done; at the snakes, rustling in the briars, making the dogs' flesh creep and their teeth grit; at their own howlings, which scare themselves; at the toads which they crush with a single snap of their jaws (why are these toads so far from the marshes?); at the trees whose gently-cradled leaves are so many mysteries that the dogs cannot understand, that they would penetrate with their steady, intelligent eyes; at the spiders suspended between their own legs, who climb the trees to escape; at the crows who have found nothing to eat all day and return to their nests with weary wings; at the rocks on the shore; at the lights on the masts of invisible vessels; at the heavy sound of the sea; at the great fish, which as they swim reveal their black backs before plunging again into the depths; and at Man who makes slaves out of dogs.

After all this they scamper over the countryside again, leaping with their bleeding feet over ditches and pathways, fields, pastures and steep rocks. You would think they were mad with rabies and seeking some vast pond in which to assuage their thirst. Their endless howling horrifies nature. Alas for the wayfarer! These friends of the cemeteries will fling themselves upon him, tear him to pieces, devour him with their blood-dripping jaws; for the dogs have sharp teeth. Wild animals, not daring to invite themselves to share this feast of flesh, hasten trembling away. After many hours the dogs, weary of racing hither and yon, almost expiring, their tongues lolling out of their mouths, throw themselves upon one another, not knowing what they are doing, and tear one another into a thousand pieces with incredible rapidity. They do not behave thus from cruelty. One day my mother, her eyes glassy-looking, said to me:

"When you are in bed and you hear the howling of the dogs in the fields, hide yourself beneath your blankets, don't make a jest of what they are doing: they have the insatiable thirst for the infinite, like you, like me, like the rest of us human beings with our long, pale faces. I will even permit you to stand at the window and see this spectacle, which is rather magnificent."

Since that time I have respected the dead woman's wish. I, even as the dogs, feel a yearning for the infinite . . . I cannot, I cannot satisfy that hunger! I am the son of a man and a woman, from what they tell me. This astounds me . . . I had thought to be more than this! Yet what difference does it make whence I come? For my part, if it had been left to me I would much rather have been the son of a female shark, whose hunger is the friend of the tempest; and of a tiger, whose cruelty is acknowledged: I would be less evil.

You who now are gazing upon me: stand back, for my breath exhales poison. No one yet has seen the green furrows in my forehead, nor the protruding bones of my emaciated face, resembling the bones of some great fish, or the rocks which cover the seashore, or the rugged Alpine mountains which I climbed often when my hair was of a different color. And when I wander with burning eyes and hair whipped by tempestuous winds, during nights of storm, lonely as a stone in the middle of the road, around the habitations of men, I cover my blighted face with a bit of velvet black as the soot that coats the chimney. No eyes may dwell upon the ugliness that the Creator, with a grin of potent hatred, has afflicted upon me.

Every morning, when the sun rises for others spreading joy and wholesome warmth everywhere, I crouch in my beloved cave in a state of despair that intoxicates me like wine: I stare into the shadowy wastes of space and I tear my breast to ribbons with my strong hands. Yet I do not feel overcome with rage! And I do not feel that I am suffering alone! But I do feel that I am breathing! Like a condemned man trying his muscles while reflecting upon their destiny, knowing that he is about to mount the scaffold, I stand upright on my straw pallet, my eyes closed, and I turn my head slowly from right to left, from left to right, for whole hours on end. I do not fall stone dead. From time to time, when my neck cannot continue to turn farther in one direction, when it stops to return in the opposite direction, I look sharply towards the horizon, peering through the few spaces left by the bushes covering the entrance to my cave. I see nothing! Nothing . . . unless it be fields whirling with trees and long files of birds winging through the air. All this disturbs my blood and my brain. . . . Who is it beating upon my head with a bar of iron like a hammer beating upon an anvil?

I propose to proclaim in a loud voice and without emotion the cold and grave chant that you are about to hear. Consider carefully what it contains and guard yourself against the painful impression it cannot fail to leave like a blight upon your troubled imaginings. Do not believe that I am on the point of death for I am not yet a skeleton and old age does not rest upon my brow. Consequently let us reject any idea of comparing me with a swan at the moment when its life is about to take wing; and see before you nothing but a monster whose face, I am happy to say, is hidden from you. Yet this face is less horrible than the soul, and nevertheless I am no criminal. . . . But enough of that.

Not long ago I saw the sea once again and trod upon the bridges of ships; my memories of it are as lively as if it had all happened yesterday. If you are able, however, be as calm as I am as you read what is to follow (for already I regret offering it to you) and do not blush for the human heart.

O octopus of the silky glance! You whose soul is inseparable from mine; you, the most beautiful creature upon the terrestrial globe; you, chieftain of a seraglio of four hundred sucking-cups; you, in whom are nobly enthroned as though in their natural habitat, by a common agreement and with an indestructible bond, the divine graces and the sweet virtue of communication: why are you not with me, your belly of quicksilver pressed to my breast of aluminum, the two of us sitting here together upon a rock by the shore as we contemplate the spectacle I adore!

Ancient ocean, crystal-waved, you resemble somewhat those bluish marks that one sees upon the battered backs of cabin-boys; you are a vast bruise inflicted upon the body of earth: I love this comparison. At the first sight of you a long breath of sadness that might be the murmur of your own bland zephyr passes over the deeply moved soul, leaving ineffaceable scars, and you recall to the memories of those who love you, though they are not always aware of it, the crude origins of man when first he made the acquaintance of the sorrow that has never deserted him. I salute you, ancient ocean!

Ancient ocean, your harmonious sphere, rejoicing the grave countenance of geometry, reminds me too much of man's little eyes, in paltriness resembling those of the boar and those of the nightbird in the circular perfection of their contour. Yet man has thought himself beautiful throughout the centuries. As for me, I presume that he believes in his beauty only from pride, but that he is not really beautiful and that he suspects this, for why does he contemplate the countenance of his fellow-man with so much scorn? I salute you, ancient ocean!

Ancient ocean, you are the symbol of identity: always equal to yourself. Essentially you never change, and if your waves are somewhere lashed

[*18*]

into fury, elsewhere they are stilled in the most complete peace. You are not like men, who linger in the street to watch two bulldogs tearing at each other's throats but who hurry on when a funeral passes; who in the morning may be reasonable and in the evening evil-tempered; who laugh today and weep tomorrow. I salute you, ancient ocean!

Ancient ocean, it might not be impossible that you conceal within your bosom future utilities for man. You have already given him the whale. You do not willingly yield up the thousand secrets of your intimate organism to the hungry eyes of the natural sciences: you are modest. Man praises himself constantly, and for what trifles! I salute you, ancient ocean!

Ancient ocean, the different species of fish that you nourish have not sworn brotherhood among themselves. Each species lives in its own place. The varying temperaments and conformations of each one explain satisfactorily what appears at first to be an anomaly. So it is with Man, who has not the same motives to excuse him. If a piece of land is inhabited by thirty million humans, these believe that they are forced to stand aloof from the existence of their neighbors who are rooted in an adjacent piece of land. To descend from the general to the particular, each man lives like a savage in his lair, rarely coming forth to visit his fellows similarly crouching in another den. The great universal family of human beings is a Utopia worthy of the meanest logic. Furthermore, from the spectacle

[*19*]

of your fruitful breasts the idea of ingratitude is suggested, for we think of those innumerable parents ungrateful enough to the Creator to abandon the fruit of their wretched unions. I salute you, ancient ocean!

Ancient ocean, your material vastness may be compared only with the active natural force that was necessary to beget your total mass. A glance is not sufficient to encompass you. To envision your entirety the sight must revolve its telescope in a continuous movement towards the four points of the horizon, just as a mathematician when he resolves an equation must examine various possible solutions before attacking the problem. Man devours nutritive substances and, in order to appear fat, makes other efforts worthy of a better cause. Let the beloved bullfrog inflate itself to its heart's desire. Be calm: it will never equal you in size. At least I suppose not. I salute you, ancient ocean.

Ancient ocean, your waters are bitter. They have exactly the same flavor as the gall distilled by critics upon the fine arts, the sciences, upon all. If there should be a man of genius they make him out an idiot. If someone should have a beautiful body he is called a hideous hunchback. Indeed, it must be that man feels his imperfections strongly (three quarters of which, incidentally, are his own fault) to criticize himself thus! I salute you, ancient ocean!

Ancient ocean, men, despite the excellence of their methods and assisted by scientific means of

investigation, have not yet succeeded in plumbing
the dizzy depths of your abyss. You have pro-
fundities that the longest and heaviest soundings
have recognized inaccessible. To do so is granted
to fish, but not to mankind. I have often asked my-
self which is the easier to recognize: the depth of
the ocean or the depth of the human heart! Often
as I stand watching the ships, my hand to my brow
while the moon swings askew between the masts,
I have surprised myself, blind to everything but
the goal I was pursuing, trying to solve this diffi-
cult problem! Yes, which is the deeper, the more
inpenetrable of the two: the ocean or the human
heart? If thirty years experience of life can to a
certain degree swing the balance in favor of one
or the other of these solutions, I should be allowed
to assert that, despite the depth of the ocean it
cannot touch, in a comparison on these grounds,
the depth of the human heart. I have known
men who were virtuous. They died at sixty
and the world never failed to exclaim: "They did
good on this earth. That is to say, they practised
charity, that is all. They were not wicked. Anyone
could do as much." Who may understand why two
lovers who idolized one another the night before
will quarrel over a single misunderstood word and
flee on the wings of hatred to opposite points of
the compass, full of love and remorse yet refusing
to see one another, each cloaked in lonely pride?
This is a miracle that occurs daily and is none the
less miraculous for that. Who may comprehend

why we delight not only in the general misfortunes of mankind but also those of our dearest friends, while at the same time we suffer for them? Here is an irrefutable example to terminate the series: man says hypocritically, yes; and thinks, no. Thus it is that the wild boars of humanity have so much confidence in one another and are not self-centered. Psychology has a long way to go. I salute you, ancient ocean!

Ancient ocean, you are so powerful that men have learned this at their own expense. In vain they have employed all the resources of their genius . . . they cannot enslave you. They have found their master. I say that they have found something stronger than they. This something has a name. This name is: the ocean! Such is the fear that you inspire in them that they respect you. In spite of that you toss their heaviest machines around with grace, elegance, and ease. You make them leap acrobatically into the heavens, and you make them plunge into the very depths of your domains: a professional tumbler would be jealous of you. Happy are they whom you do not envelop utterly in your boiling coils, swallowing them into your watery guts without benefit of railroads to find out how the fishes are doing, and more important still how they themselves are doing. Man says: "I am more intelligent than the ocean." This is possible, even more or less true. But the ocean inspires more dread in him than he in the ocean. No proof of this is necessary. That patriarchal observer, contem-

porary of the first epoch of our suspended globe,
smiles pityingly when he contemplates the naval
battles of nations. Here are a hundred leviathans
issued from the hands of humanity. The sharp
commands of the officers, the shrieks of the
wounded, the blasts of cannon, all this is a hulla-
baloo purposely created to kill a few seconds of
time. It appears that the drama is over, that the
ocean has engulfed everything into its belly. Its
mouth is enormous. The ocean must be vast to-
wards the bottom, in the direction of the un-
known! Finally to crown the stupid farce, which
is not even interesting, some travel-weary stork
appears in the air and without interrupting its flight
cries out: "This displeases me! There were some
black dots down there. I closed my eyes and they
disappeared!" I salute you, ancient ocean!

Ancient ocean, O greatest of celibates, as you
wander amid the solemn solitudes of your quiet
kingdoms you are justly proud of your native mag-
nificence and of the justifiable eulogies I am eager
to offer you. Voluptuously cradled by the gentle
flow of your majestic deliberation, which is among
the greatest of the attributes bestowed upon you
by the sovereign power, gloomily, mysteriously
you unfold over your sublime surface your incom-
parable waves with the quiet sense of your eternal
strength. They follow one another in parallel lines,
each separated from the next by a brief distance.
Scarcely has one subsided than another swells to
replace it, to the accompaniment of the melancholy

sound of breaking foam, warning us that all is foam. (So do human beings, those living waves, die monotonously one after another; but they leave no foamy music). Birds of passage rest upon the waves confidently and abandon themselves to their motion, full of graceful pride, until the bones of their wings have recovered their customary strength and they continue their aerial pilgrimage. I would that human majesty were but the reflection of your own. I ask much, and this sincere wish is a glory for you. Your moral greatness, image of the infinite, is vast as the meditations of a philosopher, as the love of a woman, as the heavenly beauty of a bird, as the thoughts of a poet. You are more beautiful than the night.

Tell me, ocean, will you be my brother? Roll wildly . . . more wildly yet . . . if you would have me compare you to the vengeance of God.

Spread out your livid claws and tear yourself out a pathway in your own bosom . . . that is good.

Roll your appalling breakers, hideous ocean, understood by me alone, and before whose feet I fall prostrate.

Man's majesty is borrowed; it shall not overcome me. You, yes.

Oh, when you advance, your crest high and terrible, surrounded by your tortuous coils as by a royal court, magnetic and wild, rolling your waves one upon the other full of the consciousness of what you are; and when you give utterance from the depths of your bosom as if you were suffering the pangs of some intense remorse which I have been unable to discover, to that perpetual heavy roar so greatly feared by men even when, trembling on the shore, they contemplate you in safety: then I can perceive that I do not possess that signal right to name myself your equal.

Hence in the presence of your superiority I would bestow upon you all my love (and none may know how much love is contained in my aspirations towards beauty) if you would not make me reflect sadly upon my fellow men, who form the most ironical contrast to you, the most clownish antithesis that has ever been seen in creation.

I cannot love you, I detest you. Why do I return to you, for the thousandth time, to your friendly arms which part to caress my burning brow, their very contact extinguishing my fever! I know not your secret destiny. All that concerns you interests me. Tell me whether you are the dwelling-place of the Prince of Darkness. Tell me this, ocean . . . tell me (me alone, for fear of distressing those who have yet known nothing but illusion) whether the breath of Satan creates the tempests that fling your salty waters up to the clouds. You must tell me this because I should love to know that hell is so close to man.

I desire that this should be the last verse of my invocation. So, just once more, I would salute you and bid you farewell! Ancient ocean, crystal-waved. . . . My eyes fill with copious tears and I have not the strength to proceed, for I feel that the

[*25*]

moment is come to return among men with their brutal aspect. But, courage! Let us make a great effort, and accomplish dutifully our destiny on this earth. I salute you, ancient ocean!

You will not see me at my last hour (I am writing this on my death-bed) surrounded with priests. I wish to die cradled upon the waves of the stormy sea or standing upon a mountain . . . my eyes directed not upwards. I know that my annihilation will be complete. Moreover, I shall expect no mercy.

Who is opening the door of my death-chamber? I said that no one should enter. Whoever you are, leave me. But if you expect to distinguish any sign of sorrow or fear on my hyena's face (I use this comparison although the hyena is more beautiful than I and more pleasant to look upon), be undeceived. Let him draw near. It is a winter night, the elements battle on all sides, and the child contemplates some crime against one of his playmates, if he is as I was during my childhood.

The wind, whose wailing has saddened the race of man since the beginning of man and of the wind, carries me off over the world on the bones of his wings, some moments before my last agony, eager for my death. I shall again gloat secretly over the innumerable examples of human wickedness (a brother loves to watch unseen the actions of his brothers). The eagle, the crow, the immortal pelican, the wild duck, the wandering crane, awakened shuddering with cold, will see me pass in the glare of lightning, a horrible and happy apparition. They will not understand what it means. On the ground, the snake, the great eye of the toad, the tiger, the elephant; in the sea, the whale, the shark, the hammer-fish, the shapeless ray, the tusked sealion, all will ask themselves what is this contradiction of the laws of nature? Man, trembling, will whimper and bow his head to the ground.

"Yes, I surpass you all in my inherent cruelty, cruelty the suppression of which does not depend upon myself. Is it for this reason that you prostrate yourselves before me thus? Or rather is it because you see me flying like a frightful comet—novel phenomenon—through blood-streaked space?"

(A rain of blood is falling from my mighty body like the ebon cloud that heralds the hurricane).

"Fear naught, my children, I shall not curse you. The evil you have done me is too great, and too great is the harm I have done you, that it should have been involuntary. You have gone your way and I have gone mine, both similar and both perverse. Necessarily we must have met in that similitude of character. The resultant shock has been fatal to both of us."

Then the people slowly raise their heads and, regaining their courage, stretch out their necks like snails to see who it is addressing them thus. Suddenly their burning, rotting faces, displaying the

most awful of passions, writhe in such grimaces
that wolves would fear them. All together they rise
like an immense spring. What curses! What shriek-
ing voices! They have recognized me. And now
the beasts of the earth unite with men and add their
weird bellowings. No more mutual hatred. The
two hatreds are turned against the common enemy,
myself. They come together with universal con-
sent. Supporting winds, raise me higher, for I fear
treachery. Yes, let us disappear little by little from
their eyes, utterly satisfied, witness once again of
the consequences of passion. My thanks, O *Rhi-
nolophus* with your snout surmounted by a horse-
shoe-shaped crest, for having awakened me with
the motion of your wings.

I perceive now that actually it has all been a
passing sickness and with disgust I feel myself re-
turning to life. Some say that you came to me to
suck out the drop of blood left in my body. Why
is this hypothesis not the reality?

A family is sitting around a lamp standing on a
table.

"My son, give me the scissors over there on the
chair."

"They are not there, mother."

"Then go and look for them in the other room.
Do you remember the time, dear master, when we

prayed to have a son in whom we should be born again and who would be the prop of our old age?"

"I remember, and God heard us. We have had nothing to complain of in our lot on this earth. Each day we bless Providence for her benefactions. Our Edward possesses all the graces of his mother."

"And the masculine qualities of his father."

"Here are the scissors, mother. I found them at last."

He returns to his work. But someone has appeared at the door and for a few moments the stranger watches the picture lying before his eyes.

"What does this scene signify? There exist many persons less happy than these are. What argument do they give themselves to explain their love of life? Take yourself off, Maldoror, from this peaceful hearth! Your place is not here."

He has gone!

"I don't know why it should be, but I feel human faculties at war in my heart. My soul is distressed, I know not why. The air is heavy."

"Wife, I feel the same myself. I fear that some ill-fortune will overtake us. Have faith in God; in Him lies the supreme hope."

"Mother, I can hardly breathe. My head pains me."

"You too, son! I will moisten your brow and your temples with vinegar."

"No, mother dear."

See how he leans back in his chair, exhausted.

"Something is going on inside me that I cannot explain. Now the slightest thing upsets me."

"How pale you are! This evening will not end before some baneful event plunges the three of us into the lake of despair!"

I hear in the distance prolonged shrieks of the most poignant agony.

"My son!"

"Oh, mother, I am frightened!"

"Tell me quickly if you are in pain."

"Mother, I am not in pain, I am not telling the truth."

The father cannot get over his astonishment.

"Those are the cries we hear sometimes in the silence of starless nights. Although we can hear these cries, whoever utters them is not near here for it is possible to hear them three leagues away carried by the wind from one city to another. I have often heard of this phenomenon but I have never before had the opportunity of judging its truth for myself. Wife, you were speaking of misfortune. If a more real misfortune existed within the long spiral of time it is the misfortune of whoever is now disturbing the sleep of his fellowmen."

I hear in the distance prolonged shrieks of the most poignant agony.

"Heaven grant that his birth be not a calamity for his country, which has thrust him from its bosom. He wanders from land to land, hated by all. Some say that he has been a victim of some special kind of madness since childhood. Others believe that he is of an extreme and instinctive cruelty, of which he himself is ashamed, and that his parents died of grief because of it. There are those who maintain that in his youth he was branded with an epithet and that he has been inconsolable for the rest of his existence because his wounded dignity perceives there a flagrant proof of the wickedness of mankind, which manifests itself during their earliest years and grows continually. This epithet was *The Vampire!*

I hear in the distance prolonged shrieks of the most poignant agony.

"They add that night and day without rest nor respite horrible nightmares cause him to bleed through the ears and mouth; and that ghosts sit at the head of his bed and, driven despite themselves by an unknown force, fling in his face, now softly, now in tones like the roar of battle, and with implacable persistence, that loathsome and persistent epithet, which will perish only when the universe perishes. Some say that love brought him to this state; or that his cries are the expression of remorse for some crime, shrouded in the night of his mysterious past. But most think that he is tortured by incommensurable pride, as Satan was, and that he would like to be God's equal."

I hear in the distance prolonged shrieks of the most poignant agony.

"My son, these are very exceptional confidences. I am sorry that you should have heard them at your age, and I hope you will never imitate that man."

"Speak, Edward. Say that you will never imitate that man."

"O beloved mother, to whom I owe the light of day, I promise, if the holy promise of a child has any value, never to imitate that man."

"Good, my son. You must obey your mother in everything."

The shrieks are heard no more.

"Wife, have you finished your work?"

"There are just a few more stitches to put in this shirt, though we have stayed up very late."

"I have not yet finished the chapter I began. Let us take advantage of the last moments of the lamp, for there is hardly any more oil, and each of us finish his work."

The child cries out:

"If God spares us!"

"Radiant angel, come to me. You shall wander among meadows from morning to night. You shall do no work. My splendid palace is built with silver walls, golden columns, and diamond doorways. You shall sleep when you will, to the strains of celestial music, and you need not say your prayers. When in the morning the sun reveals his resplendent rays and the joyous lark carries off her song with her far into the distance, you may still remain in bed until you are weary of rest. You shall walk upon the most precious carpets; you shall be constantly surrounded with an atmosphere composed of the perfumed essences of the sweetest-smelling flowers."

"It is time to repose the body and the mind. Arise, mother of my family, on your strong legs. It is just that your stiffening fingers should release the needle of overwork. Extremes are not good."

"Oh, how smooth will be your existence! I shall give you a magic ring. When you twist the jewel you will become invisible like the princes in the fairy tales."

"Put your daily tools away in the protective closet, while I clear away my things."

"When you twist it back to its original position you will reappear as nature fashioned you, O young magician. This is because I love you and hope to make you happy."

"Go away, whoever you are. Do not seize me by the shoulders."

"My son, do not fall asleep, cradled by the dreams of childhood. The evening prayer has not yet begun and your clothes are not yet carefully folded upon a chair. On our knees! Eternal Creator of the Universe, Thou showest Thine inexhaustible goodness even in the smallest things."

"Then you do not love the limpid streams where thousands of tiny fish are gliding, red, blue and silver fish? You shall catch them with so beautiful a net that it will attract them of itself until it is full. From the surface you shall see brilliant pebbles more highly polished than marble."

"Mother, see those claws. I distrust him. But my conscience is clear for I have nothing with which to reproach myself."

[*33*]

"Thou seest us prostrate at Thy feet, overcome with the sense of Thy greatness. If some prideful thought should insinuate itself into our imaginations, we reject it at once with the spittle of disdain and make unto Thee the irremissible sacrifice."

"You will bathe there with young girls who will embrace you in their arms. Then they will deck you with roses and carnations. They will have transparent butterfly wings and long waving hair floating around the sweetness of their brows."

"Even though your palace be more beautiful than crystal I shall not stir from this house to follow you. I believe you are nothing but an impostor, for you speak to me so softly, fearing to be overheard. To abandon one's parents is an ill deed. I shall never be an ungrateful son. As for your young girls, they are not so beautiful as my mother's eyes."

"Our whole life is consecrated to the praise of Thy glory. Such as we have been until this moment, so shall we be when we receive from Thee the command to depart from this world."

"They will obey your least whim and think only of your pleasure. If you desire the ever-restless birds, they will bring them to you. If you desire a coach of snow to carry you to the sun in the twinkling of an eye, they will bring it to you. What will they not bring you! They will even bring you the stag-beetle, as tall as a tower and hidden by someone on the moon, to whose tail are suspended by

silken threads birds of every species. Look to your-
self . . . heed my advice!"

"Do as you wish. I shall not interrupt my pray-
ers to call for help. Even though your body evapo-
rates when I try to thrust it aside, know that I have
no fear of you."

"Before Thee nothing is great unless it be the
flame of a pure heart."

"Think over what I have told you or you will
regret it."

"Heavenly Father, destroy the sorrows that may
descend upon our family."

"Then you will not go away, evil spirit?"

"Preserve my beloved wife who has been the
consolation of my despondency."

"Since you refuse me, I shall make you scream
and grind your teeth like a man who is hanged."

"And this beloved son of mine, whose chaste lips
have scarcely opened to the kisses of life's morn-
ing."

"Mother, he is choking me! Father, save me! I
can no longer breathe! Your blessing!"

A mighty cry of irony rises up into the air. See
how the eagles fall from the highest clouds stupe-
fied, literally blasted by the column of air.

"His heart beats no more. And my wife has died
at the same moment as the fruit of her womb —
fruit that I can no longer recognize so greatly is he
disfigured. My wife! My son! I remember a dis-
tant time when I was husband and father."

He told himself, before the scene that offered it-

self to his eyes, that he would not support this in-
justice. If the power accorded him by the infernal
demons, or rather the power he draws out of him-
self, be effective, then before the night has passed
that child should be no more.

He who knows not how to weep (for he has
always repressed his suffering within himself)
happened to find himself in Norway. In the Faroe
Islands he took part in a search for the nests of sea-
birds among precipitous crevasses, and he was
amazed that the rope, three hundred metres in
length, which supports the explorer over the abyss,
was chosen for such great strength. He saw in this
a striking example of human goodness, and he
could not believe his eyes. Had it been he who had
prepared the rope he would have nicked it in vari-
ous places so that it would break and precipitate
the hunter into the sea!

One evening he visited a cemetery, and the
youths who find their pleasure in violating the
corpses of beautiful women recently dead could,
if they would, have overheard the following con-
versation that took place together with the scene
of action that will unfold at the same time.

"Grave-digger, would you not like to converse
with me? A sperm-whale raises itself gradually out
of the sea's depths and shows its head above the

water in order to see the vessel that passes by this solitary place. Curiosity was born with the universe."

"Friend, it is impossible for me to exchange ideas with you. The soft moonbeams have been shining down upon these marble tombs for a long time now. It is the silent hour when more than one human being dreams he sees the apparition of women loaded with chains, trailing their shrouds, covered with spots of blood as an ebony sky is with stars. The sleeper cries out like one condemned to die, until he awakens and discovers that reality is three times worse than dream. I ought to finish digging this grave with my tireless spade that it may be in readiness for tomorrow. To accomplish an important task one should not do two things at once."

"He thinks that digging a grave is an important task! Do you believe that digging a grave is an important task?"

"When the wild pelican resolves to offer his breast to his children to devour, having for witness only him who was able to create so great a love that men were put to shame, although the sacrifice be great the action is understandable. When a youth sees a woman whom he adored in the arms of his friend, he smokes a cigar. He stays in his house and forms an insoluble friendship with sorrow. This action is understandable. When a pupil in a boarding-school is dominated for years which seem centuries, from morning till night and from night till morning, by an outcast of civilization whose eyes

are constantly upon him, he feels tumultuous floods
of an inveterate hatred rush to his brain like a heavy
fog until his head seems about to burst. From the
moment when he was thrown into prison until the
moment yet to come when he will be liberated his
face is yellowed by an intense fever which furrows
his brow and hollows his eyes. At night he thinks,
because he will not sleep. By day his thoughts leap
over the walls of this home of stupidity to meet
that moment when he shall escape or they shall ex-
pel him like a leper from this everlasting cloister.
This action is understandable. Digging a grave fre-
quently transcends the forces of nature. How
would you, stranger, that the pick tear up this soil,
which first feeds us and then provides us with a
commodious bed sheltered from the winter winds
that blow with such fury in these icy lands, when
he who grasps the pick in his trembling hands after
having fingered all day long the cheeks of the non-
living who enter into his kingdom, sees in the eve-
ning written in letters of flame on each wooden
cross the statement of the terrifying problem that
humanity has not yet solved: the mortality or im-
mortality of the soul. I have always preserved my
love for the Creator of the universe; but if after
death we no longer exist, then why most nights do
I see each grave open up and its tenant raise softly
the leaden cover to breathe the fresh air?"

"Cease your labors. Emotion exhausts your
strength. To me you seem as weak as a reed. It
would be foolhardy to continue. I am strong. I am

going to take your place. You, stand aside. You shall instruct me if I do wrong."

"What muscular arms, and what a pleasure it is to watch him dig the soil with such ease!"

"You must not permit a useless doubt to torment your thoughts. All these tombs, which are scattered about the cemetery like flowers in a meadow (a comparison lacking in truth) are worthy to be measured with the serene compasses of the philosopher. During the daytime dangerous hallucinations may appear; but they come chiefly at night. Consequently do not be astonished by any fantastic visions your eyes appear to see. During the daytime, when your mind is at rest, question your conscience. It will tell you with assurance that the God who created man with a portion of His own intelligence is possessed of limitless benevolence and will receive his masterpiece back into his bosom after earthly death. Grave-digger, why do you weep? Why these tears, these womanish tears? Remember well: we are aboard this dismasted vessel to suffer. It is a credit to Man that God should have judged him capable of conquering his deepest sufferings. Speak, and since according to your most cherished desires we should not suffer, tell me then of what virtue would consist (that ideal that each one of us strives to achieve) if your tongue is constructed like that of other men."

"Where am I? Have I not changed my character? I feel a strong breath of consolation passing over my unruffled brow, as the springtime zephyr reanimates the hope of the aged. Who is this man who in sublime speech has said things that the first passer-by would not have uttered? What musical beauty in the incomparable melody of his voice! I would rather hear him speak than hear others sing. Yet the more I observe him the less frank his face appears to be. The general expression of his features contrasts singularly with these words which the love of God alone could have inspired. His lightly-furrowed brow is branded with an indelible stigma. Is this stigma, which has aged him before his time, honorable or infamous? Should his wrinkles be regarded with veneration? I know not and I dread knowing. Even though he says what he does not think I believe he had his reasons for doing as he did, inspired by the ragged remnants of a charity that has been destroyed in him. He is absorbed in meditations that are strange to me, and he throws himself into arduous labor that he is not in the habit of undertaking. Sweat moistens his skin, he does not notice it. He is unhappier than the feelings inspired by the sight of a child in its cradle. O, how gloomy he is! Whence come you? Stranger, let me touch you and let my hands, which clasp seldom those of the living, pass over the nobility of your body. No matter what happens I shall know how to restrain myself. This hair is the most beautiful that I have ever touched in my life. Who would be audacious enough to deny I understand the quality of hair?"

"What do you want of me, while I am digging

a grave? The lion loves not to be interrupted at his repast. If you are ignorant of this I shall teach you. Come now, hurry! Finish whatever it is you want."

"This that shudders beneath my touch and makes me shudder myself is undoubtedly flesh and blood. It is true . . . I am not dreaming! Who are you, crouching there and digging a grave, while I like an idle dog that eats the bread of others do nothing? This is the hour of rest, or the hour to sacrifice sleep to science. In any case, no one is abroad at this hour, and every man is at home behind doors tightly closed against thieves. They lock themselves up in their rooms as best they can, while the embers in the old fireplace still warm the chamber with the last flicker of their heat. You do not behave like others. Your habits suggest a native of some distant country."

"Although I am not weary it is useless to dig the grave any deeper. Now undress me and place me in it."

"The conversation between us two for the last few moments has been so strange that I do not know how to answer you. I think he is joking."

"Yes, yes, that's right. I was joking. Pay no attention to what I said."

He collapsed and the grave-digger hastened forward to support him!

"What is wrong with you?"

"Yes, yes, it is true, I lied to you. I was weary when I laid down the pick. It was the first time I had ever done such work. Pay no attention to what I said."

"My opinion grows more and more consistent. This man suffers the most appalling sorrows. May Heaven prevent me from questioning him. I would rather remain uncertain, such is the pity he inspires in me. Moreover he would not reply, that is sure. We suffer twofold when we open up our hearts in such an abnormal frame of mind."

"Let me depart from this cemetery. I shall continue on my journey."

"Your legs would not carry you. You would lose your way as you trudged along. My duty is to offer you a rude bed—I have no other. Have confidence in me, for hospitality will not demand the violation of your secrets."

"O venerable louse with your body denuded of elytrae, once you reproached me bitterly for not sufficiently adoring your sublime intelligence, which is not an open book. Perhaps you were right, for I do not even feel gratitude towards this man. Beacon of Maldoror, where do you guide his footsteps?"

"To my house. Whether you be a criminal who has not taken the precaution of washing his right hand after committing his crime and easily recognizable by inspecting that hand; or whether you be a brother who has lost his sister; or some dethroned monarch, fleeing from his kingdom, my truly magnificent palace is worthy to receive you. It was not constructed of diamonds and precious stones because it is only a poor badly-built hut; but that famous hut has an historical past that is renewed by the present and persists without end. If it could speak it would astound you — you, who appear to be astounded by nothing. How often, even as that hut, I have seen funeral biers defile before me, hearses containing bones soon to be more worm-eaten than the beams of my door against which I was leaning. My innumerable subjects multiply daily. I do not have to take a periodical census. Here it is as with the living: each one pays a tax proportionate to the luxury of the spot chosen; and if some miser refuses to hand over his quota I have orders to act as a bailiff does: there are plenty of jackals and vultures eager for a good meal. I have seen laid out beneath cerements those who had been handsome; those who after death had lost no beauty; men, women, beggars and kings' sons; the illusions of youth, the skeletons of the aged; genius and madness; laziness and its opposite; those who were false, those who were true; the mask of the proud, the modesty of the humble; vice crowned with flowers and innocence betrayed."

"No, surely I shall not refuse your lodging, which is worthy of me, until dawn which is not far off. I thank you for your kindness. Grave-digger, it is wonderful to contemplate the ruins of cities; but it is more wonderful yet to contemplate the ruins of men!"

Maldoror

The leech's brother wandered slowly through the forest. Often he would stop and open his mouth as if to speak. But each time his throat would contract and the abortive utterance would be choked back. Finally he cried out:

"Man, whenever you find a dog collapsed in death, thrust inextricably against a flood-gate, do not as others do take up into your hand the worms that crawl out of its swollen belly, regard them in astonishment, open a clasp-knife and cut up large numbers of them, telling yourself that you too some day will be no more than this dog. What mystery are you probing? Neither I nor the four webbed feet of the sea-bear of the northern ocean have been able to solve the mystery of life. Have a care: night is falling and you have been there since morning. What will your family, what will your little sister, say when they see you return home so late? Wash your hands and take the pathway that leads to where you will sleep. . . .

"Who is that being yonder at the horizon, that creature who dares to approach me fearlessly, leaping laboriously along its crooked way? And what majesty, yet what serene gentleness! Its eyes, though mild, are profound. Their enormous pupils move with the breeze and seem to be alive. I know not this creature. As I meet its monstrous eyes my whole body shudders for the first time since I sucked at the withered paps of what is known as a mother. There is a kind of glowing halo around this being. When he gave utterance all nature was stilled, trembling. Since it pleases you to come to me as if drawn by a magnet, I shall not hinder you. How beautiful he is! It pains me to say this. You should be strong for you have a superhuman countenance, sad as the universe, beautiful as suicide. I loathe you to the fullest extent of my power and would rather see a serpent coiled about my neck from the dawn of time than I would see your eyes.

"What! It is you, toad! Fat toad! Unhappy toad! Forgive me . . . forgive me! What are you doing here on this earth where the accursed dwell? But what have you done with your fetid, viscous pustules that you should have so fair a look? When you came down from above, sent by a higher command on a mission to comfort the various existing races of men, you swept down upon the earth with the speed of a kite, your wings unwearied by that long, majestic flight . . . I saw you! Poor toad! How you made me think on the infinite, no less than on my own weakness!

" 'One more being,' I told myself, 'who is superior to those on earth; and that through divine will. But why not I too? Of what use is injustice in the supreme decrees? Is the Creator mad? He is, nevertheless, the strongest and his wrath is terrible! Since you appeared to me, prince of the ponds and marshes, covered with a glory that could derive only from God, you have in a measure comforted me. But my reeling reason totters before such greatness! Who are you? Stay, O stay longer on

this earth! Fold your white wings and cast not your
anxious eyes upward! If you depart, let us go to-
gether!'

"The toad sat himself down on his rump (so
similar to that of man!) and, while the wood-lice,
the slugs and the snails fled in terror at the sight of
their mortal enemy, gave utterance in these terms:

" 'Maldoror, listen to me. Notice my face, calm
as a mirror; and I believe my intelligence to be
equal to yours. Once you named me the prop of
your life. Since then I have not belied the confi-
dence you placed in me. It is true that I am only a
simple dweller among the reeds; but thanks to my
contact with yourself, taking from you only
what was fine in you, my mind has developed and
I may speak to you. I came to drag you back from
the abyss. Those who call themselves your friends
gaze upon you with consternation whenever they
encounter your pale and stooping figure at the the-
atre, in public places, at church, or crushing be-
tween your two muscular thighs that horse who
gallops only at night as he bears his ghostly master
enveloped in a long black cloak. Abandon these
thoughts which empty your heart like a desert;
they are more burning than fire. Your mind is so
sick that you are not aware of it and you imagine
you are normal whenever you give utterance to
words full of insanity, although redolent of infer-
nal grandeur! Unhappy one! What have you said
since the day of your birth? O sad relic of an im-
mortal intelligence, created with so much love by

God! You have begotten naught but maledictions more frightful than the aspect of a famine-stricken panther! As for me, I would rather have my eyelids glued together, my trunk armless and legless; I would sooner have murdered a man than be as you! Because I loathe you. Why do you have this character that amazes me? By what right do you come upon this earth to make a mockery of those who inhabit it, rotten derelict that you are, badgered by scepticism? If you are unhappy here, why don't you return to the sphere from which you came? One from the great city should not live as an outlander in the village. We know that there exist in space worlds more roomy than ours, where there are beings of an intelligence greater than we are able to conceive. Very well, then . . . go to them! Leave this transitory earth! Display at last your godlike substance, hitherto concealed. And without further delay direct your upward flight towards your own world, for which we have no use whatsoever, prideful thing that you are! I have not yet succeeded in identifying you as a man or a superman! Farewell then! Hope not again to discover the toad on your journey. You have been the cause of my death. As for me, I am leaving for eternity that I may implore your forgiveness!' ”

If it be ever logical to consider the appearance of phenomena, then this first canto comes to an end here. Do not be hard on one who has but tried out his lyre. It gives forth so strange a sound! Still, if you will be impartial you will already have felt a strong impression in the midst of all the imperfections. As for me, I shall go back to work to bring forth a second canto without loss of too much time. The end of the nineteenth century will see its poet (though at first he should not begin with a masterpiece but should follow the laws of nature).

He was born on the South American shores at the mouth of the Plate River, where two peoples, once enemies, now struggle to outdo one another in material and moral progress. Buenos Aires, queen of the south, and Montevideo, the flirt, offer one another the hand of friendship across the silvered waters of the great estuary. But everlasting strife has imposed his destructive empire upon the land and joyfully harvests his numberless victims.

Farewell, aged one, and if you have read me, think of me. You, youngster, do not despair, for in the vampire you have a friend despite your opinion to the contrary. Counting also the mite that produces the mange, you will have two friends.

MALDOROR

(LES CHANTS DE MALDOROR)

2

WHAT has been the fate of the first lay of Maldoror since his mouth, filled with the leaves of night-shade, gave utterance to it in a moment of medita-tion and released it throughout the kingdoms of wrath? What has become of that lay? We do not know precisely. Neither the trees nor the winds have preserved it. And Morality, who happened to be passing by ignorant of the fact that in its glow-ing pages she would find an energetic defender, saw it wending its way with a firm and direct tread towards the obscure fastnesses and the secret fibres of human consciousness. Science at least has ac-quired something from it: since its materialization, toad-faced man no longer recognizes himself and is continually lashing himself into fits of bestial rage. It is not his fault. From the dawn of time he had modestly believed that he was filled with good-ness mingled with only a minute quantity of evil. By dragging out his heart and his life-thread into the light of day I taught him the rude lesson that, on the contrary, he is made up of evil mingled with only a minute quantity of good which the law-makers have been hard put to it to conserve. I hope my bitter truths may not overcome him with ever-lasting shame, for nothing I teach him is new. But the realization of that hope would not conform with the laws of nature. What I have done, in the final analysis, is to snatch the mask from his foul and treacherous face and hurl down one by one, like balls of ivory into a bowl of silver, the sublime untruths with which he deceives himself. It is un-derstandable, then, that his countenance should ex-press lack of composure, even when reason dis-perses the shadows of pride.

It is for this reason that my hero has drawn down on himself an irreconcilable hatred, by attacking a humanity that had considered itself invulnerable, in ridiculous philanthropic tirades which are piled one upon another in his books like grains of sand, and of which sometimes when reason abandons me I almost appreciate the farci-cal but wearisome comedy. He had foreseen it. It does not suffice to engrave the image of virtue at the head of parchments in libraries.

O, human soul! There you stand now, naked as a worm, before my diamond sword! Give up your way of life, the time for false pride has passed: prostrate, I send you my prayer. There is one who observes the smallest stirrings of your guiltful life. You are enmeshed by the subtle network of his relentless insight. Do not trust him when he turns his back, for he is watching you; do not trust him when he closes his eyes, for he is still watching you. It is hard to imagine that, insofar as cunning and evil are concerned, your stern resolve should be able to outdo the child of my imagination. His slightest blow goes home. It is possible, by taking precautions, to teach those who are unaware of the fact, that wolves and brigands do not devour one another: perhaps it is not their custom. Consequently you may safely place in his hands the burden of your existence: he will conduct it in a manner known to himself. Put no trust in his intention, which he makes shine in the sunlight, of reforming you, for his interest in you is mediocre to say the least; and furthermore I shall not verge upon the whole truth in the benevolent measure of my verification. But the fact is that he loves to injure you, legitimately convinced that you will become as evil as he and that you will accompany him, when his hour shall come, into the yawning gulf of hell. His place there was long since reserved: a spot where you will find an iron gallows hung with chains and gyves. When he is borne thither by destiny the funereal pit will never have savored a more delectable prey nor will he himself have contemplated a more appropriate home.

It seems to me that I speak in an intentionally paternal manner, and that humanity has not the right to complain.

Maldoror

I grasp the quill with which I shall execute the second canto . . . a plume torn from the wing of some ruddy sea-eagle. But . . . what ails my fingers? Their joints are paralysed from the moment I commence my labors. Yet I desire to write. It is impossible! But I repeat: I desire to write down my thoughts. I have the same right as another to submit myself to that law of nature. But no, no . . . the pen is motionless! Wait: see across the countryside where the lightning flashes afar. The tempest sweeps through space. It is raining . . . always it rains . . . how it rains! The thunder crashes . . . it has struck at me through my open window and beaten me to the floor with a blow on my brow. Poor youth! Your face was already pitted enough by premature furrows and birth-disfigurement without the need of this great sulphurous scar! (I am supposing the wound is healed, which could not have happened so soon).

What is the meaning of this storm, and what signifies this paralysis of my hands? Is it a warning from on high to prevent me from writing and to reconsider to what I am exposing myself in distilling the saliva from my square mouth? Yet the storm has not filled me with fear. What care I for a legion of storms! These heavenly policemen carry on their painful duties zealously if I may judge by my wounded brow. I have no reason to thank the Omnipotent for his remarkable dexterity. He aimed his lightning in such a manner that it divided my face precisely in two, striking at my forehead where the wound was most dangerous. Let someone else congratulate him! But the storms attacked someone stronger than they. And so, hideous Eternal God with your serpent's snout, not content with having placed my soul between the fringes of madness and of frenzied imaginings that kill slowly, you decided after mature consideration that your majesty demanded that you extract from my brow a goblet of blood! But, after all, who may tell you anything? You know that I love you not, that on the contrary I hate you. Why do you persist? When will your conduct cease to manifest such outlandishness? Tell me frankly as a friend: do you not suspect, in the final analysis, that you are demonstrating naïf eagerness in your disgusting persecution, to the utter ridiculousness of which none of your seraphim would dare draw your attention? What madness possesses you? Know that if you were to permit me to exist in the shadow of your activities my gratitude would be yours.

Come now, Sultan,[1] lap up this blood that befouls my floor! The bandage is finished: the wound in my brow is stanched and bathed in salt water and I have bound it with strips of linen. The result is not infinite: four shirts, soaked in blood, and two handkerchiefs. One would not at first have thought that Maldoror contained so much blood in his arteries, for his countenance gives forth only a corpselike radiance. But what would you? That is the way of it. Perhaps this was all the blood his body

[1] Common pet name in France for a dog. (Tr.)

contained and it is probable that little remains. . . .

Enough, enough, ravenous hound! Leave the floor as it is, your belly is full. You must not continue to drink or soon you will vomit. You are well fed, go to your kennel and sleep. Figure that you are bathing in happiness, for you will not think of hunger for three long days thanks to the globules you swallowed with a satisfaction gravely obvious.

You, Leman, take a broom; I would take one too, but I lack the strength. You understand, do you not, that I have not the strength? Dry your tears or I shall assume that you have not the courage to contemplate calmly this great scar caused by a wound already forgotten by me in the night of the past time. Go to the well and fetch two pails of water. When you have washed the floor put these rags in the other room. If the washerwoman comes this evening, as she should, give them to her. But since it has been raining heavily for an hour and continues to rain I do not think she will leave her home. She will come tomorrow. If she should ask you whence came that blood, you need tell her nothing. Ah, how weak I am! But it matters little; I still have the strength to lift my pen and the courage to set down my thoughts. What has the Creator gained by tormenting me, as if I were a child, with a thunderstorm? My intention to write is undiminished. These bandages bother me, and my room reeks of blood. . . .

Let that day never dawn when Lohengrin and I should pass side by side and elbow to elbow down the street, eyes averted, like two hurried strangers. O, let me repel that thought to the ends of the earth!

The Eternal created the world such as it is. He would show much wisdom if, during the time strictly necessary to smash a woman's head with hammer blows, he would forget his sidereal majesty and reveal to us the mysteries in the midst of which our existences stifle like fish at the bottom of a boat. But he is great and noble; he prevails over us with the power of his conceptions; were he to parley with man, all man's shame would be flung back in his face. But, wretch that you are! Why do you not blush? It is not sufficient that the army of physical and moral agonies should have been born: the secret of our tattered destiny has not been divulged to us. I know him, the Omnipotent, and he should know me, too. If by chance we should be following the same pathway his piercing gaze singles me out from afar: he takes the opposite direction to avoid the triple dart of platinum that Nature gave me for a tongue!

It would please me, O Creator, if you would let me pour out my feelings. Wielding terrible irony with a cold steady hand, I warn you that my heart holds enough to pit myself against you until the end of my existence. I shall strike your hollow carcase with such violence that I guarantee to beat out the fragments of an intelligence that you would not bestow upon man because you would have been jealous of making him equal to yourself, and that you have impudently kept hidden in your guts, cunning scoundrel, as if you had not known that some day I should ferret it out with my ever-open eye, filch it from you, and share it with my fellow men. All this I have done, and now men fear you no more; they deal with you as one power with another.

Grant me death to atone for my audacity: I bare my breast and await you humbly. Come, contemptible shades of everlasting punishment! . . . pompous flutterings of overrated attributes! He has shown his incapacity to halt the circulation of my blood, which flouts him. Nevertheless, I have proof that he does not hesitate to extinguish in the flower of life the breath of other humans when they have scarcely tasted of the joys of living. It is, quite simply, atrocious, but only according to the feebleness of my opinion!

I have seen the Creator, spurring on his senseless cruelty, setting great fires in which children and old people perished! It is not I who open the attack; it is he who forces me to spin him like a top with a steel-lashed whip. Is it not he himself who furnishes me with accusations against him? My appalling zest will never be assuaged! It feeds upon insane nightmares that torture my sleeplessness.

It was because of Lohengrin that all the above was written; let us return to him. Fearing that he might eventually become as other men I resolved

first to stab him to death when he had passed the
age of innocence. But I thought it over and wisely
abandoned my resolution in time. He does not sus-
pect that his life was in danger for fifteen minutes.
All was ready and the knife had been bought. It
was a slender stiletto, for I love grace and elegance
even in the appurtenances of death; but it was long
and sharp. A single thrust in the neck carefully
piercing one of the carotid arteries, and I think
it would have been enough. I am satisfied with my
conduct: I should have regretted it later. And so,
Lohengrin, do what you will, act as you please,
shut me up for the rest of my life in a gloomy
prison with scorpions for company, or tear out one
of my eyes and fling it upon the ground, I shall
never reproach you. I am yours, I belong to you,
I live no longer for myself. The pain you might
cause me would not compare with the joy of
knowing that he who was wounding with murder-
ous hands was bathed in a more divine spirit than
his fellows! Yes, it is still good to give one's life
for a human being and thus to preserve the hope
that all men are not evil, since there was one at
least who could forcibly attract the contemptuous
disgust of my bitter sympathy!

It is midnight. There is not a single omnibus to
be seen from the Bastille to the Madeleine. But I am
mistaken: there is one suddenly approaching as if

it had arisen from the bowels of the earth. A handful of belated wayfarers examines it attentively, for it seems to resemble no other omnibus. Men are seated on the upper deck, men with the motionless eyes of dead fish. They are leaning together and seem to be lifeless, but the omnibus contains no more than the regulation number of passengers. When the coachman whips up his horses you would say that it was the whip that activated his arm rather than his arm the whip. What is this carload of weird and mute beings? Are they dwellers on the moon? From time to time one is tempted to believe so; but rather they resemble corpses.

The omnibus, anxious to reach its last stop, devours space and the pavement groans beneath it. It is vanishing! But a formless shape is pursuing it desperately amid the dust.

"Stop! I implore you, stop! My legs are swollen from walking all day . . . I have not eaten since yesterday . . . my parents have abandoned me . . . I don't know what to do . . . I am determined to return home and I should soon be there if you would make room for me . . . I am a little child eight years old and I trust you . . ."

The omnibus rushes on . . . on . . . but a formless shape is pursuing it desperately amid the dust.

One of the cold-eyed men on the bus jogs his neighbor's elbow and seems to be complaining of the metallic whimpering that reaches their ears. The other acknowledges what he hears with a slight inclination of his head and relapses again into his self-centered immobility like a tortoise into its shell. Everything in the features of the other travelers indicates the same sentiments as the first two. The cries continue to be heard for two or three minutes, more and more piercing. Windows are flung open along the boulevard and a terrified figure, lamp in hand, having cast a hasty glance down the roadway, quickly closes the shutters again and does not reappear.

The omnibus rushes on . . . on . . . but a formless shape is pursuing it desperately amid the dust.

One young man, deep in reverie, alone among these persons of stone seems to feel any pity for misfortune. He dares not raise his voice in favor of the child who hopes to overtake the coach with his small, weary legs, for the other men regard him with contempt and authority and he knows that he can achieve nothing against all of them. Elbow on knee and head in hand he asks himself, stupefied, if this is really what they call *Human Charity*. He realizes then that it is but a vain word no longer to be found even in the lexicon of poetry, and he frankly admits his error. He says to himself:

"After all, why should I concern myself over a little child? Let him well alone."

However, a burning tear rolls down the cheek of this young man who has just blasphemed. He passes his hand wearily over his brow as if to brush away a cloud whose density obscures his intelligence. He strives hard to reconcile himself with the century into which his lot has been cast; he feels that he is out of place but that he cannot escape. Terrible prison! Ghastly fate! Lombano, I have been pleased with you since that day! I watched you constantly, although my face expressed the same indifference as the other passengers'.

The young man arose indignantly and wanted to leave the omnibus to spare himself the pain of participating even involuntarily in a deed of wickedness. I made a sign to him and he came and sat down at my side.

The omnibus rushes on . . . on . . . but a formless shape is pursuing it desperately amid the dust.

The outcry is suddenly silenced, for the child has tripped over a projecting stone, and falling, has injured his head. The omnibus has disappeared into the distance and nothing remains but the silent street.

It rushes on . . . on . . . but no formless shape is pursuing it desperately amid the dust.

See that passing rag-picker crouching over his wan lantern: there is more heart in him than in all those men on the omnibus. He raises up the child. Rest assured that he will care for it tenderly and will not desert it as its parents have done.

The omnibus rushes on . . . on . . . but the piercing gaze of the rag-picker follows it relentlessly amid the dust!

Stupid and idiotic human race! You will regret such conduct. It is I who tell you this. You will regret, you will regret! My poetry will consist only in the attack by all means in my power upon Man, that wild beast, and the Creator, who should never have created such vermin. Volumes shall pile upon volumes until the end of my life, but only that one idea will be found therein . . . that one thought ever present in my consciousness!

❦

Taking my daily walk I used to pass through a narrow street. And each day a slender ten-year-old girl would follow me at a respectful distance along that street, watching me with sympathetic and curious eyes. She was tall for her age and slim. Thick black hair, parted in the middle, fell loosely over her marble shoulders. One day she was following me as usual when a muscular woman of the people seized her by the hair as a whirlwind seizes a leaf, struck her brutally twice on her proud silent face and dragged her, bewildered creature, back into the house. In vain I pretended unconcern: she persisted in pursuing me with her inopportune presence. When I would turn into another street to continue on my way she would stop and a violent struggle would take place within her at the end of that narrow street as she stood motionless as a statue of silence, gazing after me until I disappeared from her sight.

Once this girl walked ahead of me on the street, blocking the way before me. If I would hasten my stride to overtake her she would almost run to keep an equal distance between us; but if I slowed down in order to increase the distance, she, with all the grace of childhood, slowed down too. At the end of the street she turned slowly around, in such a manner as to impede my further progress. I had no time to evade her and found myself face to face with her. Her eyes were red and swollen. I could easily perceive that she wanted to speak to me but did not know how to begin. Suddenly turning pale as death she enquired:

"Would you be so kind as to tell me what time it is?"

I told her I carried no watch and hurried away.

Since that day, child of the uneasy and precocious imagination, you have seen no more in that narrow street the mysterious youth whose heavy shoes tramped wearily over the stones of the tortuous cross-roads. The vision of that flaming comet, a sorry subject for fanatic curiosity, will shine no more upon the façade of your deluded observation. And you will think often, too often, perchance forever, of him who seemed to concern himself little with either the good or the evil of this life, and wandered aimlessly with his horribly dead countenance, his bristling hair, his tottering gait, and his arms reaching out blindly into the ironic waters of the ether as if seeking there the bloody prey of hope, everlastingly tossed through the vast regions of space by the implacable snow-plow of fate! You will see me no more, I shall see you no more!

Who knows? Perchance that young girl was not what she appeared to be. Beneath her innocent exterior perhaps she concealed a deep cunning, the weight of eighteen years, and the charm of vice. We have seen peddlers of love joyfully expatriating themselves from England and crossing the Channel. They spread their wings and swirled about the glittering lights of Paris in golden swarms, and when you looked at them you would say: "But these are still children. They are not more than ten or twelve years old." Actually they were twenty years old.

Oh, in the light of that supposition, accursed be the devious ways of that gloomy street! What happens there is horrible, horrible! I believe the mother struck her because she was not plying her trade skilfully enough. It is possible that she was only a child, and if so the mother was guiltier yet. As for me I prefer not to believe this supposition, which is only an hypothesis, and would rather be loving in this romantic character a soul that had revealed itself too soon. Ah, my child, I warn you not to appear again before my eyes if ever I pass once more through that narrow street. It may cost you dearly!

Already blood and hate flood my brain in turbulent waves, I, a being sufficiently generous to love his fellow men! No, no! This I have sworn to do from the day of my birth! They do not love me! Worlds shall crash in ruins, granite rocks shall float like cormorants upon the surface of the waves, be-

fore I shall touch the infamous hand of a human
being! Away, away with that hand! Young girl,
you are no angel, you will become at last as other
women. No, no, I implore you! Never appear
again before my grim and squinting eyes. In a mis-
guided moment I might seize your arms and twist
them as one wrings water from washed linen, or
crack them like two dry branches and force you to
devour them afterwards. Taking your head be-
tween my hands, gently and caressingly, I could
sink my eager fingers into the lobes of your inno-
cent brain and, with a smile on my lips, extract
thence an efficacious ointment with which to bathe
my eyes, smarting from the everlasting sleepless-
ness of life. I could, by sewing up your eyelids,
deprive you of the spectacle of the universe and
make it impossible for you to find your way: I
should not act as your guide. I could, lifting up
your virgin body with an arm of iron, grasp you
by the legs and swing you around me like a cata-
pult, concentrate my strength in the last whirl,
and fling you against a wall. Each drop of blood
would splash upon a human breast to appall men
and set before them the example of my wicked-
ness! They would without respite tear from them-
selves shreds and strips of flesh but the drop of
blood would be indelible, glittering like a diamond.
Let your mind be at rest: I would order a half-
dozen servants to watch over the holy relics of
your body and preserve it from the voracity of
starving dogs. Doubtless the body would remain

plastered on the wall like a ripe pear and would not fall to the ground; but dogs can leap high if we don't watch out.

🐚

How sweet is that child sitting on a bench in the Tuileries Gardens! His bold eyes pursue some distant invisible object in space. He could not be more than eight years old, yet he does not amuse himself as he should. At least he should be laughing and walking with some playmate instead of being alone. But this is not his character.

How sweet is that child sitting on a bench in the Tuileries Gardens! A man, moved by a secret design, sits down beside him on the same bench with a questionable air. Who is he? I need not tell you, for you will recognize him by his tortuous conversation. Let us listen and not disturb them.

"What are you thinking about, my child?"

"I was thinking of heaven."

"It is not necessary to think about heaven. There is already enough to think about here on earth. Are you tired of life, you who were so recently born?"

"No, but everybody prefers heaven to earth."

"Well, not I. For since God made heaven as well as earth you may be sure that you will find up there the same evils as down here. After your death you will not be rewarded according to your deserts, for if they do you injustice here on this earth (as you will find out by experience later) there is no reason why they should not do you further injustice up there. It would be much better for you to give up thinking of God and to create your own justice, since it is refused you. If one of your playmates harmed you would you not be happy to kill him?"

"But that is forbidden."

"It is not as forbidden as you think. All that is necessary is to avoid being caught. The justice offered by law is worthless. It is the legal knowledge of the injured party that counts. If you hated one of your playmates wouldn't you be unhappy at the reflection that you would have the thought of him constantly before your mind?"

"That is true."

"That playmate of yours would make you unhappy all your life. For seeing that your hatred of him was passive he would continue to harm and flout you with impunity. There is only one way to put a stop to the situation: to get rid of the enemy. This is the point I wanted to establish in order to make you understand upon what foundations present society is based. Each man should create his own justice, and if he does not he is nothing more than an imbecile. He who gains the victory over his fellow man is the most cunning and the strongest. Would you not love to dominate your fellow men some day?"

"Yes, yes."

"Then be the strongest and the most cunning. You are still too young to be the strongest. But from today on you can employ cunning, the greatest weapon of men of genius. When the shepherd David struck the giant Goliath in the forehead with a stone from a catapult, is it not wonderful to observe that it was solely by cunning that David overcame his adversary, and if on the contrary they had wrestled together the giant would have crushed him like a fly? For you it is the same thing. In open warfare you could never dominate men, over whom you are desirous of imposing your will; but with cunning you can battle alone against everyone. You desire wealth, fine palaces, and glory? Or did you deceive me when you assured me you had such noble pretentions?"

"No, no, I didn't deceive you. But I would rather obtain what I desire by other means."

"In that case you will get nothing at all. Good and virtuous methods lead nowhere. You must employ more powerful levers and more subtle webs. Before you have become famous by your virtue and have reached your goal, a hundred others will have had time to scamper over your back and arrive at the height of their careers before you, so that there will be no room for your narrow ideas. You must know how to embrace the horizon of the present time more largely. Have you never heard, for example, of the great glory gained by victories? Yet victories do not make themselves. Blood must be spilled, much blood, to accomplish them and lay them at the feet of the conquerors. Without the bodies and the broken limbs that you may see in the field where the carnage raged so sensibly, there would be no war, and without war there would be no victories. You see that when one wants to become famous one must plunge one's self gracefully into rivers of blood fed by cannon-fodder. The end justifies the means. The first thing in becoming famous is to have money. Since you have none you must commit murder to get it. But, as you are not strong enough to wield a dagger, be a thief while waiting until your limbs shall have developed. And in order that they shall develop more rapidly I advise you to exercise twice daily, one hour in the morning, one hour in the evening. In this manner you may attempt crime with some chance of success as soon as you are fifteen, instead of waiting until you are twenty. The love of glory excuses all, and perhaps later on when you are master of your fellow men you will do them almost as much good then as you did them harm in the beginning!"

Maldoror perceived that the blood was boiling in the head of his young companion. His nostrils flared wide and a trace of white froth appeared about his lips. He felt the boy's pulse: it beat rapidly. His tender body was in the grip of fever. Maldoror feared the consequences of his words. He hastened away, wretched creature, annoyed that he had not been able to converse at greater length with that child. When in maturity it is so difficult to master the passions, balanced between good and evil, how is it with an inexperienced mind? And what relative amount of extra strength must we possess? The child, after three days in bed, will be restored to health. Heaven grant that maternal care will bring peace to that sensitive flower, fragile envelope of a beautiful soul!

Yonder in a grove surrounded with flowers a hermaphrodite is sleeping, slumbering deeply on the greensward, drowned in his own tears. The disc of the moon has escaped from the heaped clouds and with her pale beams caresses the sweet young face. Manly power shines from his features, yet too they betray the tenderness of a heavenly virgin. Nothing in him seems natural, not even the muscles of his body which ripple about the harmonious contours of a feminine shape. One arm is bent across his forehead, the other hand is pressed against his breast as if to restrain the pulsing of a heart closed to all confidence and charged with the heavy burden of an eternal secret. Weary of life and ashamed to walk among those who resemble him not, despair has taken possession of his soul and he travels alone like a beggar in the valley. How does he exist? Compassionate souls watch over him without his knowledge and never abandon him: he is so good! He is so resigned!

Maldoror

Sometimes he is glad to converse with sensitive persons, without touching their hands and holding himself at a distance in the fear of an imaginary danger. If they ask him why he has chosen solitude for a companion he raises his eyes towards heaven and represses painfully a tear of reproach against Providence; but he does not reply to that imprudent question that brings to snow-white eyelids the blush of a morning rose. If the conversation continues he grows restless, his eyes shift over the horizon as if seeking a loophole of escape from the presence of an invisible enemy. He raises his hand in an abrupt gesture of farewell, goes off on the wings of his aroused modesty, and disappears into the forest.

People generally take him for a madman. One day four masked men, acting under orders, threw themselves upon him and bound him firmly so that he could not move a limb. With whips they raised great welts on his back and told him to set out at once along the road to Bicêtre.[1] He began to smile under the lash and addressed these men with much feeling and intelligence concerning the many human sciences he had studied, displaying an immense erudition in one still so young; and he spoke to them of the destiny of the human race, unveiling before them the poetic nobility of his soul, until his attackers, horrified at what they had done to him, released his battered limbs from the bonds, fell on their knees

[1] An asylum for the insane.

description of poetic career

before him and implored his forgiveness, which he granted them, and took themselves off, their countenances expressing a veneration not ordinarily bestowed upon men. After that occurrence, which was much discussed, everyone guessed his secret but pretended to be ignorant of it in order not to multiply his distress; and the government granted him an honorable pension to make him forget that once they had wanted to shut him up forcibly, without verification, in a madhouse. Half this money he spends on himself, the rest he gives away to the poor.

Whenever he sees a man and a woman strolling down some grove of plane-trees he feels his body split in twain from head to foot and each new part yearns to embrace one or another of the strangers. But this is only an hallucination and reason is not slow in repossessing her empire. For this reason he mingles neither with men nor with women, for his excessive modesty, which has derived from his feeling that he is nothing but a monster, prevents him from bestowing his warm sympathy upon anyone. He would feel that he was profaning himself and others. His pride repeats to him this axiom: "Let each one be sufficient unto himself." His pride, I say, for he fears that in joining his life with that of a man or a woman he would be reproached sooner or later, as with a great crime, with the conformation of his body. So he entrenches himself behind his pride, offended by this impious supposition that exists only within himself, and he persists in remaining alone and inconsolable with his torments.

Yonder in a grove surrounded with flowers a hermaphrodite is sleeping, slumbering deeply on the greensward, drowned in his own tears. The awakened birds gaze with delight through the branches of the trees upon that melancholy countenance, and the nightingale is reluctant to unloose the crystal torrent of her song. The forest has become austere as a tomb from the nocturnal presence of the unhappy hermaphrodite.

O wandering traveler, by the adventurous spirit that inspired you in your tender youth to abandon father and mother; by the torture of the thirst you suffered in the desert; by the homeland perchance you are seeking after wandering, an exile, in strange lands; by your horse, your faithful friend, who has borne with you the exile and the intemperance of climates into which your wandering spirit led you; by the dignity a man gains through his wanderings over distant territories and uncharted seas, amid polar glaciers or beneath the torrid suns of the tropics: touch not with your hand as with the trembling of the zephyr's breath these locks of hair spread out on the ground to mingle with the green grass. Step back to a distance and you will do better. Those tresses are sacred; it is the hermaphrodite who wished it. He does not desire that human lips shall reverently caress his hair, scented by the breath from the mountain, nor his brow, which is resplendent now like the stars of the firmament. But it would be easy to believe that a star itself had descended out of its orbit while traversing space, to rest upon that majestic brow and to surround it with diamond brilliance as a halo.

Night, dismissing sadness, adorns herself in all her charms to pay homage to the slumber of this incarnation of modesty, this perfect image of angelic innocence; the murmuring of insects is suppressed. The trees bow their burdened branches over him to protect him from the dew and the night breeze, sounding its tuneful harp, sends towards him joyous harmonies through the universal silence, towards those closed eyelids which seem to take part, motionless, in the cadenced concerto of suspended worlds.

He dreams that he is happy; that his bodily nature has changed; or at least that he is being borne away upon a purple cloud to another sphere where dwell beings like himself. Alas! May his vision endure until the awakening of dawn! He dreams that flowers dance around him in great crazy wreaths, bathing him in their sweet breath, while he, locked in the embrace of a human being of enchanted beauty, sings a psalm of love. But it is only the evening mist he crushes in his arms and when he awakens they will be empty.

Sleep on, hermaphrodite, awaken not, I implore you. Why will you not believe me? Sleep . . . sleep forever. Your breast may rise and fall as you pursue the ethereal hope of happiness, that I will

[73]

allow you. But do not open your eyes! Ah, do
not open your eyes! I want to leave you thus, I do
not wish to witness your awakening. Perhaps one
of these days upon the passionate pages of some
mighty tome I shall recount your history, appalled
by what it brings forth. Hitherto I have not been
able, for each time I have tried copious tears have
fallen upon the paper and my fingers have trem-
bled, but not because of old age. But in the end
I yearn for the courage. I am incensed that I should
have no more nerve than a woman, and that I
should swoon like a girl whenever I contemplate
the depth of your misery. Sleep . . . sleep forever.
But do not open your eyes!

Farewell, hermaphrodite! I shall not forget to
pray to Heaven for you each day (were it for
myself I should not pray at all!). Let peace dwell
within your breast!

❦ ⚹

Whenever the soprano voice of a woman gives
out its vibrant and melodious tones, my eyes as
I listen to this human harmony are filled with a
latent flame and throw forth painful sparks, while
my ears seem to resound with the crash of cannon
fire. Whence could come this deep repugnance
for all that appertains to man? If the harmonies
should flow from the strings of an instrument I
listen voluptuously to these jeweled notes as they
wing their cadenced way through the elastic

waves of the air. My hearing receives only the impression of a sweetness enough to dissolve nerves and mind; an ineffable lethargy envelopes the active potency of my senses and the vital strength of my imagination with its magic opium like a veil subduing the light of day.

They say I was born deaf! In my early childhood I could not hear what was said to me. When with the greatest difficulty they succeeded in teaching me to speak, it was only by reading what they wrote down on a piece of paper that I could communicate my thoughts to them. One day (ill-fated day!) I was increasing in beauty and innocence; and the intelligence and purity of divine youth were the admiration of all and sundry. Many a conscience was stirred by contemplation of the limpid features where my soul was enthroned. They approached me with veneration for they saw in my eyes the bright glance of an angel. But I knew that the gay roses of youth could not blossom perpetually in capricious garlands on my modest and noble brow — brow that was passionately kissed by all mothers. I began to feel that the universe, with its vaulted dome studded with impassive and disturbing spheres, was perhaps not the great thing I had dreamed it to be.

Thus one day, weary of trudging up the steep pathway of the earthly journey and of passing, staggering like a drunken man, through the catacombs of life, I slowly raised my mournful eyes, ringed with great bluish circles, towards the in-

verted bowl of the firmament, and dared to try
and penetrate, young as I was, the mysteries of
heaven. Not finding what I was seeking I raised my
staring eyes higher . . . higher yet . . . until at
last I perceived a throne built of human excrement
and gold upon which was enthroned with idiot
pride and robed in a shroud made from unlaun-
dered hospital sheets, *that one* who calls himself
the Creator!

In his hand he held the decaying trunk of a man
and he lifted it successively from his eyes to his
nose and from his nose to his mouth, where one
may guess what he did with it. His feet were
bathed in a vast morass of boiling blood to the
surface of which there suddenly arose like tape-
worms in the contents of a chamber-pot, two or
three cautious heads which disappeared instantly
with the speed of arrows; for an accurate kick on
the nose was the well-known reward for such a
revolt against the law, caused by a need to breathe
the air, for men are not, after all, fish!

Like amphibians they swam between two waters
in that unclean juice! And when the Creator had
nothing left in his hands he would seize another
swimmer by the neck with the two first claws of
his foot as in a pincers and raise him up out of that
ruddy slime (delicious sauce!) This victim would
receive the same treatment as the preceding ones.
First he would devour the head, the legs, and the
arms and finally the trunk until there was not a
morsel left, for he crunched up the bones. And so

on throughout the rest of his everlasting life. From time to time he would cry out: "I created you. Hence I have the right to do what I will with you. You have done me no harm, I admit. I make you suffer for my own pleasure." And he would resume the cruel repast, his moving jaw agitating his beard, which was full of brains.

O, reader, does not this last detail make your mouth water? Who would not love to devour such brains, so tasty and fresh, taken only fifteen minutes ago from that lake of *fish*.

For a long while I contemplated that spectacle, my limbs inert and my throat dumb. Three times I almost fell to the ground like a man who suffers too strong an emotion; three times I succeeded in regaining my balance. Not a fibre of my body was still and I trembled like the lava in the interior of a volcano. At last, my heaving bosom being unable to expel the life-giving air speedily enough, my lips opened and I cried out . . . a cry so heart-rending that I myself heard it! The obstacle in my ears snapped abruptly, the eardrum cracked beneath the shock of that mass of noisy air expelled from within me so violently, and a new phenomenon took place within that organ condemned by nature. I had heard a sound! A fifth sense was born in me!

But what pleasure could I have found in the discovery? Henceforth human speech could enter my ear only with a sense of pain engendered by pity for a great injustice. When anyone spoke to me I remembered what I saw that day beyond the visible spheres and recalled the expression of my smothered feelings in a sudden shriek, the tone of which was identical with that of my fellow-creatures! I could not reply, for the tortures inflicted upon the weakness of man in that loathsome purple sea passed before my eyes, bellowing like flayed elephants and brushing my scorched hair with their fiery wings.

Later when I was better acquainted with humanity this feeling of pity was accompanied by an intense fury against that tigress's stepmother whose callous offspring know nothing but to curse and to do evil. Audacious liars! They assert that with them evil is the exception!

Now it is long since finished: I have spoken to no one for a long time. O, you, whoever you are, when you are near me let your vocal chords utter no sound; let your motionless larynx try not to rival the nightingale; and never venture to acquaint me with your soul by means of language. Preserve a religious silence interrupted by nothing. Cross your hands humbly upon your breast and cast down your eyes. I have told you that since the vision that made known to me the supreme truth, enough nightmares have avidly sucked at my throat day and night that I should still have the courage to renew even in my thoughts the sufferings I underwent in that infernal hour, the memory of which pursues me relentlessly.

O, when you shall hear an avalanche crash down

from the icy mountains; or the lioness in the midst of the waterless desert mourning for her young; or the tempest accomplishing its destiny; or the condemned man moaning in his prison on the night before his execution; or the savage octopus riding the waves and singing of his victories over swimmers and the drowning: admit that any of these majestic voices is more beautiful than man's derision!

There is an insect nourished by men at their own expense. They owe it nothing but they fear it. This insect, that loves not wine but prefers blood, would be capable by the exercise of occult powers, if its legitimate cravings were not satisfied, of swelling to the size of an elephant and crushing men like grain. It is worth observing how they respect it, how they surround it with canine veneration, how they esteem it above all other animals in creation. They accord it their head for a throne and it fastens its claws into the roots of the hair with dignity. Later on when it has become plump and very old they kill it, aping the custom of a certain ancient people, in order that it may not feel the blows of old age. They give it a magnificent funeral as if it were a hero, and the hearse that conveys it straight to the tomb is carried on the shoulders of the leading citizens. Over the moist soil turned up by the grave-digger with his skilful spade they put together colorful phrases concerning the immortality of the soul, the nothingness of life, the inexplicable will of Providence; and the marble closes down forever upon that entity now merely a corpse. The crowd disperses and soon night covers the walls of the cemetery with her shadows.

But be consoled, humans, for this sad loss. Here comes his innumerable family advancing upon you. This is a generous legacy he has left you, that your despair should be less bitter and sweetened by the agreeable presence of these snarling abortions soon to grow into magnificent lice endowed with remarkable beauty, monsters with the appearance of sages. He brooded over many dozen cherished eggs, with a maternal wing, in your hair dried out by the relentless suction of these fearful interlopers. The time soon comes when the eggs will hatch out. Never fear, they will not be slow in their growth, these youthful philosophers, into this ephemeral life. They will grow to an extent that they will make you feel with their claws and suckers.

You do not understand why they do not devour the very bones of your skull rather than contenting themselves with extracting the quintessence of your blood. Wait a moment: I shall tell you. It is because they lack the strength. Be very sure that if their jaws conformed to the measure of their infinite desires your brain, your eyeballs, your

backbone, your whole body would be devoured.
Like a drop of water. Take a microscope and
observe a louse working at the head of a young
beggar from the streets: you will be astonished.
Unfortunately they are small, these highwaymen
of the long hair. It would be useless to conscript
them into the army for they are not of the height
proscribed by law. They belong to the lilliputian
world of the runt, and the blind would not hesitate
to place them among things infinitely tiny. Alas
for the whale that should pit itself against a louse!
It would be devoured in the twinkling of an eye,
despite its size. Not even its tail would be left to
tell the news. The elephant permits caresses, but
not the louse. I would advise you not to attempt
so perilous an experiment. Beware if your hand
be hairy; yet it is enough even that it be made of
flesh and blood. It would mean the end of your
fingers. The lice would crunch them up as if they
had been put to the torture. The flesh would dis-
appear by a strange magic. Lice are incapable of
committing the amount of evil their imaginations
prompt them to. If you find a louse in your way
hurry by and do not lick the papillae of its tongue.
Some harm would come to you. It has been known
to happen. No matter, I am already satisfied with
the amount of evil the louse does to you, O human
race! I only wish it could be more.

When will you abandon this wormeaten wor-
ship of a deity who is insensible of the prayers and
generous sacrifices you offer up to him in expiatory

holocaust? Look you: he is not in the least appreciative of all those great goblets of blood and brains you spread out on your piously flower-bedecked altars before him. He does not appreciate them for earthquakes and tempests have continued to rage since the dawn of time. And yet (spectacle worthy of note!) the more indifferent he is the more you admire him. It is apparent that you mistrust his hidden attributes; and you argue that only a deity of extreme power could demonstrate such contempt towards the faithful who submit to his religion. It is for this reason that in different countries exist different gods: here a crocodile, there a whore; but when it comes to the louse, that sacred name, all peoples kneel down together in the square before the throne of that shapeless and bloody idol, universally kissing their chains of slavery. That people refusing to obey its instinct to grovel, and showing any tendency to revolt, would disappear sooner or later from the earth like an autumn leaf, annihilated by the vengeance of that inexorable god.

O louse with your shriveled eyes, as long as rivers empty themselves into the depths of seas; as long as the stars remain within their orbits; as long as empty void is without limit; as long as humanity tears itself to shreds in deadly warfare; as long as divine justice casts down its vengeful thunders upon this selfish globe; as long as man misunderstands and flouts (not without reason) his Creator and treats him with contempt, your reign in the universe will be assured and your dynasty will persist from century to century. Rising sun, I salute you, celestial liberator, man's invisible enemy. Command filth to unite with man in foul kisses and to swear to him with oaths not written in the dust that it shall remain his faithful lover until eternity. Imprint from time to time a kiss upon the robes of that famous lecheress, Filth, in memory of the important services she will not fail to render you. If she did not seduce man with her lascivious paps, it is probable that you could not exist — you, the product of that rational coupling. O son of filth! Tell your mother that if she should desert man's bed to wander off alone and without support in solitary places she would see her existence compromised. Let her entrails, which bore you nine months in their perfumed depths, stir an instant at the thought of the subsequent dangers to which their tender fruit would be submitted — fruit so tranquil and so sweet, yet already cold and ferocious. Filth, great empress, preserve before the eyes of my hatred the gradual multiplication of the muscles of your famine-stricken offspring. To achieve this end you know that you have only to adhere more closely to the flanks of man. You can do this without disturbing your modesty for you two have been joined in wedlock for a long time.

As for me, if I may be permitted to add a few words to this hymn of glory, I shall relate that I have caused to be constructed a pit four leagues square and correspondingly deep. Therein lies in its unclean virginity, a living mine of lice. It fills the bottom of the pit and thence snakes out in great dense streams in every direction. Here is how I built this artificial mine. I snatched a female louse from the hair of humanity. I was seen to lie with her on three successive nights and then I flung her into the pit. The human fecundation, which would have been ineffective in other similar cases, was accepted this time by fate and at the end of several days thousands of monsters, swarming in a compact knot of matter, were born to the light of day. The loathsome mass became in time more and more immense, in the meantime acquiring the liquid properties of mercury, and poured itself out in divers tributaries which now feed upon themselves (the birth rate is higher than the death rate), except when I fling them a new-born bastard whose mother desired its death; or an arm that I hack off during the night from some young girl, after chloroforming her. Every fifteen years the generations of lice that feed upon men decrease noticeably, and themselves predict infallibly the imminence of their complete destruction. For man, more intelligent than his enemy, succeeds in overcoming him. Then, with an infernal shovel that increases my strength, I dig out of that inexhaustible mine whole chunks of lice, big as mountains. I split them up with an axe and I transport them in the depths of the night to the city streets. There, in contact with human temperature, they dissolve

into individuals as in the first days of their forma-
tion in the tortuous galleries of the underground
mine, dig themselves a bed in the gravel and
spread out in streams through human habitations
like noxious spirits. The guardian of the house
barks dully, for it seems to him that a legion of
unknown beings is piercing the pores of the walls,
bringing terror to the beds of the sleepers. Per-
chance you may have heard at least once in your
life this kind of sad, drawn-out howl. They try to
pierce the darkness of the night with impotent eyes,
for their dog's brains cannot understand what is
going on. This singing in their ears irritates them
and they feel themselves betrayed. Millions of
enemies fling themselves thus upon cities like
clouds of locusts. There is enough for fifteen years.
They will attack man, wounding him with biting
wounds. After that lapse of time I shall send others.
When I crush up the chunks of animated matter
it sometimes happens that one fragment is more
densely packed than another. Its atoms struggle
furiously to tear away from the mass in order to
go forth and torment humanity; but the endurance
of cohesion resists. By a supreme convulsion they
generate such an effort that the rock, unable to
scatter its living contents, flings itself into the
upper atmosphere as if blown up by gunpowder,
and then falls to earth burying itself deeply in the
soil. Sometimes the thoughtful peasant observes
an aerolith cut vertically through space and dis-
appear into a field of corn. He does not know

whence comes this stone. You now have a clear and succinct explanation of the phenomenon.

If the earth were covered with lice like grains of sand on the sea shore the human race would be annihilated in the midst of terrible suffering. What a spectacle! And I, with the wings of an angel, motionless in the air, contemplating it!

※

O austere mathematics! I have not forgotten you since your learned teachings, sweeter than honey, distilled themselves through my heart like refreshing waves. Instinctively, since the day of my birth, I have aspired to drink from your spring more ancient than the sun and I still continue to frequent the courtyard of your solemn temple: I, the most faithful of your initiates.

There used to be a vacuum in my soul, a something, I know not what, dense as smoke; but wisely and religiously I mounted the steps that lead to your altar, and you dispelled that gloomy shroud as the wind blows a butterfly. In its place you set an extreme coldness, a consummate prudence and an implacable logic. With the aid of your invigorating milk my intelligence developed rapidly and assumed immense proportions in the midst of the ravishing illumination that you bestow prodigally upon those who love you with a sincere love.

[*86*]

Arithmetic! Algebra! Geometry! Imposing trinity! Luminous triangle! He who has never known you is without sense! He merits the ordeal of the most cruel tortures for in his ignorant carelessness there is a blind contempt. But he who knows you and appreciates you desires nothing more of this world's goods, is content with your magical joys and, borne upon your somber wings, desires nothing better than to ascend, lightly flying and describing an ascendant spiral, towards the curved vault of the heavens. Earth offers him nothing but illusion and moral phantasmagoria.

But you, O concise mathematics, by the rigorous fetters of your tenacious propositions and the constancy of your iron-bound laws you dazzle the eyes with a powerful reflection of that supreme truth whose imprint is manifest in the order of the universe. But the order surrounding you, represented chiefly by the perfect regularity of a square, Pythagoras' friend, is even greater; for the Omnipotent revealed himself and his attributes completely in that memorable effort that consisted in extracting from the entrails of chaos your treasures of theorems and your magnificent splendors. In ancient and in modern times more than one great human imagination saw his genius appalled by the contemplation of your symbolic figures traced upon burning paper like so many mysterious signs living with a latent breath, incomprehensible to the vulgar and profane, which were merely the radiant revelation of eternal axioms and hieroglyphics that existed before the universe and will continue to exist beyond it.

Leaning over the precipice of a fatal question-mark, he demands how it can be that mathematics contains so much imposing grandeur and so much incontestable truth, while man is filled with nothing but pride and deceit. Then this superior being, saddened and feeling even more strongly through his familiarity with your counsels, the pettiness and incomparable folly of humanity, rests his blanched head upon his emaciated hand and remains absorbed in supernatural meditations. He bends his knee to you and his reverence pays homage to your divine countenance as to the image of the Omnipotent.

During my childhood you appeared before me one moonlit night in May, in a verdant meadow by the side of a limpid stream, all three equal in grace and modesty, all three full of the majesty of queens. You took several steps towards me, your long robes floating about you like a cloud, and you lured me towards your proud breasts like a beloved son. I rushed upon you and clenched my hands upon your white bosom. Gratefully I fed myself upon your life-giving manna and I felt humanity grow and improve within me.

Since that time, O rival goddesses, I have never abandoned you. Since that time what pompous projects, what sympathies, that I had thought to be engraved upon my heart as upon marble, have you not slowly erased from my undeceived reason

as the dawn effaces the shadows of night! Since
that time I have seen death, with the intention
visible to the naked eye of populating his tombs,
ravaging battlefields steeped in human blood and
planting morning flowers over funereal skeletons.
Since that time I have assisted at the revolutions
of our globe; earthquakes and volcanoes with their
flaming lava, the simoom of the desert and ship-
wrecks of the storm have all witnessed my pres-
ence as impassive spectator. Since that time I have
seen many a generation of human beings raise in
the morning their wings and their eyes to space
with the inexperienced joy of the chrysalis saluting
his last metamorphosis; and I have seen them
die in the evening before sunset, their heads droop-
ing like wilted flowers swayed by the plaintive
whisper of the wind.

But you are unchanging. No change, no enven-
omed wind, touches the steep rocks and wide
valleys of your identity. Your modest pyramids
will endure longer than the pyramids of Egypt,
those ant-hills erected by stupidity and slavery.
The end of all centuries will yet see, standing upon
the ruins of time, your cabalistic ciphers, your
terse equations, and your sculptural lines, en-
throned at the vengeful right hand of the Omni-
potent, while in despair like jets of water the
stars will sink into the eternity of a horrible and
universal night; and while man, grimacing, thinks
of settling his accounts with the last judgment.

I thank you for the numberless services you

have rendered me. I thank you for the unfamiliar qualities with which you have enriched my intelligence. Without you I might perhaps have been overcome in my struggle against man. Without you he would have rolled me in the dust and made me kiss his feet. Without you he would have ploughed my flesh and bones with a treacherous claw. But I watched out for myself like an expert athlete. You gave me the coldness that exhales from your sublime conceptions, free from passion. I used it to reject disdainfully the ephemeral joys of my brief journey and to thrust from my door the sympathetic but deceptive overtures of my fellow men. You gave me the stubborn prudence that is disclosed at every step in your admirable methods of analysis, synthesis and of deduction. I used it to confound the pernicious cunning of my mortal enemy, skilfully to attack him in my turn and to plunge into man's viscera a sharp dagger that will remain forever buried in his carcass, for it is a wound from which he will never recover.

You gave me logic, which is the very soul of your wise instruction. With its syllogisms, the labyrinths of which are made more understandable by their very complication, I felt my intelligence redouble its daring strength. With the aid of that terrible ally I discovered in humanity as I plunged into its depths, beside the reefs of hatred, black and loathsome evil crouching amid deleterious miasmas, contemplating its navel. I was the first to discover in the shadow of his entrails that disastrous vice of wickedness, more powerful in him than good.

With the envenomed weapon you lent me I forced to descend from his pedestal, built by the cowardice of men, the Creator himself! He ground his teeth and submitted to this ignominious insult, for his adversary was stronger than he! But I tossed him aside like a bundle of string that I might descend from my flight. The thinker Descartes once uttered the reflection that nothing solid had ever been built upon you. It was an ingenious way of demonstrating that it is not given to everyone to discover your inestimable value all at once. Indeed, what could be more solid than your three principal qualities already mentioned which arise interlaced like a unique crown from the summit of your colossal architecture? You are a monument that grows unceasingly with daily discoveries from your mines of jewels and from scientific explorations through your superb domains.

O sacred mathematics, could you not through your perpetual activity console the remainder of my days for the wickedness of man and the injustice of the Most High!

"O lamp of silver, my eyes discern you in the air, companion of the cathedral dome, and I seek the reason for your suspension there. They say that your beams illumine the darkness of night

for the crowds who come to worship the Omnipo-
tent and that you show the repentant the path to
the altar. Listen, this is quite possible; but need you
render such services to those to whom you owe
nothing? Leave the columns of the basilica plunged
in gloom; and when a gust from the tempest amidst
which whirls the devil penetrates with him, spread-
ing terror, into the holy place, instead of struggling
bravely against the envenomed blast extinguish
yourself suddenly beneath its feverish breath in
order that, unseen, he may select his victims among
the kneeling believers. If you will do that I
shall owe you all my happiness. When you shine
thus, shedding your flickering yet adequate beams,
I dare not respond to the promptings of my nature
but lurk beneath the sacred porch peering through
the half-opened doors at those who escape my
vengeance in the bosom of the Lord.

"O poetic lamp! you who would be my friend
if you could understand me, why, whenever my
feet in the dark hours touch the stone-paved aisles
of churches, do you commence to shine in a man-
ner which, I must confess, seems to me peculiar?
On such occasions your beams become tinted with
the white radiance of electricity; the eye can no
longer bear to look upon you; and you illuminate
the Creator's hovel with a new and powerful flame
as if you were prey to a holy anger. Then when I
retire from the scene having uttered my blasphe-
mies you dwindle again to your previous modest and
pale gleam, convinced that you have accomplished

an act of justice. Tell me, would it be because you
understand the convolutions of my heart that
whenever I happen to appear where you are keep-
ing your vigil you hasten to draw attention to my
pernicious presence and to point out to the wor-
shippers the spot where the enemy of man has
appeared? I incline towards this opinion, for I too
begin to understand you; and I know who you are,
ancient sorceress, who keep so watchful a vigil in
the sacred mosques where your peculiar master
struts like a rooster.

"Vigilant wardress, you have taken upon your-
self a foolish mission. I warn you: the first time
you point me out to the discretion of my fellows
by the amplification of your phosphorescent
beams, since I do not fancy this optical phenom-
enon which in any case is not mentioned in any
textbook of physics, I shall seize you by the skin
of the breast and hook you by the nape of your
scurvy neck with my scaly claws and fling you
into the Seine. I do not claim that when I am doing
nothing to you, you wittingly behave in a manner
annoying to me. In the Seine I will permit you to
shine as long as it pleases me; there you will flout
me with an inextinguishable smile; there, con-
vinced of the incompetence of your lawless oil,
you will piss it forth with bitterness."

Having spoken thus Maldoror does not leave
the cathedral but stands staring at the lamp in that
holy place. He thinks he sees some kind of provo-
cation in the attitude of that lamp that irritates

him to the highest degree by its untimely presence. He tells himself that if there is any soul concealed within that lamp it is cowardly not to reply sincerely to a straightforward attack. He beats the air with his sinewy arms and wishes that the lamp could be transformed into a man; he promises himself that he would put him through a bad quarter-hour. But the means by which a lamp changes into a man are unnatural. He does not resign himself to this but goes seeking on the floor of that wretched pagoda a flat stone with sharp edges. This he flings violently through the air . . . the chain is cut through the middle like grass before the scythe and the religious instrument falls to the ground spreading its oil upon the flagstones. He seizes the lamp to carry it outside but it resists and begins to increase in size. He seems to see wings sprouting from its sides and its upper part takes on the form of an angel's bust. It tries to take flight but he restrains it with a firm hand. One does not often see a lamp and an angel united in the same body. He recognizes the shape of the lamp; he recognizes the form of the angel; but he cannot distinguish them in his mind. Indeed, in reality they are joined together and form together one free and independent body. But he feels that some cloud has veiled his eyes and caused him to lose slightly the excellence of his eyesight. Nevertheless he prepares himself bravely for the struggle, for his adversary has no fear.

There are naive persons who assert that the

sacred door closed of its own accord, swinging on its battered hinges, in order that none should witness that impious struggle the vicissitudes of which were about to develop within the precincts of that violated sanctuary.

The cloaked man, while undergoing cruel punishment from an invisible sword, strove to draw the angel's face to his mouth. He thought only of that and all his struggles were to that end. The lamp-angel weakens and seems to feel a presentiment of its destiny. Its struggles become feebler and the moment is imminent when its adversary will be able to embrace it at his ease, if that is what he intends to do.

Now the moment is come. Exerting his muscles he compresses the throat of the angel, who can no longer breathe, and crushes her against his loathsome breast. For a moment he feels pity for the fate awaiting this heavenly being, of whom he would have willingly made a friend. But he reminds himself that it is an envoy of the Lord and he can no longer restrain his wrath. It is irrevocable: something horrible is about to enter the cage of time! He bends down and applies his salivated tongue to that angelic cheek despite the imploring glances of his victim. For several moments he passes his tongue over that cheek. Oh! Look! Look there! The pink and white cheek has turned black, black as coal! It exhales a miasma of putrefaction. This is gangrene, no further room for doubt. The gnawing disease extends over the whole face and from there continues its ravages until soon the whole body is reduced to a great loathsome wound. Maldoror himself appalled (for he did not realize his tongue contained so virulent a poison) snatches up the lamp and flees from the church. Once outside he perceives in the air a blackish shape that bears itself wearily on singed wings up towards the regions of heaven. They look upon one another while the angel ascends towards the serene heights of virtue and Maldoror, on the contrary, descends into the vertiginous abyss of evil. What a look passes between them! All that humanity has thought in sixty centuries and much more that it will think could easily have been contained therein, so much do they say to one another in that supreme farewell! But one is aware that these are thoughts more elevated than those which spring from human intelligence; in the first place because of the persons involved and then because of the circumstances. That look binds them together in an eternal friendship.

Maldoror is astonished that the Creator can have missionaries with such noble souls. For an instant he believes himself mistaken and asks himself whether he should have followed the ways of evil as he has done. But the shadow passes and he remains firm in his resolution. And it would be glorious, according to him, sooner or later to conquer the All-in-All and to reign in his place over the entire universe and over legions of angels as beautiful as that one.

The ascending angel gives Maldoror to under-
stand that he will resume his original form as he
mounts toward Heaven; lets fall a tear to refresh
the brow of *that one* who afflicted him with gan-
grene; and disappears little by little like a vulture
amid the clouds. The culprit turns his attention to
the lamp, cause of the preceding events. He rushes
through the streets to the Seine like a madman and
flings the lamp over the parapet into the river.
For a few seconds it whirls around, then finally
sinks down into the muddy waters.

Since that day, each evening at sundown a bril-
liant lamp appears floating gracefully upon the
surface of the river. Instead of handles it bears two
tiny angel's wings. It proceeds slowly upon the
waters, passes beneath the arches of the Pont de
la Gare and the Pont d'Austerlitz and continues
its silent course down the Seine to the Pont de
l'Alma. There it turns and retraces its journey
with ease, arriving at its point of departure at the
end of four hours. This procedure continues all
through the night. *Its beams white as electric light*
eclipse the gas lamps that border the two banks
of the river, between which the lamp advances like
a queen, alone, impenetrable, *with an inextin-
guishable smile, and its oil does not pour itself
bitterly forth.*

At first boats would pursue it, but it frustrated
these vain efforts, escaped all the hunters, by
plunging like a flirt beneath the waters and re-
appearing at a distance. Now when the super-

stitious boatmen see it they row in the opposite direction and they silence their chanties.

When you are crossing a bridge at night be very careful: you are sure to see that lamp shining here or there. But they say it does not show itself to everyone. When someone with a guilty conscience crosses a bridge, it suddenly extinguishes its beams and the passer by, appalled, seeks it desperately and in vain on the surface of the river. He knows what this means. He would believe that he had seen the heavenly radiance, but he tells himself that this light came from some ship or from the reflection of the gas-lights, and he is right. . . . He knows that he is the cause of the disappearance of that lamp, and plunged in sorrowful meditations he hastens his step homewards. Then the silver lamp reappears upon the surface and continues its course in capricious and elegant arabesques.

Hear the thoughts of my childhood when I would awaken, humans of the red rod:

"I have just awakened, but my mind is still benumbed. Each morning I feel a heaviness in my head. Rarely do I find rest at night for I am tormented by frightful dreams when I succeed in falling asleep. By day my mind wearies itself with weird meditations while my eyes wander at random through space. And at night I cannot sleep.

When, then, should I sleep? For Nature must claim her rights. Inasmuch as I scorn her she makes my face pale and my eyes burn with the bitter flame of fever. As for myself I should ask nothing more than surcease from the continual draining of my mind in meditation. But even when I struggle against it my dismayed senses constrain me invincibly towards it. I discovered that other children are like me; but they are even paler and their brows are lowered like those of our older brothers, men.

"O Creator of the Universe, I shall not fail to offer you this morning the incense of my childish prayers. Sometimes I forget it and I have noticed that on such days I have felt happier than usual. My breast swells free of all constraint and I breathe more easily the spiced air of the fields. While when I perform the wearisome duty commanded by my parents of addressing you daily with a canticle of praises accompanied by the inseparable boredom that the task of inventing them causes me, then I am sad and irritable the rest of the day because it seems to me illogical and unnatural to say what I do not think and I seek to retreat into the vast solitudes. If I ask them to explain the reason for this strange condition of my soul, they make no reply.

"I want to love you and worship you but you are too powerful and there is fear in my praises. If you can destroy or create worlds by a mere manifestation of thought, my feeble prayers could serve you no useful purpose. If when it pleases you, you can send cholera to ravage cities, or death to bear away in his talons without distinction the four ages of life, I wish to form no alliance with a friend so formidable.

"Not that hatred directs the thread of my argument; but on the contrary I fear your known hatred which, by a capricious command, may emerge from your heart and become vast as the wings of the Andean condor. Your questionable amusements are not within my scope and I should probably be their first victim. You are the Omnipotent. I do not contest that title since you alone have the right to bear it, and since your desires with their consequences disastrous or auspicious have no limit except with yourself. And this is precisely why it would be painful to me to walk beside you in your cruel garment of sapphire, not as your slave, but liable to become so from one minute to another.

"It is true that whenever you search within yourself to examine your royal conduct, if a phantom of a past injustice committed against that unhappy humanity that has always obeyed you as your most faithful friend erects before you the motionless vertebrae of a vengeful spine, your haggard eyes let fall an appalled tear of belated remorse and as your hair rises up on your scalp you utter a resolution, that you believe to be sincere, to lay aside forever among the brambles of nothingness the inconceivable sport of your tiger's imagination, which would be laughable if it were not lamentable. But I know too that constancy has not planted the harpoon of its eternal permanence in your bones like a tenacious marrow, and that you fall again often enough, you and your thoughts both covered with the black leprosy of error, into the funereal lake of gloomy curses. I would like to believe that these latter are unconscious (though even so they would be no less envenomed) and that good and evil, united, issue forth impetuously from your royal and gangrenous bosom like a waterfall from a rock by the secret spell of a blind force. But nothing offers me proof of this.

"I have seen too often your filthy teeth snap with rage and your august countenance, covered with the fungus of time, blush like a flaming coal because of some microscopic futility that man had committed, to be able to pause longer before the signpost of that silly hypothesis.

"Daily with joined hands I send up to you the accents of my humble prayer, because I must. But I implore you that your Providence pay no attention to me; cast me aside like a grub groveling in the soil. Know that I should prefer to nurture myself greedily upon the marine growths of wild unknown islands, borne by tropical waves within their foamy bosoms, than to know that you are observing me and that you insert into my consciousness your grinning scalpel. It has just now revealed to you all my thoughts and I hope that your prudence applauds the good sense of which they retain the ineradicable imprint.

"Apart from these reservations placed upon the kind of relationship more or less intimate that I should maintain with you, my mouth is ready at no matter what hour of the day to exhale like an artificial gale the flood of lies exacted strictly from each human by your vainglory from the moment that the bluish dawn arises seeking light in the satin folds of the twilight, even as I, excited by the love of virtue, seek the good. My years are few, yet I feel already that virtue is nothing but a collection of sonorous verbiage. I have found it nowhere. You leave your character too open; you should conceal it with more skill. Yet perchance I am mistaken and you do this on purpose, for you know better than others how to conduct your own behavior. Men find their glory in imitating you; for this reason sacred virtue does not recognize her temple in their wild eyes: like father, like son. Whatever one may think of your intelligence, I speak only as an impartial critic. I ask no better than to have been led into error. I do not wish to show you the hatred I bear towards you, a hatred I gloat over lovingly like a cherished daughter. For it is better to hide it from your eyes and to take upon myself before you only the aspect of a strict censor charged with the control of your impure actions. You will thus sever all active commerce with it, you will forget it, and you will destroy completely that ravenous flea gnawing at

your liver. I would rather have you listen to words
of reverie and sweetness. . . .

"Yes, it is you who created the world and all in
it. You are perfect. You lack no virtue. You are
most powerful, everyone knows. Let the entire
universe intone hourly your everlasting hymn!
The birds bless you as they wing their way
through the country. The stars belong to you. . . .
So be it!"

After such beginnings does it surprise you to
find me what I am?

the ineffable

I sought a soul that might resemble mine and
I could not find it. I rummaged in all the corners
of the earth: my perseverance was useless. Yet I
could not remain alone. There must be someone
who approved of my character; there must be
someone who had the same ideas as myself.

It was morning. The sun rose in his magnificence
at the horizon and behold! a young man also
appeared at whose presence flowers sprang up in
his path. He approached me and held out his hand:
"I have come to you because you sought me. Let
us bless this happy hour." But I replied: "Go! I
did not call you. I have no need of your friend-
ship."

It was evening. Night was beginning to spread
the blackness of her veil over nature. A beautiful

woman whom I was barely able to perceive also exerted over me her bewitching influence and gazed upon me with compassion, not daring to speak. I said: "Come closer that I may distinguish clearly the outlines of your face, for the starlight is not strong enough at that distance." Then, with a modest bearing, she drew nearer to me over the greensward. As soon as I had seen her I exclaimed: "I perceive that goodness and justice dwell in your heart. We could not live together. Now you are admiring my beauty, which has distracted more than one woman. But sooner or later you would regret having consecrated your love to me, for you do not know my soul. Not that I would ever be unfaithful to you: she who delivers herself to me with so much abandon and confidence, with the same confidence and abandon I give myself to her. But remember this and never forget it: wolves and lambs do not look upon one another with friendly eyes."

What then did I desire, I who rejected with such disgust all that was most beautiful in humanity! I know not. I was not yet accustomed rigorously to take stock of the phenomena of my mind by means of the methods recommended by philosophy.

I sat down upon a rock by the sea. A ship had just set out from the shore at full sail, when an imperceptible dot appeared on the horizon and came nearer and nearer, growing rapidly, hurled forward by the squall. The storm was about to open its attack and already the heavens were overcast with a blackness almost as hideous as the heart of man.

The vessel, which was a great warship, dropped all her anchors in order to avoid being swept on to the rocky coast. The wind blew furiously from every point of the compass, tearing the ship's sails into ribbons. Thunder crashed and lightning glared but could not muffle the sound of lamentations arising from the foundationless house, now a floating sepulchre. The surging masses of water had not succeeded in breaking the anchor chains, but they had opened a way into the sides of the vessel. It was an enormous breach, for the pumps were impotent to impede the masses of salt water that broke foaming over the bridge like mountains.

The distressed ship fired off her alarm guns but slowly and with majesty she foundered.

Whoever has not witnessed the foundering of a ship in the midst of a hurricane while the brilliance of lightning alternates with the most profound darkness and the souls on board are overcome with that despair you know so well, knows nothing of the tragedy of life. Finally a great universal shriek of agony escapes from within the vessel, while the sea redoubles its terrible attacks. Human strength giving itself up has inspired that cry. Each man enfolds himself in the garment of resignation and commits his soul into the hands of God. They huddle together like a flock of sheep.

The distressed ship fires off her alarm guns but slowly and with majesty she founders.

[*105*]

Maldoror

All day they have toiled at the pumps. Useless effort. The dense implacable night has fallen to put the finishing touch to this gracious spectacle. Each man tells himself that once he is in the water he will be no longer able to breathe; for, no matter how far back he may search his memory, he does not recollect any fish among his ancestors. But he urges himself to hold his breath as long as possible in order to prolong his life by two or three seconds: this is the vengeful irony he would offer death.

The distressed ship fires off her alarm guns but slowly and with majesty she founders.

He does not know that the ship as she sinks causes a powerful circumvolution of billows; that muddy ooze mingles with the troubled waters, and that a force rising from below — counter-effect of the tempest that rages above — stirs the element into choppy and violent activity. Thus despite the provision of self-control that he musters before-hand, the man about to be drowned, after more mature consideration, should be happy if he prolong his life amid the whirlpools of the watery gulf by as much as half an ordinary breath, in order to give good measure. It would be impossible for him to achieve his supreme desire and flout death.

The distressed ship fires off her alarm guns but slowly and with majesty she founders.

An error. She fires off no more alarm guns, she is not foundering. The cockleshell has been completely swallowed up. O heaven! How may I live after having reveled in such voluptuousness! It has been given to me to witness the death-agonies of several of my fellow men! Minute by minute I followed the vicissitudes of their anguish. Now it would be the bellowing of some old woman driven mad by fear; now the solitary whimpering of a suckling infant would drown out the voice of the ship's command. The ship was too far off for me to distinguish clearly the cries borne upon the gale, but I drew nearer by an effort of will and the optical illusion was complete. Every fifteen minutes, when a gust of wind stronger than the others raised its sad moan amidst the cries of the terrified petrels, split the vessel lengthwise and increased the outcries of those about to be offered in a holocaust to death, I jabbed a pointed iron into my cheek, secretly thinking: "They suffer more!" At least I had thus a basis for comparison.

From the shore I apostrophized them and flung curses and threats at them. It seemed to me that they must have heard me! It seemed to me that my hate and my words, covering the distance, violating the laws of acoustics, must have arrived distinctly to their ears already deafened by the roar of the enraged sea! It seemed to me that they must have thought of me and breathed forth their vengeance in impotent rage.

From time to time I cast my eyes towards the cities, sleeping upon the solid earth; and seeing that no one suspected a ship was foundering a few miles from the shore with a crown of birds of prey and a pedestal of aquatic giants with empty bellies,

I took courage and hope returned to me. I was certain that the ship would be lost! They could not escape! In an excess of precaution I had gone to obtain my double-barreled pistol in order that with one bullet in the shoulder to break his arm I could prevent any drowning man from climbing up the rocks and saving himself from imminent death.

At the most furious moment of the tempest I saw a forceful head with hair on end swimming through the waters with desperate efforts. He swallowed liters of water, tossing about like a cork, and disappeared beneath the surface. But soon he reappeared, hair streaming, and fixing his eye upon the shore seemed to defy death. His calm was admirable. A gaping, bloody wound, caused by a sharp projection from some hidden reef, gashed his intrepid and noble countenance. He could not have been more than sixteen years old; for faintly, by the flashes of lightning that illumined the night, I could perceive the peach-bloom on his upper lip. And now he was only a few hundred yards from the cliff and I could see him clearly. What courage! What indomitable spirit! How the steadiness of his head seemed to flout destiny as it clove vigorously through the waves that parted reluctantly before him. I had made up my mind in advance. I owed it to myself to keep my promise: the last hour had sounded for all, none should escape. That was my resolution, nothing should change it. A sharp detonation was heard and the head disappeared forever.

I did not relish this murder as much as one might think. And it was precisely because I was sated with perpetual killing that thenceforward I did it simply from a habit impossible to relinquish but yielding only the slightest pleasure. The feeling was blunted, hardened. What pleasure could I feel at the death of that one human being when there were more than a hundred about to offer me the spectacle of their last struggles against the waves, once the ship had sunk? With this one death I had not even the thrill of danger, for human justice, cradled by the hurricane of that frightful night, slumbered in houses a few steps away.

Today when the years weigh heavily upon me I make this statement sincerely, as a supreme and solemn truth: I was not as cruel as men afterwards related; but sometimes their own wickedness wreaks its ravages for years on end. So I recognized no further limits to my fury. I was seized with an access of cruelty and I became terrible to any being who fell within range of my haggard eyes, as long as he belonged to my own race. Were it a horse or a dog I let it go free: did you hear what I just said? Unhappily, on the night of that storm I was in the grip of one of those rages and my reason had flown (for ordinarily I was just as cruel but more cautious); and everything that fell at that time into my hands, perished. I make no pretence of excusing myself for my misdeeds. The fault lies not entirely with my fellow men. I simply state the facts as I await the last judgment, scratching the nape of my neck in anticipation. What care I for the last judgment! My reason never deserts me, as I said a moment ago to confuse you. And when I commit a crime I know what I am doing. I would not act in any other manner!

Standing upon the rock while the hurricane lashed my hair and my cloak, I watched with ecstacy the power of the storm furiously attacking the ship beneath a starless sky. I followed triumphantly all the vicissitudes of the drama, from the moment when the vessel dropped her anchors until the moment when it was swallowed up in that fatal garment that dragged those who were clothed in it as in a cloak down into the entrails of the sea. But the moment was approaching when I myself was to be involved as an actor in these scenes of disrupted nature.

When the spot where the vessel had striven showed clearly that she had gone to spend the rest of her days at the bottom of the sea, many of those who had been swept overboard began to reappear on the surface. They clutched at one another in two's and three's, not saving their lives by this move for they impeded one another's movements and sank like leaky pitchers.

What is this army of marine monsters cutting swiftly through the waves? There are six of them. Their fins are vigorous and open up a passage through the heaving seas. Of all these human beings who stir their four limbs in that shifting continent the sharks rapidly make one eggless omelet, which they share among themselves according to the law of the strongest. Blood mingles with the waters and the waters mingle with blood. Their savage eyes adequately illumine the scene of carnage.

But what is this further disturbance in the waters, yonder, on the horizon? It looks like an approaching waterspout. What powerful strokes! I realize what it is. An enormous female shark is coming to take part in the duck-liver pasty and to eat cold boiled beef. She is furious for she arrives ravenous. A battle takes place between her and the other sharks over the few palpitating limbs floating here and there, saying nothing, on the surface of that crimson cream. To left and to right she slashes with her teeth, dealing mortal wounds. But three living sharks surround her still and she is forced to twist in every direction to outwit their maneuvers.

With a mounting emotion hitherto unknown to him the spectator on the shore follows this new kind of naval engagement. His eyes are fixed upon that brave female shark with her deadly teeth. He hesitates no longer, brings his gun to his shoulder, and, with his usual skill, lodges his second bullet in the gill of one of the sharks as it shows itself for a moment above the waves. Two sharks are left, their fury redoubled. From the summit of the rock the man with the brackish saliva throws himself into the sea and swims toward the pleasantly-colored canvas, gripping in his hand that steel knife that never leaves him. From now on each shark has an enemy to deal with. He advances upon his weary adversary, and, taking his time, buries his sharp blade into its belly. The moving fortress disposes easily of the last enemy.

The swimmer and the female shark rescued by him find themselves together. For a while they look at one another eye to eye; and each is astonished to find so much ferocity in the aspect of the other. They swim around in circles, neither losing sight of the other, and each murmurs to himself: "Hitherto I have been mistaken: here is someone more evil than I." Then with common consent they glide toward one another, with a mutual admiration, the female shark parting the waters with her fins, Maldoror beating the waves with his arms; and they hold their breaths, each desirous of contemplating for the first time his living portrait. Arriving within three yards of each other, effortlessly, suddenly they come together like two magnets and kiss with dignity and gratitude in an embrace as tender as that of a brother or a sister.

Carnal desire soon follows this demonstration of friendship. Two sinewy thighs clasp tightly about the viscous skin of the monster like two leeches; and arms and fins interlace about the body of the adored object which they surround with love, while their throats and breasts soon fuse into one glaucous mass exhaling the odors of seawrack.

In the midst of the tempest that continues to

[*112*]

rage, illumined by its lightnings and having for a
nuptial couch the foamy waves, borne upon an
undertow as in a cradle, and rolling upon one
another towards the depths of the ocean's abyss,
they join together in a long, chaste and hideous
coupling!

At last I had found someone who resembled me!
Henceforth I should not be alone in life! She had
the same ideas as I! I was face to face with my first
love!

The Seine is bearing away a human body. In
these circumstances she takes on a solemn aspect.
The swollen corpse floats on the waters; it dis-
appears beneath the arch of a bridge; but farther
on it appears again, turning slowly upon itself
like a millwheel and sinking at intervals. With the
aid of a pole a boatman drags it to the shore. Before
taking it to the morgue they leave it for a while on
the bank in an attempt to bring it back to life. A
crowd assembles around the body. Those who can-
not see because they are behind jostle as much as
they can those who are in front. Each one says:
"I should not have drowned myself." They pity
the young suicide, they admire him, but they do
not imitate him. Yet he found it very natural to
give himself to death, having decided that nothing
on earth could please him and aspiring to higher

things. His face is distinguished, his clothes are expensive. Is he seventeen years old? That is young to die!

The paralysed crowd continues to cast their fixed eyes upon him. Night is falling. Everyone retires silently. No one dares to turn over the drowned man in order to empty him of the water that fills his belly. They fear to appear too sensitive, and no one moves, each with his head buried in his shirt collar. One goes off, shrilly whistling an absurd Tyrolean tune; another cracks his finger-joints like castanets.

Harassed by his gloomy thoughts, Maldoror passes by on his horse with the speed of light. He sees the drowned man: it is enough. Immediately he pulls up his horse and descends from the saddle. He raises up the young man without disgust and makes him throw up a quantity of water. At the thought that this inert corpse might revive beneath his hands, he feels his heart beat faster and his courage redoubles. Vain effort! Vain effort, I said, and it is true. The cadaver remains inert and lets itself be turned every. which way. Maldoror chafes its temples; he massages this limb and that limb; for an hour he breathes into the unknown's mouth, pressing his lips against the other's. At last he seems to feel beneath the hand that he has placed upon the youth's breast a faint beating. The drowned man is alive!

At that supreme moment one could have noticed that several furrows disappeared from the horseman's brow, removing ten years from his age. But alas! the furrows will return, perhaps tomorrow, perhaps as soon as he has departed from the banks of the Seine.

Meanwhile the drowned man opens lustreless eyes and thanks his rescuer with a wan smile. But he is still weak and can make no movement.

What a fine thing it is to save someone's life! And how that act atones for sins!

The man with the lips of bronze, until then engrossed in snatching him back from death, looks at the youth more narrowly, and the features appear to be not unknown to him. He tells himself that between this asphyxiated man with the fair hair, and Holzer, there is very little difference. See how they embrace effusively! But it matters little. The man with the jasper eyes adheres to keeping up his appearance of severity. Saying nothing he lifts up his friend, sets him behind on the saddle, and the courser gallops off.

O Holzer, you who believed yourself to be so reasonable and so strong, have you not seen by your own example how hard it is during an access of despair to preserve the sang-froid of which you brag? I hope you will never again cause me another such sorrow; and I for my part promise you never to attempt my life.

There are certain hours in the life of lousy-

haired man when he fixes his staring eyes upon
the green membranes of space; for he seems to
hear before him the ironic mockery of a phantom.
He staggers and bends his head: what he hears
is the voice of his conscience. Then he rushes from
the house with the speed of a madman and tears
through the rugged plains of the countryside. But
the yellow phantom does not lose sight of him and
pursues him with an equal speed.

Sometimes on a stormy night while legions of
winged octopi, in the distance resembling crows,
hover above the clouds and fly stiffly towards the
cities of men on a mission to warn them to alter
their conduct, the gloomy-eyed pebble sees two
beings pass by beneath the flashes of lightning,
one behind the other; and, wiping away a furtive
tear of compassion flowing from his frozen eye
he cries out: "Certainly he deserves this; it is
only justice." Having spoken thus he resumes his
ferocious attitude and continues to watch the
man-hunt, trembling nervously, and the wide lips
of the vagina of darkness whence flow unceasing-
ly like a river immense shadowy spermatozoa
which take flight into the lugubrious ether con-
cealing, with the vast manipulation of their bat's
wings, the whole of nature and the solitary legions
of octopi, grown dejected at the aspect of these
obscure and inexplicable fulgurations.

But meanwhile the steeplechase continues be-
tween the two indefatigable runners, and the phan-
tom belches forth torrents of flame upon the

scorched back of the human antelope. If during the accomplishment of this duty he meets Pity trying to block his path, he accedes with repugnance to her pleas and lets the man escape. The phantom clicks his tongue as if to tell himself that he is about to give up the pursuit and retires to his kennel to await further orders. His voice, the voice of the damned, reaches to the uttermost limits of space; and when his appalling cries penetrate the heart of man, the latter would rather have, they say, death for his mother than remorse for his son. He buries his head up to the shoulders in the earthy complications of a hole; but conscience dissipates this ostrich's trick. The excavation evaporates like a drop of ether; light appears with its train of rays like a flock of curlews descending upon lavender bushes and the man finds that he is again confronting himself with ghastly, staring eyes.

I have seen him making for the seashore, climbing a jagged sea-begirt promontory, and precipitating himself like an arrow into the waves. Now comes the miracle: the cadaver reappears the next day floating on the surface of the ocean which bears the fragment of flesh back to the shore. The man releases himself from the mould hollowed out by his body in the sand, squeezes the water out of his dripping hair, and resumes the journey of life, his head muted and bowed.

Conscience judges our thoughts and our most secret actions severely and makes no mistakes. As she is often incapable of preventing evil, she persists in trailing man like a fox, especially after dark. From her vengeful eyes, that ignorant science calls *meteors*, livid flames are diffused, re-volve upon one another, and articulate mysterious words. . . . that he understands! Then his bed is crushed beneath the tremors of his body, over-whelmed by the weight of insomnia, and he hears the sinister breathing of vague night noises. The angel of sleep himself, mortally wounded in the brow by a mysterious stone, abandons his task and returns to heaven.

Very well, this time I present myself to defend Man; I, the scorner of all the virtues; I, who have not been able to forget the Creator since the glori-ous day when, upsetting the stand upon which rested the annals of heaven whereby I know not what infamous chicanery were consigned *His* power and *His* eternity, I applied my four hundred suckers to his armpits, making him cry out horribly. The cries changed into serpents as they left his mouth and went to lie in ambush in the brushwood and in ruined walls by day and by night. Those cries now cringe and writhe in count-less coils with small flat heads and treacherous eyes; and they have sworn to lie in wait for human inno-cence; and when innocence goes walking in the tangled woodlands or over the hills or among the sand dunes, she soon changes her ideas. If, that is, there be still time; for sometimes man becomes aware of the poison introduced into the veins of his leg through an almost imperceptible bite before he has had time to retrace his steps and take to his heels. It is thus that the Creator, preserving an admirable sangfroid even in the face of the most atrocious sufferings is able to extract harmful germs from the bosoms of earth's inhabitants.

How astounded he was when he saw Maldoror, changed into an octopus, bear down upon his body with eight enormous arms any one of which solid lashes could easily have reached around the circumference of a planet! Taken unawares he struggled for a few moments against that viscous embrace, which contracted and contracted. . . .

I feared some dirty trick on his part. After having abundantly nourished myself upon the globules of that holy blood, I detached myself abruptly from his majestic body and hid myself in a cave, which subsequently became my home. Here, after a fruitless search, he could not find me. This was all long ago; but I think he knows where I am now. He avoids my place and we both live like two neighboring monarchs who are aware of one another's respective powers, cannot overcome one another, and are weary of the useless battles of the past. He fears me and I fear him. Each, while unconquered, has sustained some severe injuries from his adversary, and we let it go at that. However, I am ready to resume the struggle whenever he so desires. But he had better not await some favorable moment for his secret plans. I shall always be on the look-out and keeping my eye on him. Let him never again inflict the earth with

conscience and its tortures. I have taught mankind
what weapons they may use to combat it advan-
tageously. They are not as yet familiar with it,
but you know that as far as I am concerned it is
no more than a straw driven by the wind. That is
as much as I make of it. If I wished to profit by the
occasion that presents itself here of elaborating
these poetic discussions, I might add that I would
attach more importance to the straw than to con-
science; for straw is useful to the cow chewing
her cud, while conscience knows nothing beyond
showing her steel talons.

These claws sustained a severe setback the day
they came up against me. As conscience was sent
by the Creator I thought it proper not to permit my
passage to be obstructed by it. If it had approached
me with the modesty and humility proper to its
rank, and from which it should never have de-
parted, I would have listened to it. I did not like
its pride. I held out my hand and crushed the talons
between my fingers. They fell into dust beneath
the increasing pressure of this new kind of mortar.
I stretched out my other hand and tore off its head.
Then I chased that female conscience out of my
house at the end of a whip and I have not seen
her since. I kept her head as a souvenir of my
victory. . . .

With a head in my hand, gnawing the skull, I
stood on one foot like a heron at the edge of a
precipice slashed into the flanks of a mountain.
I was seen descending into the valley while the

flesh of my bosom was still and calm as the lid of a tomb!

With a head in my hand, gnawing the skull, I swam down to the most dangerous depths of the ocean, among deadly reefs, and plunged deeper than the currents to assist like a foreigner at the battles between marine monsters. I swam from the shore farther than my piercing gaze could see, and hideous stingrays with their paralysing magnetism prowled around my limbs as they cut through the waves with robust movements, not daring to approach me. I was seen to return safe and sound to the beach, and the flesh of my bosom was still and calm as the lid of a tomb!

With a head in my hand, gnawing the skull, I climbed the steps of a high tower. Weary-limbed, I reached the dizzy summit. I gazed upon the countryside and the sea; I gazed upon the sun and the firmament; thrusting with my foot at the granite, which remained immovable, I defied death and divine punishment with a supreme howl and flung myself like a paving-stone into the jaws of space. Men heard the painful and reverberating crash that resulted from the encounter of the earth with the head of conscience, which I had dropped in my flight. I was seen to descend with the leisure of a bird, borne upon an invisible cloud, and pick up the head in order to force it to be witness of a triple crime that I was to commit that same day, while the flesh of my bosom was still and calm as the lid of a tomb!

Maldoror

With a head in my hand, gnawing the skull, I betook myself to the place where stand the posts that support the guillotine. I placed the smooth grace of the necks of three young girls beneath the blade. As executioner, I pulled the string with the apparent experience of an entire lifetime and the triangular steel, falling slantwise, sliced off three heads that regarded me meekly. Next I placed my own head beneath the heavy razor and the executioner prepared to accomplish his duty. Three times the blade descended between its grooves with a new vigor; three times my material body, especially at the base of the neck, was shaken to its foundations as when one dreams of being crushed by a falling building. The stupefied populace let me pass as I removed myself from that grisly spot. They saw me elbow my way through the undulating waves of the crowd, and bestir myself, full of life, head held erect, while the flesh of my bosom was still and calm as the lid of a tomb!

I did say that I would defend mankind this time. But I fear my apologia would not be the expression of truth, and consequently I prefer to be silent. Humanity will applaud this measure with gratitude!

It is time to apply the brakes to my inspiration and to pause for a while by the wayside, as when one looks upon the vagina of a woman. It is good to look back over the course already traveled, and then, the limbs rested, to rush on again with an impetuous bound. To accomplish a journey in one single breath is not easy, and the wings weary much during a high flight without hope and without remorse. No, let us lead no deeper into the explosive mines of this impious lay the haggard pack of swots and busybodies! The crocodile will not change one word of the vomit that issued from within his skull! Too bad if some furtive shadow, inspired with the praiseworthy ambition of revenging a humanity unjustly attacked by me, surreptitiously should open the door of my room, brushing against the wall like a sea-gull's wing, and plunge a dagger into the side of the plunderer of celestial flotsam and jetsam! Clay might as well dissolve its atoms in that manner as in another.

MALDOROR

3

LET us recall the names of those imaginary angel-
like beings whom my pen during the second lay
has drawn from a brain shining with a radiance
derived from those beings themselves. They are
still-born on the scorched paper like sparks the
rapid extinction of which the eye can hardly fol-
low. Leman! . . . Lohengrin! . . . Lombano! . . .
Holzer! . . . For an instant you appeared, cov-
ered with the insignia of youth, within my
enchanted horizon. But I let you fall back into
chaos like diving-bells. You will never return. It
is enough that I have retained the memory of you.
You must make room for other substances, less
beautiful perhaps, to which the stormy overflow
of a love that has resolved never to appease its
thirst with the human race will give birth. A raven-
ous love, that would devour itself if it did not seek
its nourishment in celestial fictions: creating, in
the long run, a pyramid of seraphim more numer-
ous than the insects that swarm in a drop of water,

it will interweave them into an ellipse that it will cause to revolve around itself. Meanwhile if the traveler, pausing before the appearance of a cataract, will raise his head he will see in the distance a human being borne towards the cavern of hell by a garland of living camellias! But . . . silence! The floating image of the fifth ideal traces itself slowly, like the blurred folds of an aurora borealis, upon the vaporous surface of my intelligence, and takes on a more and more precise consistency. . . .

Mario and I were riding along the beach. Our horses, necks outstretched, clove through the membranes of space and struck sparks from the pebbles on the beach. An icy blast struck us full in the face, penetrated our cloaks, and swept back our hair on our twin heads. The sea-gull tried in vain to warn us by his outcries and the agitation of his wings of the possible proximity of the storm, and cried out: "Where are they off to at that mad gallop?" We said nothing; plunged in meditation we let ourselves be carried away by that furious race. The fisherman, seeing us pass by swift as an albatross, and realizing that he was seeing before him the *two mysterious brothers* as we had been called because we were always together, hastened to cross himself and hide with his paralysed dog in the deep shadows of a rock.

The inhabitants of the coast had heard tell of many strange things concerning these two persons, who appeared on earth amid clouds during periods

of great disaster, when a frightful war threatened
to plant its harpoon in the breasts of two enemy
countries, or when cholera was preparing to
hurl out from its sling putrefaction and death
through entire cities. The oldest beachcombers
frowned gravely, affirming that the two phan-
toms, whose vast black wingspread every one had
noticed during hurricanes above the sandbanks
and reefs, were the evil genius of the land and the
genius of the sea, who promenade their majesty up
in the air during great natural revolutions, united
by an eternal friendship the rarity and glory of
which have given birth to the astonishment of
unlimited chains of generations.

It was said that, flying side by side like two
Andean condors, they loved to soar in concentric
circles amid the layers of atmosphere close to the
sun; that in these places they fed upon the pure
essence of light; but that they resigned themselves
only reluctantly to reversing the inclination of
their vertical flight towards the dismayed orbit
where the human globe turns deliriously, inhab-
ited by cruel spirits who massacre one another on
battlefields (when they are not killing one another
secretly in their cities with the dagger of hatred or
ambition) and who feed upon beings as full of life
as themselves and placed a few degrees lower in
the scale of existence.

Or again, when the pair firmly resolved, in order
to excite men to repentance by the verses of
prophecy, to swim in great strokes towards the

sidereal regions where the planet stirs in the midst of the dense exhalations of avarice, pride, curses and mockery, given off like pestilential vapors from the loathsome surface, seeming no larger than a ball and almost invisible because of the distance, they did not fail to find occasions on which they repented bitterly of their benevolence, misunderstood and spurned, and hid themselves in the depths of volcanoes to converse with the tenacious fire that boils in the vats of the central vaults, or at the bottom of the sea to rest their disillusioned eyes in the contemplation of the most ferocious monsters of the deep, which to them appeared as models of gentleness compared with the bastards of humanity.

When night fell with her propitious gloom they rushed from the porphyry-crested craters and from the subaqueous currents, and left well behind them the craggy chamber-pot where the constipated anus of the human cockatoo wriggles: left it so far behind that they could no longer distinguish the suspended silhouette of the filthy planet. Then, aggrieved by their fruitless attempt, the angel of the land and the angel of the sea kissed, weeping, amid the compassionate stars and under the eye of God! . . .

Mario and he who galloped at his side were not unaware of the vague and superstitious rumors that were recounted during their evening vigils by the fishermen whispering around the hearth behind closed doors and windows, while the night-wind, desirous of warming itself, making its plaint heard around the thatched cottage, shaking the frail walls that are surrounded at the base by fragments of crushed shells washed up by the dying ripples of the waves.

We did not speak. What do two hearts that love say to each other? Nothing. But our eyes expressed all. I warn him to wrap himself more closely in his cloak, and he points out to me that my horse goes too far ahead of his. Each takes as much interest in the life of the other as in his own life. We do not laugh. He tries to smile at me, but I perceive that his countenance bears the weight of terrible impressions engraved there by meditation, constantly inclined towards the sphynxes that lead astray, with oblique glances, the great anguish of mortal intelligence. Seeing that his attempt is useless he turns aside his gaze, gnaws his earthly chains with the saliva of rage and stares into the horizon that flees at our approach.

In my turn I try to remind him of his golden youth which asks nothing better than to parade like a queen through the palace of pleasures. But he notices that my words emerge from my shrunken mouth with difficulty, and that the years of my own springtime have passed, sad and glacial like an implacable dream that stalks over banquet tables and beds of satin where the pale priestess of love slumbers paid with the glitter of gold, the bitter pleasures of disenchantment, the pestilential furrows of age, the terrors of solitude, and the torches of pain. Seeing that my attempt is useless, I am not surprised I am unable to make him happy.

The Omnipotent appears before me armed with his instruments of torture, in the whole resplendent halo of his horror; I turn away my eyes and stare into the horizon that flees before our approach.

Our horses gallop along the coast as if they were fleeing from the human eye....

Mario is younger than I. The humidity of the weather and the salty foam that splashes up over us bring the contact of cold to his lips. I tell him: "Beware! . . . Beware! . . . Close your lips, press them together. Do you not see the sharp talons of cold-chap furrowing your skin with burning wounds?" He stares at me and replies with motions of his tongue: "Yes, I see them, those green claws. But I will not disturb the natural position of my mouth to repel them. Look, to see if I lie. Since it seems to be the will of Providence I shall conform to it. But its will could have been better." And I cry out: "I admire that noble vengeance!" I want to tear out my hair, but he forbids me with a severe glance and I obey him with respect.

It is growing late and the eagle is returning to its nest hollowed out in the anfractuosity of a rock. My brother says to me: "I am going to loan you my coat to shield you from the cold. I do not need it." I reply: "Woe unto you if you do as you say. I do not wish that another suffer in my place, especially you." He makes no reply, because I am right. But then I set out to console him because of the too impetuous tone of my words. . . .

Our horses gallop along the coast as if they were fleeing from the human eye. . . .

I raise up my head like the prow of a vessel thrown up by a huge wave and I say to him:

"Are you weeping? I ask you this, king of fogs and snows. I see no tears on your face, beautiful as the cactus-flower, and your eyes are dry as a river-bed; but I perceive in the depths of your eye a vat full of blood in which boils your innocence, stung in the neck by a large species of scorpion. A violent wind blows upon the fire that heats the cauldron and spreads gloomy flames even outside your sacred eye-socket. I brought my hair close to your rosy brow and I smelled a smell of burning because the hair had caught fire. Close your eyes, for if you do not your countenance, reduced to cinders like lava from a volcano, will fall in ashes into the hollow of my hand."

He turns towards me paying no heed to the reins he holds in his hand and contemplates me tenderly while slowly raising and lowering his lily-white eyelids like the rising and falling of the sea. He wants to reply to my audacious question and this is what he says:

"Pay no attention to me. Even as the river-mists climb along the hillsides and having arrived at the summit, melt into the atmosphere in the form of clouds; even so has your anxiety on my account insensibly increased without reasonable motive, and

forms over your imagination the deceptive outline
of a desolate mirage. I assure you that there is no
fire in my eyes, although I do have a feeling as if
my head were plunged into a helmet of blazing
coals. How do you suppose the flesh of my inno-
cence should be boiling in a vat, since I hear noth-
ing but the feeblest and most confused outcries,
that to me are nothing but the wailing of the wind
as it passes over our heads? It is impossible that a
scorpion should have taken up residence and fast-
ened its sharp pincers into the depths of my jagged
eye-socket. I think they are rather powerful tongs
that crush the optic nerve. However I am of your
opinion that the blood filling the vat was extracted
from my veins by an invisible executioner during
last night's sleep. I waited for you a long time, be-
loved son of the ocean; and my sleep-heavy arms
engaged in a vain combat with one who entered
the vestibule of my house. . . . Yes, I feel that my
soul is padlocked in my body and cannot free itself
to flee far from coasts beaten by the human sea and
be no longer witness to the livid pack of sorrows
that pursues the human izard without respite
across morasses and the abyss of vast despondency.
But I make no complaint. I received life like a
wound, and I have forbidden suicide to heal the
gash. I wish the Creator to contemplate this yawn-
ing crevice every hour of his eternity. This is the
punishment I inflict upon him. Our steeds slow
down the speed of their bronze feet; their bodies
tremble like a hunter surprised by a flock of

peccaries. They must not listen to what we are saying. By dint of attention their intelligences might increase and they would be able to understand us. Woe unto them! For they would suffer more! Indeed, think only of the wild boars of humanity: does not the degree of intelligence that separates them from other beings of the creation seem to have been accorded them only at the irremediable price of incalculable sufferings? Imitate my example and plunge your silver spurs into the flanks of your steed. . . ."

Our horses gallop along the coast as if they were fleeing the human eye.

See the madwoman as she passes by dancing and vaguely recalling something. Children pursue her with stones as if she were a blackbird. She brandishes a stick and makes as if to pursue them, then continues on her way. She left a shoe behind and does not notice it. Long spider's legs crawl at the nape of her neck: these are nothing but her hair. Her face resembles no human countenance and she bursts into shrieks of laughter like a hyena. She lets fall rags of phrases of which, if they were knit together, very few would have any clear significance. Her gown, torn in several places, flutters about her bony and filthy legs. She wanders on like a poplar leaf borne upon a whirlwind of unconscious associations, she, her youth, her illusions and her former happiness remembered now through the mists of a ruined mind. She has lost her pristine grace and beauty; her bearing is mean and her breath reeks of brandy.

If men were happy on this earth, there would be cause for astonishment. The madwoman makes no reproaches, she is too proud to complain and will die without having revealed her secret to those who interest themselves in her but whom she has forbidden ever to address a word to her.

Children pursue her with stones as if she were a blackbird.

She has dropped a roll of paper from her bosom. Someone picks it up, locks himself in his room all night, and reads the manuscript that follows:

After many sterile years Providence sent me a daughter. For three days I kneeled down in churches in unceasing gratitude to the great name of him who had at last fulfilled my hopes. I nourished her who was more than my life with my own milk. I saw her growing rapidly, endowed with all qualities of soul and body. She said to me: "I should like to have a little sister to play with. Ask God to send me one, and to reward him I will weave him a garland of violets, peppermint and geraniums." All the answer I made was to raise her to my breast and kiss her lovingly.

"She was already interested in animals and asked me why the swallow was content to brush the abodes of humans with his wings, not daring to en-

ter in. But I placed a finger on my lip as if to tell
her to be silent regarding this grave question, the
elements of which I did not want her to understand
as yet in order not to do violence to her childish
imagination by a strong feeling; and I hastened to
change the subject, one painful to discuss for any
being belonging to a race that has extended an un-
just domination over other animals of the creation.

"When she spoke to me of the tombs in the cem-
etery, telling me that she could breathe the pleas-
ant perfumes of cypress and everlasting-flower in
that atmosphere, I refrained from contradicting
her. But I told her that the cemetery was a bird-
town, that there the birds would sing from dawn
until twilight, and that the tombs were their nests
where they slept at night with their families, lift-
ing up the marble covers.

"I sewed all the dear little garments she wore, as
well as the laces with their thousand arabesques,
reserved for Sunday. In winter she had her special
place by the hearth; for she took herself very seri-
ously, and, during the summer the meadows knew
the gentle pressure of her footstep when she ven-
tured forth with her silken net fastened to the end
of a rush to catch the independent little humming-
birds and butterflies with their provoking zig-zags.
"What have you been up to, little vagabond, while
supper has been waiting an hour and your spoon
grows impatient?" But she would cry out, flinging
her arms about my neck, that she would never
roam again. Next day she would be off again,

through the daisies and mignonettes; amid the
sun's rays and the whirling flight of ephemeral
insects; knowing only the prismatic goblet of
life, and not yet the gall; happy in being larger
than a titmouse; laughing at the warbler for not
singing as well as the nightingale; slyly sticking out
her tongue at the rascally crow, who watched her
paternally; and graceful as a young cat.

"I was not to enjoy her presence for long. The
time was approaching when she should in an un-
foreseen manner bid farewell to the magic of life
and abandon forever the company of the turtle-
dove, the hazel-grouse and the green-finch, the
prattle of the tulip and the anemone, the advice of
the water-grasses, the keen spirit of frogs and the
freshness of streams. They told me what had hap-
pened, for I was not by when the event took place
that resulted in the death of my daughter. Had I
been there I should have defended that angel at the
price of my own blood. . . .

"Maldoror was passing by with his bulldog. He
saw a young girl sleeping in the shade of a plane
tree and at first he took her for a rose. . . . None
may say which idea rose first to his mind: whether
it was the appearance of that child or the resolution
in which this resulted. He undressed rapidly, like
a man with a purpose. Naked as a stone, he
threw himself upon the young girl's body and
lifted up her dress to commit an attack upon her
virtue . . . in the full light of the sun! No embar-
rassment for him! Let us not dwell upon this im-

pure act. His spirit dissatisfied, he hurried back into his clothes, glanced cautiously up and down the dusty deserted pathway, and ordered the bulldog to strangle the bloodstained child with the movement of its jaws. He pointed out to the mountain dog the spot where the suffering victim breathed and wailed, and retired into the background in order not to witness the entrance of those sharp teeth into the rosy veins.

"Carrying out that order appeared to be difficult for the bulldog. He thought his master had commanded him to do what had already been done, and this wolf with the monstrous muzzle contented himself with violating the virginity of that delicate child in his turn. From her lacerated stomach the blood ran again down her legs and upon the meadow. Her cries mingled with the animal's yelps. The child held up the golden cross that she wore about her neck that he might spare her; she had not dared to present it before the savage eyes of him who first conceived the idea of profiting by the weakness of her age. But the dog knew well that if he disobeyed his master a knife thrown from beneath a sleeve would abruptly open up his entrails without warning.

"Maldoror (how hateful to pronounce that name!) heard the agonies of pain and was amazed that the victim should be so tenacious of life and not yet dead. He approached the sacrificial altar and saw the conduct of his bulldog, abandoned to its lowest instincts and lifting up its head above the child as a drowning man raises his above the angry waves. He gave the dog a kick that split open one of its eyes. The maddened animal rushed off through the countryside dragging after him for a distance, that though short was still too long, the suspended body of the girl which was detached only by grace of the violent movements of the flight; but he was afraid to attack his master, who was not to see him again.

"Maldoror drew from his pocket an American knife with ten or a dozen blades serving various purposes. He opened up the angular paws of that steel hydra and, armed with this for a scalpel, seeing that the greensward had not yet disappeared beneath the stain of so much spilled blood, he hastened without changing color to rummage bravely within the vagina of the unhappy child. From that enlarged hole he removed successively the interior organs: the intestines, the lungs, the liver, and finally the heart were torn from their foundations and dragged out into the light of day through that awful opening. The sacrificer perceived that the girl, like a drawn chicken, had been long dead. He ceased the increasing perseverance of his ravages and left the cadaver to sleep again beneath the shade of the plane tree.

"The knife was found thrown away nearby. A shepherd, witness of the crime whose author was never discovered, told of it a long time afterwards when he felt sure the criminal had safely reached the frontier and he had no further fear of the certain revenge that would be his reward if he revealed what he had seen.

"I pitied the madman who perpetrated this heinous crime, unforeseen by the lawmakers and without precedent. I pitied him, for it is probable that he was not in his right mind when he wielded the multiple-bladed knife ploughing through the wall of the stomach from top to bottom. I pitied him because if he was not mad his shameful conduct should hatch out a great hatred against his fellows for so furiously attacking the flesh and arteries of an inoffensive child, who was my daughter. I assisted at the burial of those human fragments with mute resignation. And daily I go to pray over a grave."

At the conclusion of his reading the unknown finder of the manuscript could no longer keep his senses and fainted. When he came to he burned the manuscript. He had forgotten this memory of his youth (habit encrusts the memory); and after twenty years' absence he returned to that fatal country. He will not buy a bulldog! He will speak with no shepherds! He will not sleep in the shade of the plane trees! . . .

Children pursue her with stones as if she were a blackbird.

Tremdall has shaken for the last time the hand of him who is leaving voluntarily, forever fleeing, forever pursued by the image of mankind. The Wandering Jew says that if the earth's scepter were held by the crocodile he would not flee thus. Tremdall, standing above the valley, has raised one hand to his eyes to concentrate the solar rays and make his sight more piercing, while his other hand palpates the bosom of space, the arm horizontal and motionless. Leaning forward, a statue of friendship, he watches with eyes mysterious as the sea the high boots of the traveler climbing up the side of the hill, aided by his iron-feruled staff. The earth seems to crumble beneath Tremdall's feet, and even had he so desired he could not have restrained his tears and his feelings:

"He is far away. I see his silhouette mounting a narrow pathway. Where is he going with that heavy step? He does not even know himself. . . . Yet I am certain I am not sleeping. What is that approaching and going to meet Maldoror? How huge the dragon is . . . larger than an oak! You would say that his whitish wings, attached to him by tough ligaments, had nerves of steel so easily do they cleave the air. His body is that of a tiger with a long serpent's tail. I have not been accustomed to see such things. What is that upon his brow? I see a word written there in symbolic language, a word I cannot decipher. With a final sweep of his wings the dragon comes up to him the tone of whose voice I could plainly recognize, and utters these words:

" 'I was expecting you, and you me. The hour

has come; here I am. Read upon my brow my name written in hieroglyphic symbols.'

"But Maldoror has scarcely perceived the dragon before he has changed himself into an enormous eagle and now prepares for battle, clacking his curved beak contentedly as if to say that, single-handed, he would devour the dragon's hind end. See how they circle one another in ever-diminishing orbits, each judging the other's tactics, before they begin to fight. They are doing well. The dragon seems to me to be the stronger. I hope he gains the victory over the eagle. I shall suffer strong emotions in witnessing this spectacle in which a portion of my being is involved. Potent dragon, I will encourage you with my cries if necessary, because it is in the eagle's own interest that he should be crushed.

"What are they waiting for? I am in mortal terror. Come now, dragon, you begin the attack. You have just given him a sharp blow with your talons: that's not so bad. I assure you the eagle must have felt it; the beauty of his feathers, blood-stained, is carried off by the wind. Ah! The eagle tears out one of your eyes with his beak, and you have only torn his flesh. You should have prevented that. Bravo, get your revenge and break one of his wings! It goes without saying that your tiger's teeth are good. If only you could get near enough to the eagle while he circles in space and shoots down towards the ground! I notice this eagle inspires you with caution, even when he is falling.

He is on the ground, he cannot rise. The aspect of all those gaping wounds intoxicates me. Fly close to the ground around him and finish him off if you can with blows of your scaly serpent's tail. Courage, excellent dragon! Bury your strong talons in him and let blood mingle with blood to form a waterless stream. This is easy to say but not to do. The eagle has concocted a new strategic plan of defence, profiting by the unforeseen chances of this memorable battle. He is cautious. He is sitting down firmly in an unshakable position on his remaining wing, his two thighs and his tail that hitherto has served him as a rudder. He is ready to defy efforts more extraordinary than those he has met so far. Now he will twist and turn as swiftly as the tiger without any sign of fatigue; now he will lie down upon his back with his two powerful claws in the air and stare up at his enemy with cool irony. I must know in the end who will be the victor. The battle cannot last forever. I am thinking of the consequences that will result from it! The eagle is terrible and makes tremendous leaps that shake the earth, as if he were about to take flight, but he knows this is impossible. The dragon is suspicious: he thinks that at any moment the eagle will attack him on the side where he lacks an eye.... Alas for me! This is what happens. How did the dragon allow himself to be seized by the breast? Useless for him to employ cunning and force. I see that the eagle, clinging to him with all his limbs like a leech despite the fresh wounds he is receiving even at the root of the neck, is burying his beak deeper and deeper into the dragon's belly. Only his body can be seen. He seems to be quite at his ease and does not hurry to get out. Doubtless he is seeking something, while the tiger-headed dragon utters howls that awaken the forests. Now the eagle is withdrawing his head from that cavern. Eagle, how repulsive you are! You are redder than a lake of blood! Although you hold in your beak a palpitating heart you are so covered with wounds that you can scarcely stand up on your plumed claws, and you stagger, without opening your beak, near the dragon who is dying in frightful agony. The victory has been difficult. No matter — you gained it: one must at least report the truth. . . . In shedding your eagle's shape you act according to the laws of reason, as you put a distance between yourself and the dragon's body.

So, Maldoror, you have conquered! So, Maldoror, you have conquered *Hope*! Henceforth, with deliberate steps, you must enter upon a career of evil! In spite of the fact that I am, so to speak, indifferent to suffering, the last blow you gave the dragon has not failed to affect me. Judge for yourself whether I suffer! But you frighten me. See . . . see in the distance that man in full flight! Upon him, O excellent earth, curses have put forth their bristling foliage. He is accursed and he curses. Whither are you pointing your sandals? Where are you going, hesitating like a somnambulist on a roof? May your perverse destiny achieve itself!

Maldoror

Maldoror, farewell! Farewell until eternity, where you and I shall not find ourselves together!

🌿

It was a day in springtime. Birds were uttering their chirruping song and mankind, going about their various chores, were bathed in the sanctity of weariness. Everything was working towards its destiny: the trees, the plants, the sharks. All — except the Creator!

He was stretched out by the wayside, his clothing in ribbons. His lower lip hung down like a sleepy cable. His teeth were unbrushed and dust mingled with the flaxen waves of his hair. Stunned by a heavy drowsiness, crushed against the stones, his body was making useless efforts to get up. His strength failed him, and he lay there feeble as an earthworm, impassive as the bark of a tree. Streams of wine filled the ruts hollowed out by the nervous jerking of his shoulders. Swine-snouted sottishness covered him with protective wings and cast loving eyes upon him. His slack-muscled limbs groveled in the dust like blind masts. Blood flowed from his nostrils: as he fell he had struck his face against a post. . . . He was drunk! Horribly drunk! Drunk as a flea that has swallowed three barrels of blood during the night! He aroused the echoes with words that I will not repeat here. If the Supreme Drunkard does not respect himself I must respect mankind. Did you know that the Creator got drunk! Pity on that lip, befouled in the goblets of an orgy!

A passing hedgehog stuck its spines into his back and said: "That for you. The sun is half way through its orbit. Work, sluggard, and eat not the bread of others. Wait a while and you'll see what will happen if I should summon the cockatoo with his crooked beak."

A woodpecker and a screech-owl, passing by, buried their beaks in his belly, saying: "That for you. What are you doing here on earth? Did you come to offer this lugubrious farce to the animals? I assure you neither the mole nor the cassowary nor the flamingo will imitate you."

A passing ass gave him a kick in the temple, saying: "That for you. What did I ever do to you that you should have given me such long ears? All creatures down to the cricket scorn me."

A passing toad spat in his face, saying: "That for you. If you had not given me such a huge eye and had I seen you in the state you are in now, I would have chastely concealed the beauty of your limbs beneath a shower of buttercups, myosotis and camellias, in order that none should see you."

A passing lion inclined his royal visage, saying: "As for me I respect him, although his splendor appears to be momentarily eclipsed. You others, affecting haughtiness when actually you are nothing but cowards since you attacked him while he was sleeping, would you be happy in his place if

you were subjected to the insults of passers-by —
insults you have not spared him?"

A passing man stopped before the displaced
Creator and, amid the applause of the crab-louse
and the viper, defecated for three days upon that
august countenance. Woe unto mankind for that
insult! For he had no respect for an enemy laid
out in a mess of filth and blood and wine, defense-
less and almost inanimate! . . .

Eventually the sovereign God, awakened at last
by all these vicious insults, got himself up from the
ground as best he could and staggered over to a
large stone where he sat down, his arms pendant
like a consumptive's testicles. He looked around
him with glassy, lack-lustre eyes upon the whole of
nature, which belonged to him.

O mankind! You are wicked children; but I im-
plore you to spare that Great Being, who has not
yet slept off his disgusting liquor, and, not having
the strength to support himself erect, has fallen
heavily back on to the rock where he was sitting
like a wayfarer.

Notice that beggar passing by. He saw that the
dervish was holding out a skinny arm, and, without
knowing upon whom he was bestowing his char-
ity, he threw a piece of bread into that hand be-
seeching pity. The Creator acknowledged the gift
with an inclination of his head.

O, you will never know how difficult a thing it
becomes to be holding constantly the reins of the
universe! Sometimes the blood rushes to the head

as one strains to wrest a new comet from nothingness, with a new race of beings. The Intelligence, stirred to its very foundations, escapes like one overcome in battle, and may very well fall for once in life into the aberrations of which you have been a witness!

A red lantern, vice's ensign, suspended at the end of a rod swung its carcass beneath the whip of the four winds above a massive and worm-eaten doorway. A foul corridor, smelling of human thighs, gave on to a courtyard where cocks and hens, thinner than their own wings, scratched for food. In the wall that served as an enclosure for the courtyard divers openings had been frugally executed, each covered by a grating. The building was covered with moss. Doubtless at one time it had been a convent, but now it served as an abode for all those women who daily would exhibit the interior of their vaginas in exchange for a little money to any who would enter.

I was standing on a bridge with piers that were plunged in the muddy waters of a moat. From its height I contemplated the minutest architectural details of the interior of that age-toppling structure on the landscape. From time to time the grating of one of the openings would lift with a grinding sound as if by the upward impetus of a hand that violated the nature of the metal. A man's head would appear at the opening, then his shoulders upon which would fall fragments of dislodged plaster; then his body covered with cobwebs would follow. Laying his hands like a crown on the filth of every description with which the ground was encumbered while he extracted his legs from the interstices of the grating, he would straighten himself up to his natural posture and go to dip his hands in a broken-down tub, the soapy water of which had seen entire generations rise and fall. Then he would hurry away from those slums as quickly as possible to breathe the purer air of the city's center. After the client had departed a naked woman would struggle out in the same manner and make her way to the tub. Then the cocks and the hens would come running up in flocks from various parts of the courtyard, attracted by the seminal odor, knock her to the ground despite her struggles, trampling over her body as if it had been a dunghill, and peck at the flaccid lips of her swollen vagina until the blood came. The hens and the cocks, satiated, would return to scratch in the courtyard grass; the woman, now clean, would rise trembling to her feet covered with wounds, as when one awakens after a nightmare. She would let fall the rag she had brought with her to wipe her legs, having no further need of the communal tub, and return to her lair to await another job.

The sight of all this inspired me, too, with the desire to enter that house! I was about to descend from the bridge when I saw upon the entablature of a pillar the following inscription in Hebrew characters:

"You who pass over this bridge, go not yonder. There crime fraternises with vice. One day his friends awaited in vain a young man who crossed that fatal threshold."

Curiosity was stronger than fear. In a few moments I found myself standing before one of the openings, the grating of which was solidly barred. I tried to peer into the interior through that dense sieve. At first I could see nothing; but it was not long before I could distinguish the objects in the gloomy chamber, thanks to the fading light of the sun disappearing below the horizon.

The first and only thing I saw was a light-coloured rod composed of cones thrust into one another. This rod was moving about! It was walking round the room! Its violence was such that the floor shook beneath it. With its two ends it tore huge gashes in the walls, and resembled a battering-ram beating against the walls of a besieged city. Its efforts were useless for the walls were built of freestone. I saw this rod, when it struck against the wall, bend like a steel blade and bound back like an elastic ball. So it was not made of wood! Then I noticed it coiled and uncoiled with ease, like an eel. Although as tall as a man it did not hold itself erect. Sometimes it tried to do this and exhibited one of its ends at the grating. It bounded about impetuously, fell

again to the ground, and could not stave in the ob-
stacle. I examined it more and more narrowly and
finally I perceived that it was a hair! After another
violent struggle with the material that hemmed it
in like a prison, it laid itself down on a bed that was
in that room, its root resting on the sheets and its
pointed end against the bed's head. After a few
moments of silence broken by irregular sobs, the
hair spoke as follows:

"My master left me in this room. He does not
come to seek me. He rose from this bed where I am
lying and combed his perfumed hair, not dreaming
that I had already fallen to the ground. Yet if he
had gathered me up I would not have found that
simple act of justice in any way astonishing. He has
abandoned me in this confining room after having
been enfolded within the arms of a woman. And
what a woman! The sheets are still moist from their
lukewarm contact and in their disorder bear the
imprint of a night spent in love."

And I asked myself who his master could be!
And I applied my eye to the grating even more en-
thusiastically!

"While all of nature was wrapped in chaste
slumber he was coupling with a degraded female
in impure and lascivious embraces. He lowered
himself so far as to permit her withered and sapless
cheeks, despicable because of their habitual shame-
lessness, to approach his august countenance. He
did not blush, but I blushed for him. It is quite cer-
tain that he was happy to pass the night with this

fly-by-night bride. The woman, astounded by the majestic aspect of this guest, seemed to be enjoying incomparable sensations and covered him with frenzied kisses."

And I asked myself who his master could be! And I applied my eye even more enthusiastically to the grating!

"I, meanwhile, felt envenomed pustules increasing in numbers owing to the unaccustomed ardor of my master for the pleasures of the flesh, and surrounding my root with their mortal gall, absorbing with their suckers the generative substance of my life. The more my master and the woman abandoned themselves in their mad transports, the more I felt my strength decline. At the moment when fleshly desires attained the paroxysm of fury I became aware that my root was collapsing upon itself like a soldier wounded by a bullet. The torch of life was extinguished in me and I broke away from his illustrious head like a dead branch. I fell to the ground, without courage, without strength, without vitality, but with a feeling of deep pity for him to whom I belonged, with everlasting sorrow for his voluntary aberration!"

And I asked myself who his master could be! And I applied my eye to the grating even more enthusiastically!

"If at least he had taken to his soul the innocent bosom of a virgin. She would have been worthier of him and the degradation would have been less. He kissed with his lips that soiled brow, upon which men have trampled with dusty feet! He inhaled with shameless nostrils the emanations of those two moist armpits! I saw the skin of these contract in shame, while for their part the nostrils refused to accept that infamous respiration. But neither he nor she paid any attention to the solemn warnings of the armpits nor to the ghastly and dismal aversion of the nostrils. She raised her arms higher and he buried his face in their hollows. I was forced to be an accomplice of that profanation. I was forced to be a spectator of that unprecedented contortion, to assist at the unnatural alloy formed of those two beings whose diverse natures were separated by an immeasurable gulf."

And I asked myself who his master could be! And I applied my eye to the grating even more enthusiastically!

"When he was satiated with the odor of that woman he wanted to rip out her muscles one by one. But since she was a woman he spared her and preferred to inflict suffering upon a member of his own sex. He summoned from the neighboring cell a young man who had come to this house to spend a few carefree moments with one of these women, and commanded him to stand before him. I had been lying on the ground for a long time. Not having the strength to raise myself up on my burning root I could not see what they were doing. All I know is, the young man was hardly within arm's reach when ribbons of flesh began to fall from the foot of the bed and come to rest beside me. They whispered to me that they had been ripped from the youth's shoulders by my master's claws. The youth, at the end of several hours during which he had wrestled with a power greater than his own, arose from the bed and departed majestically. He was literally flayed alive from head to foot; along the stone floor he dragged his skin, turned inside out. He told himself that his own character was full of goodness, that he loved to believe that his fellow men also were good; that for this reason he had aquiesced to the distinguished stranger's request when he was summoned by him; but that never by any possible chance had he expected to be tortured by an executioner. "By such an executioner!" he added after a pause. Finally he made his way to the grating which, out of pity, split itself down to the level of the ground before that body denuded of epidermis. Without throwing away his skin, which might still be useful to him if only as a cloak, he attempted to leave this cutthroat den. Once he was outside the room I could not see whether he had the strength to reach the exit. O, how the cocks and the hens kept their distance, in respect, despite their hunger, from that long train of blood upon the saturated ground!"

And I asked myself who his master could be! And I applied my eye to the grating even more enthusiastically!

"Then he who should have paid more attention to his dignity and his justice raised himself up wearily on his elbow. Alone, gloomy, disgusted

and hideous! He resumed his clothing slowly.
Nuns, buried for centuries in the catacombs of the
convent, having been rudely awakened by the
sounds of that horrible night that reverberated in
a cell situated above the vaults, took each other by
the hand and came to form a funereal circle about
him. While he sought the ruins of his former
splendor, while he washed his hands with saliva
and dried them in his hair (it was better to wash
them with saliva than not to wash them at all after
an entire night spent in vice and crime), the nuns
intoned pitiful prayers for the dead, as when some-
one is lowered into the grave. And indeed the
young man could not have survived the tortures
inflicted upon him by a divine hand, and his agony
terminated during the chanting of the nuns . . ."

I remembered the inscription on the pillar, and
I understood what had happened to the pubescent
dreamer whose friends still awaited him every day
since the moment of his disappearance. . . . And I
asked myself who his master could be! And I ap-
plied my eye to the grating even more enthusias-
tically!

"The walls stood back to let him pass. The nuns,
seeing him take flight into the air with the wings
he had kept concealed beneath his emerald robe,
silently replaced themselves beneath the lids of the
tombs. He departed for his celestial abode, leaving
me here. That is not fair. The other hairs remained
on his head and I lie in this lugubrious room on a
floor covered with clotted blood and shreds of dry

meat. This room is accursed since he entered it. No one comes in here. Yet I am imprisoned. This is the end, then! Never again shall I see the angelic legions marching in dense phalanxes, nor the heavenly orbs wandering in the gardens of harmony. Very well, so be it. I shall know how to bear my sorrow with resignation. But I shall not fail to inform mankind of what took place in this cell. I shall give them permission to reject their dignity like a worn-out garment, since they have the example of my master. I shall advise them to suck the penis of crime, since *another* has already done it."

The hair fell silent. . . . And I asked myself who his master could be! And I applied my eye to the grating even more enthusiastically!

Forthwith a peal of thunder exploded and a phosphorescent glow pervaded the room. I drew back despite myself, thanks to I know not what warning instinct, and though I was withdrawn from the grating I heard another voice, this time fawning and soft for fear of being overheard:

"Stop leaping so! Silence! . . . Silence! . . . what if someone should hear you? I will replace you among the other hairs, but first let the sun sink below the horizon so that night may cover your retreat. I did not forget you. But someone might have seen you leave and I should have been compromised. O, if you only knew how I have suffered since that moment! When I returned to heaven my archangels surrounded me with curiosity. They would not ask me the reason for my absence. They who had never dared to contemplate me now endeavored to divine the enigma, casting stupefied glances upon my dejected visage, although they did not plumb the depths of the mystery, and whispered to one another thoughts in which was suspicion of some unaccustomed change in me. They wept silent tears; they felt vaguely that I was no longer the same, that I had become inferior to my identity. They would have liked to have known what disastrous resolution caused me to cross the frontiers of heaven and descend upon earth to taste of ephemeral pleasures which they themselves held in profound contempt. They observed upon my brow a drop of sperm and a drop of blood. The former had sprung from the courtesan's thighs! The latter had gushed from the martyr's veins! Hateful stigmata! Unremovable stains! My archangels found hanging on the thickets of space the flaming remnants of my opal tunic, floating there over the gaping peoples of the earth. They were not able to repair it, and my body remains naked before their innocence: memorable punishment for lost virtue. See the furrows that have traced a bed for themselves in my discolored cheeks: it is the drop of sperm and the drop of blood trickling slowly down my withered wrinkles. When they arrive at the upper lip they make a terrific effort and penetrate into the sanctuary of my mouth, attracted like a magnet by my irresistible gullet. They suffocate me, those two implacable drops. Hitherto I had believed myself to be the Omnipotent. But no, I must bow my head before Remorse who cries out to me: 'You are nothing but a miserable wretch!'

"Stop leaping so! Silence! . . . Silence! . . . What if someone should hear you? I will replace you among the other hairs, but first let the sun sink below the horizon so that night may cover your retreat. . . .

"I saw Satan, the great enemy, disentangle the bony structure of his body from his larval torpor and, up on his feet, triumphant, sublime, harangue his reassembled legions — and, as I well deserve, hold me up to derision. He said that he was much astonished that his haughty rival, caught *in flagrante delictu* by the success at last attained by perpetual espionage, could so far demean himself as to kiss the robes of human debauch after a long voyage through the hazards of the ether, and to cause the death of a member of humanity. He said that this young man, crushed in the toils of my refined tortures, might perhaps have become a genius and comforted mankind on earth with admirable songs of poetry, of courage, against the blows of misfortune. He said that the nuns of the convent-brothel had not been able to resume their slumber, that they wander about the courtyard gesticulating like automata, crushing the buttercups and lilacs beneath their feet; that they have become mad with indignation, but not mad enough to forget the cause of this disease in their brains. . . . (Here they come in their white shrouds; they do not speak together; they hold one another by the hand. Their hair falls in disorder upon their naked shoulders; bunches of black flowers droop upon their breasts. Nuns, return to your vaults; night has not yet quite descended; it is only the twilight. . . O hair! You see it yourself: I am assailed on all sides by the maddened sense of my depravity!) He said that the creator, who boasts of being the Providence of all that exists, conducted himself with a good deal of wantonness, not to say more, in offering such a spectacle to the starry worlds; for he affirmed his plan to report to the orbicular planets just how I maintain by my own example virtue and goodness in the vastness of my kingdoms. He said that the great esteem in which he had held so noble an enemy had fled from his imagination and that he would prefer to place his hand upon the breast of a young girl, though that would be an execrable act of wickedness, than to spit in my face covered as it is with a triple coat of blood and sperm mingled, in order not to contaminate his slobbering sputum. He said he believed himself justly to be superior to me, not by vice, but by virtue and modesty; not by crime, but by justice. He said that I ought to be tied to a hurdle because of my countless crimes; that I ought to be burned over a slow fire in a fiery brazier and thrown into the sea, if the sea would receive me. That, since I boasted of being just, I, who had condemned him to everlasting punishment for a trifling revolt that had had no serious consequences, I should then practice strict justice upon myself and judge impartially my iniquitous conscience. . . .

"Stop leaping so! Silence! . . . Silence! . . . What if someone heard you! I will replace you among the other hairs, but first let the sun sink below the horizon so that the night may cover your retreat."

He fell silent for a moment. Although I could not see him I understood from this necessary pause that a surge of emotion swelled his bosom as a whirlwind sweeps up a school of whales. Divine bosom, soiled one day by the bitter contact of the nipples of an unchaste woman! Royal soul delivered over in a moment of forgetfulness to the crab of debauch, the octopus of weakness of character, the shark of individual abjection, the boa of absent morality, and the monstrous snail of idiocy! The hair and its master embraced one another closely like two friends who meet after a long absence. The Creator continued in his role of accused appearing before his own tribunal:

"And mankind: what will they think of me, of whom they have so high an opinion, when they learn about the vagaries of my conduct, the hesitation of my footsteps, among these dirt-encrusted labyrinths of matter and the direction of my gloomy path through the stagnant waters and clammy rushes of the morass where, in the mists, shadow-footed-crime moans and blanches. I see I shall have to work hard for my rehabilitation in the future in order to reconquer their esteem. I am the

All-High; and yet, on one count, I remain inferior to men whom I created with a little sand! Tell them an audacious lie, tell them I never left heaven, that I have been constantly shut up with the cares of the throne, among the marbles and statues and mosaics of my palaces. I appeared before the heavenly sons of men and said to them: 'Drive evil out of your homes and let the cloak of virtue enter your abode. He who shall raise his hand against one of his fellows, inflicting a mortal wound in his breast with the homicidal steel, let him not expect the effects of my mercy and let him fear the scales of justice. He will go to hide his sadness in the woods, but the rustling of the leaves across the glades will sing the ballad of remorse in his ears and he will flee from that spot, stung in the hip by the briar, the holly and the blue thistle, his swift steps impeded by the suppleness of creepers and the sting of scorpions. He will make his way to the pebbly beach, but the rising tide with its spindrift and its dangerous approach will inform him that they are aware of his past; and he will precipitate his blind course towards the summit of a cliff, while the strident equinoctial winds, forcing themselves into the natural grottoes of the gulf and the quarries carved out of the echoing rock, will bellow like vast flocks of buffaloes of the pampas. The lighthouses of the coast will pursue him as far as the limits of the north with their sardonic beams, and the fireworks of the maremma, simple vapors in combustion, will make the hairs of his pores quiver and make green the irises of his eyes in their fantastic dances. May chastity thrive in your cottages and dwell in safety within the shadows of your fields. It is thus that your sons will become beautiful and obey their parents with gratitude; if not, sickly and stunted like parchment in a library, they will advance with great strides led by revolt against the day of their birth and the clitoris of their impure mother.' How may mankind obey these severe laws if the legislator himself is the first to break them? And my shame is as vast as eternity!"

I heard the hair forgive his master humbly for having confined him, since he had acted from caution rather than from thoughtlessness. And the last pale rays of the sun lighting my eyes retired from the mountain ravines. Turning towards him, I saw him fold himself up like a shroud. . . .

Stop leaping so! Silence! . . . Silence! . . . What if someone should hear you! He will replace you among the other hairs. And now that the sun has set on the horizon, crawl both of you, cynical, ancient and soft hair, out of this brothel, while the night, spreading her shadows over the convent, covers the retreat of your furtive footsteps across the plain. . . .

At that moment the louse, suddenly appearing from behind a promontory and stretching up its claws, said to me: "What do you think of that?" But I had no desire to answer him. I took my departure and made my way to the bridge. I effaced the original inscription and replaced it with this one:

"It is painful to retain like a dagger such a secret in the heart. But I swear never to reveal what I witnessed when I entered this terrible dungeon for the first time."

I threw the knife I had used to carve these letters over the parapet; and, making certain hasty reflections upon the childhood of the Creator, who, alas! would assuredly be inflicting suffering upon humanity for a long time to come (eternity is long), either by cruelties practised upon mankind or by the vile spectacle of the canker occasioned by great vice, I closed my eyes like a drunken man at the thought of having such a being for an enemy, and resumed my way sadly through the mazes of the streets.

MALDOROR

(LES CHANTS DE MALDOROR)

4

It is a man or a stone or a tree about to begin the
fourth canto. When your foot slips on a frog you
have a feeling of disgust; but when you lightly
stroke the human body the skin of your fingers
scales off like the laminations of a block of mica as
one fractures it with a hammer; and even as the
heart of a shark still palpitates with tenacious vital-
ity after it has been dead for an hour, so our en-
trails are still moved long after the contact. To
such an extent does man inspire his fellow man
with horror! Perhaps I am mistaken in advancing
this proposition; but perhaps also I am right. I
know of, I can conceive, a sickness more terrible
than the eyes swollen after long meditations upon
the strange character of mankind: but I am still
seeking it ... and I have not found it! I do not con-
sider myself less intelligent than another, yet who
would dare assert that I had succeeded in my inves-
tigations? What a lie would issue from his mouth!
The ancient temple of Denderah is located an

hour and a half's journey from the left bank of the Nile. Nowadays countless phalanxes of wasps have taken over its gutters and cornices. They swarm around the columns like the dense waves of a head of black hair. Solitary inhabitants of the chilly portal, they guard the entrance as a hereditary right. I compare the humming of their metallic wings with the incessant collisions of icebergs thrown against one another during the breaking up of the polar seas. But if I consider the conduct of him upon whom Providence has bestowed the throne of this earth, the three pinions of my sorrow give rise to a louder murmur!

When a comet appears suddenly in the heavens during the night after an absence of eighty years, it exhibits before the terrestrial inhabitants and the crickets its brilliant and vaporous tail. Doubtless it has no consciousness of its long journey. It is not thus with me: reclining on my bed, while the indentations of a dismal and arid horizon arise vigorously in the depths of my soul, I am absorbed in dreams of compassion and I blush for mankind!

Cut in two by the icy blast, the sailor, having finished his night watch, hastens to regain his hammock: why is this consolation denied me? The idea that I have voluntarily fallen as low as my fellow men and that I have less right than another to utter complaints concerning our lot, which remains chained to the hardened crust of a planet, and concerning our perverse soul, transfixes me like a horse-shoe nail.

You have seen explosions of fire-damp annihilate entire families; but their sufferings were brief because death was almost instantaneous amid the falling ruins and deleterious gases: I go on existing, like basalt! In the middle as in the beginning of life, angels resemble themselves: how long it has been since I ceased to resemble myself!

Mankind and I, confined within the limits of our intelligence, as often a lagoon is within a belt of coral islands, instead of uniting our strength to defend ourselves against bad luck and ill-fortune, we flee from one another, trembling with hatred, taking opposite directions, as if we had wounded one another with the points of daggers! You would say the one understands the contempt he inspires in the other; egged on by the incentive of a relative dignity we each take pains not to conduct our adversary into error; each stays on his own side and is aware that a peace proclaimed would be impossible to preserve. So be it! Let my war against mankind endure through eternity, since each recognizes in the other his own degradation . . . since the two are mortal enemies. Whether I gain a disastrous victory or whether I succumb, the battle will be good: I, alone, against humanity. I shall not employ weapons made of wood or iron; I shall kick aside the strata of minerals extracted from the earth: the powerful and seraphic sonority of the harp will become beneath my fingers a formidable talisman.

In more than one ambuscade, man, that sublime

ape, has already pierced my breast with his por-
phyry lance: a soldier does not exhibit his wounds
however glorious they may be. This terrible com-
bat will bring down much sorrow upon the heads
of the two parties: two friends striving obstinately
to destroy one another: what a drama!

Two columns that it was not difficult and yet
less possible to take for two baobab trees appeared
in the valley, larger than two pins. As a matter of
fact they were two enormous towers. And although
two baobab trees do not resemble at the first glance
two pins, or even two towers, nevertheless while
skilfully manipulating the strings of caution it may
be affirmed without fear of error (for if that affirm-
ation were to be accompanied by a single morsel of
fear it would not be an affirmation; although the
same name expresses these two phenomena of the
mind that present characteristics sufficiently clear-
cut that they are not easily confused) that a baobab
tree does differ so very much from a column that
the comparison should be forbidden between these
two architectural forms . . . or geometric forms . . .
or the one or the other . . . or neither the one nor
the other . . . or rather, massive and elevated forms.
I have just found, I make no pretense of maintain-
ing the contrary, the correct adjectives for the sub-
stantives column and baobab tree: let all men un-
derstand it is not without joy mingled with pride
that I make the remark to those who, having raised
their eyebrows, have made the most praiseworthy
resolution to con these pages while a candle burns

if it is at night, or while the sun shines if it is day-
time.

And again, should even a higher power com-
mand us in the clearest and most precise terms to
hurl into the abyss of chaos the judicious compari-
son that everyone has certainly been able to savor
with impunity, even then and especially then, let
none lose sight of this principal axiom, that the
habits contracted through the years, books, the
contact with his fellow men, and the character in-
herent in all who develop in a swift efflorescence,
would impose upon the human spirit the irrepar-
able stigma of a relapse into the criminal use (crim-
inal, by placing one's self momentarily and spon-
taneously at the point of view of the higher power)
of a rhetorical figure that many despise, but to
which many pay homage.

If the reader finds this sentence too long, will he
please accept my excuses; but let him expect from
me nothing mean. I can acknowledge my faults;
but not increase their gravity by my cowardice.

My arguments will sometimes come up against
the bells of folly and the serious appearance of
what in the final analysis is nothing but the gro-
tesque (although, according to certain philoso-
phers, it were somewhat difficult to distinguish be-
tween buffoonery and melancholy, life itself
being a comedy-drama or a drama-comedy); how-
ever it is permitted to us all to kill flies and even
rhinoceroses in order to rest from time to time from
too much tedious labor. To kill flies here is the

most expeditious manner, though not the best: you crush them between your two first fingers. Most writers who have gone deeply into this subject have calculated with a good deal of plausibility that it is preferable in many cases to cut off their heads.

If anyone reproach me for speaking of pins, as a radically frivolous subject, let him observe without coming to any foregone conclusions, that the greatest effects are often produced by the smallest causes. And, to avoid spilling any further over the edge of this piece of paper, do we not see that this laborious morsel of literature I have been composing since the commencement of this stanza would be perhaps less appreciated if it had taken as its basis some intricate question of chemistry or internal pathology? Besides, all tastes are in nature; and when at the beginning I compared columns to pins with so much accuracy (indeed I did not realise that anyone would some day reproach me with it), I based my observation upon the laws of optics which have established that the more the vision is separated from an object, the more the image diminishes upon the retina.

Thus it is that that which the inclination of our minds towards farce takes for a wretched piece of wit exists most of the time in the mind of its author as an important truth proclaimed with majesty! O, that inane philosopher who burst into peals of laughter when he saw a donkey eating a fig! I am inventing nothing: ancient books have related in the greatest detail this voluntary and shameful spoliation of human nobility. I do not know how to laugh. I have never been able to laugh, though I have tried many times. It is very difficult to learn how to laugh. Or rather I think a feeling of repugnance toward that monstrosity forms an essential distinction of my character. Very well then, I witnessed something even funnier: I saw a fig eating a donkey! And yet I did not laugh: frankly there was no movement of any buccal portion. The desire to weep seized upon me so strongly that my eyes let fall a tear. "Nature! Nature!" I cried, sobbing, "The sparrow-hawk rends the sparrow, the fig eats the donkey, and the tapeworm devours mankind!"

Without resolving to go any further, I ask myself whether I spoke of a way to kill flies. Yes, I did, didn't I? It is no less true that I did not speak of the destruction of the rhinoceros! If certain of my friends claim the contrary I shall not listen to them and I shall remind myself that praise and flattery are two great stumbling-blocks. However, in order to appease my conscience as much as possible I cannot prevent myself from remarking that this dissertation upon the rhinoceros would have carried me beyond the bounds of patience and composure, and, in itself probably (let us even have the hardihood to say certainly) would discourage present generations. Not to have spoken of the rhinoceros after the fly! At least for a passable excuse I should have mentioned promptly (and I did not do it) that unpremeditated omission, which will astonish no one who has delved deep into the contradictions real and inexplicable that inhabit the lobes of the human brain. Nothing is unworthy of a simple and dignified intelligence: the least phenomenon of nature, if it contain mystery, becomes for the sage inexhaustible material for reflection. If anyone sees a donkey eating a fig or a fig eating a donkey (these two events occur but rarely, unless it be in poetry), be sure that having reflected for two or three minutes in order to select his line of conduct, he will abandon the way of virtue and go to laughing like a cockerel!

Again, has it not been proven exactly that cockerels open their beaks on purpose to imitate mankind and make a tortured grimace? I call grimace among birds that which bears the same name among men. The cockerel does not depart from his natural characteristics, less from incapacity than from pride. Teach them to read and they revolt. They are no parrots to go into ecstacies before their ignorant or unpardonable weakness! O, execrable degradation! How like a goat one is when one laughs! The calm of the brow disappears to give place to two enormous fishes' eyes which (is it not deplorable?) . . . which . . . begin to blaze like lighthouses!

It frequently may happen to me that I should enunciate solemnly the most clownish propositions, but I do not find that this becomes a reason

peremptorily sufficient to enlarge the mouth! I
cannot help laughing, you will reply. I accept that
absurd explanation, but in that case make it a
melancholy laugh. Laugh, but weep at the same
time. If you cannot weep with your eyes, weep
with your mouth. If this is still impossible, urinate.
But I warn you that some kind of liquid is neces-
sary here to slake the dryness that cloven-featured
laughter bears in its flanks. As for me, I shall not
permit myself to be abashed by the impudent
clucking and original bellowing of those who
always find fault with a character not resembling
their own, because this is one of the countless in-
tellectual modifications that God, without aban-
doning a primordial type, created to control the
bony structures.

Hitherto poetry has followed the wrong road.
Raising itself up to heaven or groveling upon the
ground, it has misunderstood the principles of its
existence, and has been, not without reason, con-
stantly flouted by honest folks. It has not been
modest . . . the finest quality that can exist in an
imperfect being! As for me, I would exhibit my
qualities; but I am not hypocrite enough to conceal
my vices! Laughter, evil, pride, folly, will appear
each in its turn between sensibility and love of
justice and will serve as examples for the stupe-
faction of mankind. Each will recognize himself
not as he should be but as he is. And perchance
this simple ideal, conceived in my imagination, will
however transcend all that poetry has hitherto

considered greatest and most holy. For, if I permit
my vices to be revealed in these pages, one will
believe even more strongly in the virtues which
I make shine here and of which I place the halo
so high that the greatest geniuses of the future will
express a sincere gratitude to me. Thus hypocrisy
will straightway be chased out of my dwelling.
There will be in my lays an imposing evidence
of strength in order to set at naught the opinions
received.

He sings for himself and not for others. He does
not weigh the measure of his inspiration in the
human scales. Free as the storm, one day he will
be wrecked upon the indomitable coast of his
terrible will! He fears nothing, unless it be him-
self! In his supernatural battles he will success-
fully attack mankind and the Creator, as when
the sword-fish buries his harpoon in the whale's
belly. Accursed be he, by his children and by my
own relentless hand, who persists in misunder-
standing the implacable kangaroos of laughter and
the audacious lice of caricature! . . .

Two enormous towers appeared in the valley;
I said this in the beginning. Multiplying them by
two, the product was four . . . but I could not
clearly see the reason for this arithmetical opera-
tion. I continued on my way with fevered brow,
crying out incessantly: "No . . . No . . . I can-
not see clearly the reason for this arithmetical
operation!" I heard creaking of chains and mourn-
ful wailing. Let no one find it possible whenever

he should pass by that spot to multiply the towers by two so that the product should be four! Some persons suspect that I love humanity as if I were its own mother and had carried it nine months in my perfumed entrails. For this very reason I shall never return to that valley where stand the two units of the multiplicand!

A gibbet rose from the ground. A man was suspended from it by his hair, his hands tied behind his back. His legs had been left free to increase his torments and make him wish for anything rather than the binding of his arms. The skin of his forehead was so stretched by the weight of the hanging that his face, condemned by the circumstances to the absence of its natural expression, resembled the stony concretion of a stalactite. For three days he had suffered this torture. He cried out:

"Who will untie my arms? Who will untie my hair? I disjoint myself in movements that do nothing but drag the roots out of my scalp all the more. Hunger and thirst are not the chief causes of my inability to sleep. It is impossible that my existence should be prolonged beyond the limits of another hour. Someone come and slit open my throat with a sharp stone!"

Each word was preceded and followed by intense shrieks. I rushed forward from the bushes where I was taking shelter and hastened towards the puppet or flitch of bacon attached to the gibbet. But from the opposite direction two drunken women came dancing. One carried a sack and two whips with leaden lashes, the other a barrel full of tar and two brushes. The greying hair of the elder woman floated on the wind like the rags of a torn veil, and the feet of the other clattered like the tail of a tuna on a ship's poop-deck. Their eyes shone with a flame so strong and black that I thought at first these two women did not belong to my own species. They were laughing with so egotistical a self-possession, and their features inspired so much repugnance, that I doubted not for a single moment that I was face to face with two of the most hideous specimens of the human race. I re-concealed myself behind the bushes and kept silent like the *acantophorus serraticornis*, which shows only its head outside its nest. The women approached with the swiftness of a flood. Applying my ear to the ground I distinctly perceived the sound of the lyrical concussion of their tread.

When the two female orang-outangs arrived beneath the gibbet they sniffed at the air for a few seconds. They showed by their exaggerated gestures the really remarkable amount of stupefaction which resulted from their experience when they became aware that nothing had changed here: the arrival of death, according to their desires, had not occurred. They had not deigned to raise

[*174*]

their heads to see if the boloney was still in the same place. One of them said:

"Is it possible that you are still breathing? You have nine lives, my beloved husband."

As when two choristers in a cathedral intone alternately the verses of a psalm, the second woman replied:

"So you won't die, my gracious son? Tell me what you did (surely some witchcraft) to scare away the vultures? Indeed, your carcase has grown so thin! The breeze swings it like a lantern."

Each of the women took a brush and tarred the man's hanging body . . . each took a whip and raised her arm . . . I marveled (it would have been absolutely impossible not to have reacted as I did) at the eager exactitude with which the metallic lashes, instead of sliding over the surface as when one fights with a negro and makes useless efforts, worthy of a nightmare, to seize him by the hair, applied themselves, thanks to the tar, to the very interior of the flesh, slicing out furrows as deep as could reasonably be permitted by the obstacles presented by the bones. I guarded myself from the temptation to find voluptuous pleasure in that spectacle, which was extremely curious, but less profoundly comical than one had any right to expect. And yet, despite good resolutions made in advance, how could one refrain from appreciating the strength of those women, the muscles of their arms? Their skill, which consisted in striking the most sensitive parts of the body such as the

face and the abdomen, will be mentioned by me
only if I aspire to relate the entire truth! Unless,
by applying my lips one against the other, chiefly
in a horizontal direction (but everyone knows
that this is the most usual manner to bring about
this pressure), I prefer to preserve a silence swollen
with tears and mysteries to the distressing mani-
festation of which it will be impossible to conceal,
not only as well but even better than my words
(for I think I am not mistaken, although one cer-
tainly should not deny in principal, under the pain
of breaking the most elementary rules of skill, the
hypothetical possibilities of error), the disastrous
results occasioned by the fury which sets in motion
the dry metacarpus and sturdy joints: even if one
should not adopt the point of view of an impartial
observer or an experienced moralist (it is almost
as important that I learn I do not admit, at least
altogether, this more or less fallacious restriction),
doubt, in that respect, would not have the facili-
ties for extending its roots; for I do not at the
moment suppose it to be within the hands of a
supernatural power, and it would irrevocably
perish, perhaps not suddenly, due to the lack of
a sap fulfilling the conditions simultaneously of
nutrition and absence of poisonous matter. It is
understood, or if not do not read me, that the
actor on my stage is merely the timid personality
of my own opinion: far be it from me, however,
to think of relinquishing rights that are incontest-
able! It is certainly not my intention to combat

that affirmation, in which shines the criterion of certitude, that it is a simple means of making one's self understood: it would consist, I interpret it with only a few words but they are worth more than a thousand, in not arguing: it is more difficult to put into practice than the common run of mortals prefers to think generally. Argue is the grammatical word, and many persons will find that it would be better not to take issue, without a voluminous file of proofs, with what I have just set down on this paper. But the thing differs notably, if it is permitted to grant to one's own instinct that it employs a rare sagacity in the service of its circumspection, when it formulates judgments which otherwise would appear, be assured of it, of an impudence verging upon the boastful.

To close this little incident, which itself is deprived of its matrix by a flippancy as irremediably deplorable as it is inevitably full of interest (which no one will have failed to verify, on condition he has sounded his most recent memories), it is good, if one has one's faculties in perfect equilibrium, or better still, if the balance of idiocy does not outweigh too much the scale in which repose the noble and magnificent qualities of reason, that is to say, in order to make things clearer (for until now I have been nothing if not concise, a fact that many will not admit because of my prolixity which is only imaginary since it achieves its goal of hunting down with the scalpel of analysis the fugitive appearances of truth to their ultimate entrenchments), if the intelligence predominates sufficiently over deficiencies under the weight of which it has been partially smothered by habit, nature and education, it is good, I repeat for the second and last time, for, by dint of repetition we shall finish, and this is true more often than not, by misunderstanding one another, to return with my tail between my legs (if it be even true that I have a tail) to the dramatic subject embedded in this stanza.

It is useful to drink a glass of water before undertaking the continuation of my work. I prefer to drink two rather than go without it altogether. Thus, in the middle of a chase after a runaway slave through the forest, each member of the gang, at a suitable moment, hangs his gun upon the creepers and all unite in the common need to slake their thirst and appease their hunger in the shade of a clump of trees. But the pause lasts only a few seconds, the pursuit is taken up again with fury and the sound of the tally-ho soon echoes again. And, even as oxygen is recognizable by the property it possesses, without pride, to relight a match presenting a few glowing points, thus one will recognize the accomplishment of my duty by the haste I display to return to the question.

When the two females found that it was impossible to hold their whips, which weariness let fall from their hands, any longer, they judiciously put a stop to the gymnastic labor which they had been performing for nearly two hours, and withdrew, with a joy that was not devoid of threats for the future. I made my way toward him who was calling to me for help with his glazed eye (for loss of blood was so great that weakness prevented him from speaking, and my opinion, although I am no doctor, was that a hemorrhage had broken out in the face and abdomen), and I cut off his hair with a pair of scissors, after having unbound his arms. He told me that one evening his mother had called him into her room and ordered him to disrobe and spend the night with her in one bed, and that, without awaiting his reply the matron had divested herself of all her clothes while at the same time she outlined before his eyes the most immodest gestures; and that upon this he had retired from the room. Furthermore, because of his continued refusal, he had attracted to himself the wrath of his wife, who had deluded herself with the hope of reward had she been able to succeed in urging her husband to lend his body to the passions of the old woman. They resolved by a conspiracy to suspend him from a gibbet prepared in advance in some unfrequented spot, and let him die by inches, exposed to every misery and danger. It was not without many and considered reflections, full of almost insurmountable difficulties, that they finally succeeded in guiding their choice to the refined tortures which had not been terminated until the unhoped for succor of my intervention.

The liveliest marks of gratitude emphasized his

every expression, lending to his confidences not the least of their value. I carried him to the nearest cottage; for he had fainted and I left the peasants only after I had deposited my purse with them to purchase comforts for the wounded man, and after I had made them promise to lavish the evidences of a persevering sympathy upon the unfortunate as if he had been their own son. In my turn I told them of the occurrence and made for the door to resume my way; but after having gone a few hundred yards I mechanically retraced my steps, re-entered the cottage, and exclaimed: "No, no . . . do not think that this surprises me!"

This time I finally went away for good; but the soles of my feet could not set themselves down with any sureness: another would not have been able to perceive this!

The wolf no longer passes beneath the gibbet which the joined hands of a mother and a wife erected one spring day, as when he used to take in his bewitched imagination the path to an illusory meal. When he sees on the horizon that head of black hair, cradled by the wind, he does not encourage his power of inertia but takes flight with incomparable swiftness. Must we see in this psychological phenomenon an intelligence superior to the ordinary instinct of mammals? Without vouching for anything and without even conjecturing, it seems to me that this animal understood what crime is. How could he fail to understand it when human beings themselves have rejected to this indescribable point the empire of reason in order to allow to subsist in place of this dethroned queen nothing but ferocious vengeance!

✤

I am filthy. Lice gnaw me. Swine, when they gaze upon me, vomit. Scabs and scars of leprosy have scaled off my skin, which exudes a yellowish pus. I know not the waters of rivers nor the dew from the clouds. From my nape, as from a dunghill, an enormous toadstool with umbelliferous peduncles is growing. Seated upon a shapeless throne I have not stirred hand nor foot for four centuries. My toes have taken root in the soil and have grown up around my belly in a kind of lush growth, neither plant nor flesh, where dwell vile parasites. Nevertheless my heart is beating. Yet how could it beat if the rottenness and the reek of my cadaver (I dare not say my body) did not abundantly nourish it?

In my left armpit a family of toads has taken up residence, and when they stir they tickle me. Take care that one of them does not escape and come scratching with its mouth at the interior of your ear: it could penetrate into your brain.

In my right armpit there is a chameleon who eternally pursues the toads in order that he may not die of hunger: everyone must live. But when one party has completely foiled the tricks of the other, they find nothing better than calmly to go about sucking the delicate grease that covers my sides: I am used to it.

An evil viper has devoured my penis and taken its place. The villain has made a eunuch out of me. Ah! If only I had been able to defend myself with my paralysed arms, but I fear they have been transformed into logs of wood. However that may be, I can affirm that the red blood no longer circulates in them.

Two little hedgehogs of mature development flung to a dog, which did not refuse it, the contents of my testicles; and having carefully washed out the epidermis they have set up housekeeping within.

My anus has been taken over by a crab. Encouraged by my inertia he guards the entrance with his pincers and causes me much pain!

Two jellyfish deserted the sea, suddenly enticed by a hope in which they were not disappointed. They inspected narrowly the two fleshy portions which form the human backside, and, attaching themselves to these convex globes, they have so squashed the flesh by their constant pressure that nothing is left but these two monsters from the kingdom of viscosity, alike in color, form, and ferocity.

Speak not of my spine, for that is a sword! Yes, yes . . . I was not giving you my attention . . . your demand is just. You wish to know, do you not, how a sword comes to be thrust vertically into my back? I do not recollect very clearly myself. However, should I decide to treat as a memory what may be but a dream, then know that man, when he discovered I had sworn an oath to live motionless and diseased until I should have overcome the Creator, crept up on tip-toe behind me, yet not so softly that I did not hear him. I was aware of nothing more for a brief moment. Then this keen blade buried itself up to the handle as between the two shoulder-blades of a bull in the ring, and my skeleton shuddered like an earthquake. The blade cleaves so powerfully to my body that no one so far has been able to extract it. Athletes, mechanics, philosophers, doctors, have each tried in his turn with various methods. They knew not that the evil done by man was not to be undone! I forgave them the depth of their native ignorance and greeted them with a flicker of my eyelids.

Traveler, when you approach me I implore you to offer me no single word of consolation: you would undermine my courage. Leave me to warm my stubbornness at the flame of voluntary martyrdom. Leave me . . . I will not inspire pity in you. Hatred is stranger than you think; its behavior is inexplicable like the broken appearance of a stick when it is thrust into water. Even as you see me now I am able still to venture forth up to the very walls of heaven, chief of an army of murderers, and return to take up this posture again and to meditate anew upon noble projects of vengeance. Farewell, I will not detain you longer; and, that you may instruct and preserve yourself, dwell in your mind upon the fatal destiny which has led me to revolt, when perchance I was born a good man!

You will tell your son of what you have seen, and, taking him by the hand, let him admire the beauty of the stars and the wonders of the universe, the nest of the red-throat and the temples of the Lord. You will be astonished to see him so amenable to the counsels of paternity and you will reward him with a smile. But, when he thinks he is not observed, look at him and you will see him spit his saliva upon virtue. He has cheated you, he who is descended from the human race, but he will never deceive you again: you shall know what the future will make of him. O, unhappy father, make ready to accompany the halting steps of your old age to the ineradicable scaffold that will slice off the head of a precocious criminal, and the sorrow that shall point out to you the path that leads to the tomb.

On the wall of my room what shadow outlines with an incomparable power the phantasmagoric projection of its shriveled silhouette? When I set upon my heart this mute and delirious interrogation it is less for the majesty of form, for the picture of reality, than that the sobriety of style conducts itself in such a manner. Whoever you

are, defend yourself, for I am about to fling in
your teeth a terrible accusation: those eyes do
not belong to you . . . where did you steal them?
One day I saw a fair woman passing before me;
she had eyes like yours: you tore them from
her.

I see that you would make people believe in
your beauty; but no one is deceived — I less than
others. I tell you this in order that you may not
take me for a blockhead. A whole series of rapa-
cious birds, lovers of others' meat and defenders of
the utility of pursuit, beautiful as the skeletons
which are shed by the panoccos of Arkansas,
swarm around your brow like accepted and sub-
missive servitors. But is it a brow? It is not difficult
to allow a good deal of hesitation before believing
it. It is so low that it is impossible to verify the
proofs, numerically exiguous, of its equivocal ex-
istence. It is not for amusement that I tell you this.
Perhaps you have no brow, you who parade over
the wall like a badly-reflected symbol of a fan-
tastic dance the feverish trembling of your lumber
vertebrae. Who, then, scalped you? If it was a
human being, because you shut him up for twenty
years in a prison and who escaped to prepare a
revenge worthy of his retaliation, he has done
rightly and I applaud him; only, I have one reserva-
tion, he was not severe enough. Now you resemble
a Red Indian prisoner, at least (note this first)
owing to your expressive lack of hair. Not that it
may not grow again, since physiologists have dis-

covered that even severed brains reappear finally in the case of animals. But my thought, halting before a simple statement which is not, according to the little I know of it, devoid of a tremendous voluptuousness, does not go, even in the most daring consequences, as far as the limits of a wish for your recovery, but remains, on the contrary, based, by the employment of its more than suspicious neutrality, upon the consideration (or at least the wish, as a warning of greater sorrows, of what can be for you only a momentary privation of the skin that covers the top of your head. I hope you have understood me.

And even, if chance permits, by a miracle absurd but not at times unreasonable, that you find that precious skin which the religious vigilance of your enemy has kept as an intoxicating souvenir of his victory, it is almost extremely possible that, even if one had studied the law of probabilities only in connection with mathematics (for we know that analogy easily transfers the application of that law to other domains of the intelligence), your just though somewhat exaggerated fears of a partial or total chill would not refuse the important and even unique opportunity that would present itself in so opportune, though abrupt, a manner, to preserve the different parts of your brain from contact with the atmosphere, especially during winter, with a head-dress which rightly belongs to you since it is natural, and that it would be permitted to you, moreover (it would be incom-

prehensible for you to disown it) to keep it con-
stantly on your head, without running the always
disagreeable risk of infringing the simplest rules
of an elementary convention.

Is it not true that you listen to me attentively?
If you listen further, sadness will be a long way
from quitting the interior of your red nostrils. But
as I am very impartial and do not hate you as
much as I should (if I am mistaken, tell me so),
despite yourself you lend an ear to my discourse
as if impelled by a superior force. I am not as
wicked as you: that is why your genius bows
down of its own accord before mine . . . Indeed,
I am not as wicked as you! You just threw a glance
at the city built on the side of that mountain. And
now what do I see? . . . All the inhabitants are
dead! I have as much pride as anyone else, per-
haps, and this is another vice, even more. Very
well, listen . . . listen, if the confession of a man
who remembers having lived a half century in
the form of a shark among the submarine cur-
rents that extend along the African coast inter-
ests you sufficiently to give him your attention,
if not with bitterness, at least without the ir-
reparable error of showing the disgust I inspire
in you. I will not throw at your feet the mask
of virtue in order to appear before your eyes
as I really am; for I have never worn it (if that is
an excuse at all); and if from the very beginning
you will observe my features attentively you will
recognize me as your respectful disciple in per-

versity, but not as your formidable rival. Since I
do not dispute the palm of wickedness with you,
I think that no one else does: he should first have
to be a match for me, which is not easy.... Listen,
unless you are only the feeble condensation of a
mist (you are hiding your body somewhere and
I cannot find it):

One morning I saw a little girl stooping over a
pool to pluck a pink water-lily and exhibiting a
precocious experience in the manner of placing
her feet firmly at the water's edge. She was leaning
toward the water when her eyes encountered mine
(it is true that as far as I was concerned this was
not without premeditation). Instantly she reeled
like a whirlpool begotten by the tide around a rock,
her limbs failed her, and, marvelous thing to see,
phenomenon that took place as truthfully as I
speak to you now, she fell to the bottom of the
lake: the strange consequence was that she gath-
ered no nymphaeaceae. What is she doing down
there? I have not troubled to find out. Doubtless
her will, which was drawn up under the flag of
deliverance, is offering a furious battle against
decomposition!

But you, O my master, populations of cities are
suddenly destroyed beneath your gaze like ants'
nests crushed by the heel of an elephant. Have I
not just been witness of a demonstration? See . . .
the mountain is no longer happy . . . it stands there
alone like an old man. True, the houses still exist;
but it is no paradox to affirm, in a low voice, that

you could not say as much concerning the people who no longer exist. Already the emanation from their bodies assails me. Don't you smell it? See those birds of prey waiting until we go away before beginning their gigantic meal; they arrive in a perpetual cloud from the four corners of the horizon. Alas, they had already arrived, for I saw their rapacious wings tracing a monument of spirals around you, as if to inspire you to hasten the crime. Does not your sense of smell receive the faintest effluvium? The imposter is no more than that ... Your olfactory nerves are at last assailed by the perception of the aromatic atoms; they arise from the annihilated city, although I should have no need to inform you of that ...

I would like to kiss your feet, but my arms enfold only a transparent vapor. Let us seek the undiscoverable body, which, however, my eyes perceive: it deserves countless marks of sincere admiration from me.

The phantom is making a game of me: he is helping me to find his own body. If I sign to him to stay in his own place, he returns an identical sign. ... The secret is out. But not, I must state frankly, entirely to my satisfaction. All is explained, the large as well as the small details; the latter are unimportant to place before the mind, as, for example, the tearing out of a fair-haired woman's eyes: that amounts to practically nothing!

Do I not recall that I too was scalped, although

it was only for five years (the exact length of time had escaped me) that I shut a human being up in a prison in order to witness his sufferings because he had refused, and justly, his friendship, which he would not bestow upon beings like myself? Since I claim to be unaware that my eye can kill, even to the planets spinning in space, he who claims that I have not the faculty of memory will not be in error.

All that is left for me to do is smash that mirror in pieces with the aid of a rock. . . . This is not the first time that the nightmare of a temporary loss of memory has taken up residence in my imagination when, by the inflexible laws of optics, it has happened to me to be confronted with the non-recognition of my own reflection!

I was asleep on a cliff. He who has chased an ostrich all day through the desert without being able to catch it has had no time to take nourishment or close his eyes. If this man is reading me now he is, strictly speaking, able to guess what a slumber was weighing me down. But when the storm has thrust a vessel with the palm of its hand vertically to the bottom of the ocean; if, on the raft, there remains only one man of the entire crew, broken by weariness and every kind of privation; if the billows toss him around like a bit of flotsam for hours longer than the life of a man; and, if a frigate, ploughing later on through these desolate waters of a foundered keel, catches sight of the unfortunate who parades his emaciated carcase upon the ocean, and brings him assistance that is almost too late; I think this drowned man would understand even better the degree to which the heaviness of my senses was carried. Hypnotism and chloroform, when they take the trouble, can also sometimes bring about similar lethargic catalepsies. They bear no resemblance to death: it would be a great lie to say so. But let us get on with the dream, in order that those impatient persons who are starving for this kind of reading do not commence to bellow like a school of macrocephalic whales fighting over a pregnant female.

I dreamed I had entered into the body of a hog, that it was not easy to extricate myself, and that I was wallowing in the most foul mires. Was this a reward? I no longer belonged to humanity, one of my greatest desires! Thus I understood the interpretation and I felt from it a joy more than profound. However, I actively sought the deed of virtue I had done to deserve such a token of favor on the part of Providence. Now that I have gone over in my memory the various phases of that frightful flattening against the granite's belly, during which the tide passed twice without my being aware of it over that irreducible mixture of inert matter and living flesh, it is perhaps not without utility to proclaim that this degradation was

probably merely a punishment inflicted upon me
by divine justice. But who knows his own intimate
desires or the causes of his pestilential joys? The
metamorphosis never appeared to me as anything
but the lofty and magnanimous echo of a perfect
and long-awaited happiness. At last it had come,
the day when I should become a hog! I tried out
my teeth on the bark of trees; I contemplated
my snout with delight. There was not remaining
the least morsel of divinity. I was capable of rais-
ing my soul up to the excessive elevation of that
ineffable sensuality.

Listen to me, and do not blush, inexhaustible
caricatures of the beautiful who take the laugh-
able braying of your superlatively contemptible
souls so seriously, and who do not understand why
the Omnipotent, in a rare moment of excellent
buffoonery which certainly does not violate the
great general laws of the grotesque, took one day
the wonderful pleasure to inhabit a planet with
singular microscopic beings known as *humans*,
made of stuff resembling ruddy coral: indeed,
you have good reason to blush, bones and fat,
but listen to me. I do not invoke your intelli-
gence: you would make it bleed by the horror you
inspire in it. Forget it, and be consistent to your-
selves. . . . No more constraint. When I wanted
to kill, I killed; it even happened often and none
restrained me from it. Human laws still pursued
me with their vengeance, although I did not attack
the race that I had abandoned so calmly. But my

conscience made me no reproaches. During the day I fought with my new fellow creatures, and the earth was saturated with countless layers of clotted blood. I was the strongest and I bore away all the victories. Agonising wounds covered my whole body but I pretended not to notice them. Earthly animals avoided me, and I remained alone in my resplendent grandeur. How great was my astonishment when, after having swum across a river in order to leave behind me the countries depopulated by my rage and to reach other territories in which to instill my customs of murder and carnage, I tried to walk upon that flowery shore! My feet were paralysed; no movement came to betray the truth of that forced immobility. Amid supernatural efforts to continue on my way I awoke and realized that I had again become a man. Providence thus gave me to understand, in a manner not inexplicable, that it did not wish my sublime projects to be realized even in dreams. To return to my original shape was for me a sorrow so great that I still weep over it at night. My sheets are constantly moist, as if they had been dipped in water, and I have them changed every day. If you do not believe me, come and see me; you will verify by your own experience not the probability but the truth itself of my assertion.

How many times after that night spent under the stars, on a cliff, have I not mingled with a herd of swine to re-experience, as my just due, my disrupted metamorphosis!

Maldoror

It is time to take our leave of these glorious memories, which leave behind them only the pale milky voice of everlasting regret.

❦

It is not impossible to witness an abnormal deviation in the latent or visible functioning of the laws of nature. Indeed, if everyone would go to the ingenious trouble of interrogating the various phases of his existence (without forgetting a single one, for it could be that very forgotten one which was destined to furnish the proof of what I am advancing), he would remember, not without a certain surprise that would be comical in other circumstances, how, on such and such a day, to speak first of objective things, he witnessed some phenomenon that seemed to transcend and positively did transcend the known ideas furnished by observation and experience, as, for example those rains of frogs the magical appearance of which was not at first understood by scientists. And how, on such another day, to speak in second and last place of subjective things, his mind presented to the scrutinizing gaze of psychology I will not go so far as to say an aberration of reason (which nevertheless would be no less curious; on the contrary, it would be even more so), but, at least, in order not to make any difficulties for certain cold persons who would never pardon me for the flagrant lucubrations of my exaggeration, an unfamiliar state, often very serious, which indicates that the limit accorded by good sense to imagination is sometimes, despite the ephemeral pact concluded between these two forces, unhappily transcended by the presence of the will, but, more often than not also, by the absence of its effective collaboration: let us bring to the support of this a few examples, of which it will not be difficult to appreciate the aptness. I present two: the transport of rage and the disease of pride.

I warn whoever is reading me that he beware of forming a vague idea, and, for stronger reasons, a false one, of the beauties of literature I shed in the excessively swift development of my phrases. Alas! I would develop my arguments and my comparisons slowly and with much magnificence (but who disposes of his own time?), in order that everyone should understand better, if not my dismay, at least my stupefaction when, one summer evening, as the sun seemed to be sinking towards the horizon, I saw swimming in the sea with large webbed feet in the place of the usual extremities of the arms and legs, bearing a dorsal fin proportionately as long and as slender as that of a dolphin, a strongly-muscled human being; and I also saw that many schools of fish (I noticed in this procession, among other inhabitants of the deep, the torpedo, the anarnak of Greenland, the sting-ray) were following with the most evident marks of the highest admiration. Sometimes he would dive, and his viscous body would reappear almost immediately two hundred yards away. Porpoises, who, in my opinion did not steal their reputation as good swimmers, could scarcely follow at a distance this new species of amphibian. I do not think the reader will have any cause to regret it if he bring to my narrative not so much the harmful obstacle of a stupid credulity as the supreme service of a deep confidence arguing legitimately with secret sympathy concerning the poetic mysteries, only too few to his mind, which I take it upon myself to reveal to him whenever the occasion presents itself, as it has indisputably today, closely impregnated with the tonic odors of aquatic plants brought by the refreshing breeze to the stanza which contains a monster who has appropriated to himself the distinctive characteristics of the webfoot family. Who speaks here of appropriation? Let everyone know that mankind, by his complex and multiple nature, is not ignorant of the methods by which to enlarge his horizons: he lives in water like the sea-horse; in the upper layers of the atmosphere like the osprey; and under the ground like a mole, a woodlouse and the sublimity of the earth-worm.

Such is the outline more or less precise (but more rather than less) of the exact criterion of the extremely strengthening consolation that I endeavored to awaken in my spirit when I decided that the human being whom I saw at a great distance swimming with his four limbs over the

surface of the waves as never the most superb
cormorant swam, had perhaps acquired the trans-
formation of the extremities of his arms and legs
only as the expiatory punishment for some un-
known crime. It was not necessary for me to
torment my brain to manufacture in advance the
melancholy pills of pity; for I did not know
whether that man, whose arms beat the bitter
waves alternately, while his legs thrust aside the
aqueous strata with a power such as that possessed
by the spiral weapon of the narwhal, had not
voluntarily appropriated those extraordinary
shapes, rather than that they had been imposed
upon him as a chastisement. According to what
I learned later, here is the simple truth: pro-
longation of existence in that fluid element had
insensibly brought about in that human creature
who had exiled himself voluntarily from the
craggy continents the important but not essential
changes I had remarked in the object that a more
or less confused glance had caused me to take,
from the primordial moments of his apparition,
(through an unqualifiable flippancy, the errors of
which engender the so wearisome sentiment that
will be easily understood by psychologists and
lovers of prudence) for a fish of strange shape,
not yet described in the naturalists' classifications;
but perhaps in their posthumous works, although
I have no excusable claim to support this latter
supposition, imagined as it is under too many hypo-
thetical conditions. Indeed, this amphibian (for

amphibians exist, without any room for denial)
was visible to me only, which may not be said for
the fish and the cetaceans: for I noticed that certain
peasants who had stopped to stare at my face,
troubled by that supernatural phenomenon, and
who tried vainly to explain to themselves why
my eyes were constantly fixed with a perseverance
that seemed to be invincible but actually was not,
upon a spot in the sea where they themselves
could distinguish nothing but an appreciable and
limited quantity of schools of fish of all species,
stretched open their great mouths possibly as wide
as those of whales. This made them smile, but not
as I did, turn pale, they said in their picturesque
dialect; and they were not stupid enough not to
notice that, precisely, I was not watching the
bucolic evolutions of the fish, but that my gaze
was fixed upon something much farther on. Me-
chanically turning my eyes towards the remark-
able spread of those powerful mouths I told myself
that unless there should be found in the totality
of the universe a pelican large as a mountain, or
at least as a promontory (admire, if you please,
the finesse of the restriction which loses no inch
of territory), no beak of bird of prey or savage
jaws of wild animal would be capable of tran-
scending, or even of equaling, any one of those
gaping, but too lugubrious, craters. And yet,
although I allow for the sympathetic usage of
metaphor (this rhetorical figure renders much
more service to human aspirations towards the

infinite than ordinarily those who are imbued
with prejudices or false ideas, which are the same
thing, try to understand), it is none the less true
that the laughable mouths of those peasants were
opened wide enough to swallow three cachalots.
Let us contract our thought still further, let us be
serious, and let us be content with three little new-
born elephants.

With a single arm-stroke the amphibian left a
kilometer of frothy furrow behind him. During
the very brief moment when the arm remained
suspended in the air before once again burying
itself in the waves, the spread fingers, united by
means of a fold of skin in the form of a membrane
seemed to reach out towards the limits of space
and seize the stars. Standing on my rock, I used my
hands for a megaphone and cried out, while the
crabs and shrimps fled to the darkness of the most
secret crevices:

"O you, whose swimming surpasses the long
wings of the frigate-bird, if you still under-
stand the meaning of the great outcries which, like
a faithful interpretation of its intimate thoughts,
mankind furiously directs toward you, condescend
to pause for a moment in your swift progress
and relate to me summarily the phases of your
truthful history. But I warn you, you have no need
to address me if your daring plan is to give birth
in me to the friendship and veneration I felt for
you when I saw you for the first time accomplish-
ing, with the grace and strength of a shark,

your indomitable and rectilinear pilgrimage."

A sigh, which froze me to the bone and shook the rock upon which the sole of my foot was resting (unless it was I staggering because of the rude penetration of the sonorous waves which carried to my ears such a cry of despair), penetrated to the very entrails of the earth: the fish plunged beneath the waves with the sound of an avalanche. The amphibian dared not approach the beach too closely; but as soon as he was assured that his voice carried with sufficient clarity to my ear-drum, he reduced the motion of his webbed hands in such a manner as to maintain his torso, hung with sea-wrack, above the moaning waves. I saw him bow his head as if to invoke by solemn command the wayward pack of memories. I dared not interrupt him in this sacredly archeological occupation: plunged in the past, he resembled a reef. Finally he began to speak as follows:

"The centipede lacks not enemies; the fantastic beauty of his multiple feet, instead of winning him the sympathy of animals, is for them perhaps only the powerful stimulant of a jealous irritation. And I should not be surprised to learn that this insect is exposed to the most intense hatred.

"I shall conceal from you the place of my birth which has no bearing on my story: but the shame reflected upon my family has bearing on my duty. My father and mother (may God forgive them!) after a year of waiting saw Heaven grant their prayers: twins, my brother and I, were born. All

the more reason for love between us. But this was
not so. Because I was the handsomer of the two and
the more intelligent, my brother hated me and
made no effort to conceal his feelings. Conse-
quently my mother and father lavished most of
their love on me, while through my sincere and
constant friendship I tried to appease a soul that
had no right to revolt against him who had come
from the same womb. My brother's fury knew
no limits, and he so slandered me with the most
unbelievable calumnies that the hearts of our
mutual parents were closed to me. For fifteen years
I lived in a dungeon with maggots and slimy water
for food. I will not relate to you in detail the
unheard-of tortures I endured during that long and
unjust sequestration. Now and then during the
day one of the three torturers whose turn it was
would enter abruptly, armed with pincers, tongs
and various other instruments of torture. The
shrieks elicited from me by these torments left
them unmoved; the abundant loss of blood made
them smile. O, my brother, I have forgiven you —
you, the primary cause of all my ills! It must be
that blind rage finally opens its own eyes. I
made many reflections during my everlasting im-
prisonment. How my hatred developed towards
all humanity in general you can well imagine.
Progressive etiolation, solitude of body and soul,
had not yet caused me to lose my mind com-
pletely, to the point of bearing any resentment
against those whom I had never ceased to love:

triple pillory of which I was the slave. I succeeded by cunning in gaining my liberty! Disgusted by the inhabitants of dry land, who, although they called themselves my fellow men, appeared hitherto to resemble me in nothing (if they found that I did resemble them, why did they harm me?), I made my way to the pebbly beach, firmly resolved to give myself to death if the sea were to offer me memories of a life fatally lived. Do you believe your own eyes? Since the day I fled the paternal roof I have not been as unhappy as you think inhabiting the sea and its crystal grottoes. Providence, as you see, has given me in part the structure of a swan. I live in peace with the fish and they procure for me the nourishment I need as if I were their ruler. I will give a special whistle, if it will not annoy you, and you will see how they will reappear."

It happened as he had predicted. He resumed his royal swimming surrounded by his retinue of subjects. And, although at the end of a few seconds, he had completely disappeared from sight, with a telescope I could still distinguish him on the distant horizon. He swam with one hand, while with the other wiped his eyes which the terrible strain of approaching terra firma had injected with blood. He had acted in this manner to do me pleasure. I flung the revealing instrument against the steep escarpment: it bounded from rock to rock and the waves received its scattered fragments: such was the last demonstration and the supreme farewell by which I made obeisance, as in a dream, before a noble and unfortunate intelligence! Yet everything that happened was real, that summer night.

Each night, spreading my wings into my tortured memory, I evoked the image of Falmer . . . each night. His fair hair, his oval face, his noble features, were still engraved upon my imagination . . . indestructibly . . . especially his fair hair. Away, away with that hairless head, polished like a tortoise-shell. He was fourteen and I only one year older. Let that mournful voice be still! Why does it come to denounce me? But it is myself speaking. Using my own tongue to emit my thought, I notice that my lips move and that it is I who am speaking. And it is I who, relating a tale about my childhood, and feeling remorse penetrate my heart . . . it is I myself, if I make no mistake . . . it is I myself speaking . . . .

I was only one year older. . . .

Who is this to whom I refer? It is a friend I had in past time, I think. Yes, yes, I have already told his name. . . . I will not spell out again those six letters, no, no. It is also useless to repeat that I was one year older. Who knows? Let us repeat it, however, but in a laborious murmur. . . .

I was only one year older. . . .

Even then the pre-eminence of my physical strength was rather a motive for defending along the rough highway of my life him who had attached himself to me, than to mistreat a being visibly weaker than I. . . . For indeed, I believe he was weaker than I. . . .

Even then. . . .

It was a friend I had in past time, I think. . . .

The pre-eminence of my physical strength. . . .

Each night. . . .

Especially his fair hair. . . .

There is more than one human being who has seen bald heads: old age, disease, sorrow (the three together or taken separately) explain this negative phenomenon in a satisfactory manner. Such, anyway, is the reply that would be made to me by a scientist if I were to ask him about this matter. . . .

Old age, disease, sorrow. . . .

But I am aware (I, too, am a scientist) that one day, because he had seized my hand just as I was raising my dagger to pierce a woman's breast, I grasped him by the hair in a grip of steel, and whirled him around in the air with such speed that his hair remained in my hand, and his body, flung out by centrifugal force, smashed against the trunk of an oak tree. . . .

I am aware that one day his hair remained in my hand. . . .

I, too, am a scientist. . . .

Yes, yes, I already mentioned his name. . . .

I am aware that one day I perpetrated this in-

famous deed, while his body was flung out by
centrifugal force. . . .

He was fourteen. . . .

When, in an access of mental aberration, I rush
through the fields, holding pressed to my heart a
bloody thing that I have preserved for a long time
like a revered relic, the little children who pursue
me . . . the old women and little children who
pursue me with stones raise lamentable outcries:
"There is Falmer's hair!"

Away, away with that hairless head, polished
like a tortoise-shell. . . .

A bloody thing. . . .

But it is myself speaking. . . .

His oval face, his noble features. . . .

Indeed, I believe he was weaker than I. . . .

Old women and little children. . . .

For indeed I believe . . . what am I trying to
say? . . . for indeed I believe he was weaker
than I. . . .

In a grip of steel. . . .

That crash, that crash: did it kill him? Were his
bones splintered against the tree . . . irreparably?
Did that crash, engendered by the vigor of an
athlete, kill him? Was his life spared although his
bones were splintered . . . irreparably?

Did that crash kill him? . . .

I fear to know what my closed eyes did not
witness. . . .

Indeed. . . .

Especially his fair hair. . . .

Indeed, I rushed away into the distance with a conscience that was to be in the future implacable. . . .

He was fourteen. . . .

With a conscience that was to be implacable. . . .

Each night. . . .

When a young man who aspires to glory, leaning over a desk high up in a building at the silent hour of midnight, hears a rustling for which he can find no cause, he turns his head, burdened by meditation and dusty manuscripts, in every direction; but nothing, no indication of what might be causing the sound he hears so feebly, yet so distinctly. Finally he realizes that the smoke from his candle, taking flight toward the ceiling, causes almost imperceptible vibrations through the surrounding air, rustling a paper nailed to the wall. . . .

High up in a building. . . .

Just as a young man who aspires to glory hears a rustling for which he can find no cause, so I hear a melodious voice pronouncing in my ear: "Maldoror!" But, before putting an end to his apprehension, he thought he heard the wings of a mosquito. . . .

Leaning over his desk. . . .

Yet I am not dreaming. What if I am stretched out on my satin bed? Coolly I make the perspicacious remark that my eyes are open, although it is the hour of pink dominoes and masked balls. Never . . . Oh, no, never . . . did the Seraphic accents of a mortal voice pronounce with such dolorous elegance the syllables of my name!

A mosquito's wings. . . .

How friendly his voice is . . . Has he then forgiven me?

His body crashed against the trunk of an oak tree. . . .

"Maldoror!"

MALDOROR

(LES CHANTS DE MALDOROR)

5

LET the reader not be angry with me if my prose has not had the good fortune to please him. You maintain that my ideas are at least singular. What you say there, respectable man, is the truth; but, a partial truth. And what an abundant source of error and misapprehension all partial truth is! Flocks of starlings have a way of flying natural to them, which seems to be governed by a uniform and regular tactic like that of a disciplined army obeying with precision the voice of a single general. The starlings obey the voice of instinct, and this instinct prompts them always to draw in toward the center of the group, while the rapidity of their flight carries them unceasingly beyond that point; so that this multitude of birds, thus united by a common tendency toward the same hypnotic point, coming and going unceasingly, circulating and recrossing in every direction, forms a sort of agitated whirlpool, the entire mass of which, without following any particular direction, seems to have a general movement of evolution upon itself resulting from the particular circulatory motions of each of its members, and in which the center, perpetually tending to increase, but continually held in, is repulsed by the contrary strains of the environing lines that bear upon it, and constantly more compressed than any one of these lines, which are themselves compressed the more as they approach closer to the center. Despite this singular manner of eddying, the starlings do not cleave through the air with any less rare a swiftness, and gain noticeably each second a precious step toward the end of their fatigue and the goal of their pilgrimage.

In the same way you, reader, pay no attention to my odd manner of singing each of these lays. But be persuaded that the fundamental accents of poetry preserve none the less their intrinsic sway over my intelligence. Let us not generalize exceptional facts, I ask no more: yet my character is in the order of possible things. Undoubtedly, between the two extreme terms of your literature as you understand it, and mine, there exists an infinitude of intermediary steps of which it would be easy to multiply the sub-divisions; but there would be no useful purpose in this, and there would be the danger of narrowing and falsifying an eminently philosophical conception which ceases to be rational as soon as it is no longer understood as it was conceived, that is to say, amply.

You know how to unite enthusiasm with an internal coldness, observer with the concentrated disposition; in the final analysis, as far as I am concerned, I find you perfect. Yet you refuse to understand me!

If you are unhealthy follow my advice (it is the best I have at your disposition), and go take a country walk. Sorry recompense, wouldn't you say? When you have taken the air, come seeking me again with your mind rested. Do not weep; I wish you no harm. Is it not true, my friend, that up to a certain point your sympathy has been with my songs? Then what prevents you from climbing the rest of the steps? The frontier between your taste and mine is invisible; you will never be able to grasp it, proof that the frontier itself does not exist. Reflect then (I skim only lightly over the subject here) that it would not be impossible that you had signed a treaty with obstinacy, that pleasant daughter of a mule, that rich source of intolerance. If I did not know that you are no blockhead I would not reproach you thus. It is useless for you to encrust yourself with the cartilaginous shell of an axiom that you believe to be unbreakable. There are also other unbreakable axioms that proceed in parallel with yours. If you have a definite taste for caramel (admirable farce of nature) no one will conceive of it as a crime; but those whose intelligence, more energetic and capable of greater things, prefers pepper and arsenic have good reasons for their conduct without any intention of imposing their peaceful domination upon those who tremble with fear before a shrew-mouse or the speaking expression of the surfaces of a cube. I speak from experience, not playing here the part of an instigator.

And just as rotifers and tardigrades may be heated almost to boiling-point without necessarily losing their vitality, it will be the same for you if you can assimilate, with caution, the acrid suppurating serosity which is released slowly by the irritation set up by my interesting lucubrations. What! Have we not succeeded in grafting upon the back of a live rat the tail detached from the corpse of another rat? Try then in the same manner to transfer to your imagination the various modifications of my cadaverous argument.

But be wise. At the time of this writing new vibrations agitate the intellectual atmosphere: it is simply a question of having the courage to confront them face to face. Why do you make that grimace? And you even accompany it with a gesture that none could imitate with a long apprenticeship. Be convinced that habit is necessary in everything; and since the instinctive repulsion that manifested itself during my first pages has noticeably diminished in depth in inverse ratio to your application to the reading, like a boil that one lances, we must hope, although your head still aches, that your recovery will soon have reached its final stages. To me there is no doubt that you are already bordering upon complete convalescence; yet, alas! your face is still very thin!

But . . . courage! In you there is an uncommon spirit, I love you, and do not despair of your complete deliverance provided you absorb certain medications which will surely hasten the disappearance of the last symptoms of sickness. For an astringent and tonic food you will first tear off your mother's arms (if she be still in existence), you will cut them up in small pieces, then devour them in one day, your face betraying no sign of emotion. If your mother is too old, choose another chirurgical subject, younger and fresher, whose scalp will have value, and who balances easily upon the tarsal bones in walking: your sister, for example. I cannot help but deplore her fate, and I am not one of those in whom a cold enthusiasm only makes a pretence of goodness. You and I will shed for her, for that beloved virgin (though I have no proof of her virginity), two irrepressible tears, two tears of lead. That will be all. The most emollient potion I can prescribe for you is a basin full of lumpy blennorrhagic pus in which was first dissolved a hairy ovarian cyst, a follicular chancre, an inflamed prepuce skinned back from the gland by paraphimosis, and three red slugs.

If you follow my prescriptions my poetry will receive you with open arms, as a louse performs resection with its kisses upon the root of a hair.

Maldoror

I saw before me an object standing upon a hill.
I could not clearly make out its head, but already
I was aware that it was of no ordinary shape, with-
out, nevertheless, being able to distinguish pre-
cisely the exact proportion of its contours. I dared
not draw near to this motionless column; and even
had I possessed the ambulatory claws of more than
three thousand crabs (not to mention those which
serve for the prehension or mastication of food),
I still would have stayed in the same place if an
occurrence, quite futile by itself, had not de-
manded a heavy tribute from my curiosity, which
was on the verge of bursting its bonds.

A beetle, rolling along the ground with its man-
dibles and antennae a ball of which the principal
elements were composed of excrement, was ad-
vancing rapidly toward the aforementioned hill,
making every effort to advertise its desire to take
that particular direction. This articulated animal
was not very much larger than a cow! If you
don't believe what I say, come to me and I will
satisfy the most incredulous by the evidence of
good witnesses. I followed the beetle at a distance,
obviously intrigued. What was it going to do with
that great black ball?

O reader, who pride yourself (and not errone-
ously) upon your perspicacity, would you be
capable of telling me? But I do not wish to subject
your well-known passion for riddles to a violent
test. Let it suffice for you to know that the
mildest punishment I could inflict upon you would

be to inform you that this mystery would not be
revealed to you (it will be revealed to you) until
later, at the end of your life, when you are engag-
ing in philosophical discussion with the pangs of
death at your bedside . . . and perhaps even at
the end of this stanza.

The beetle had arrived at the base of the hill.
I had followed in his footsteps and I was still at
some distance from the scene; for just as the
stercoraceae, restless birds who seem always to
be starving, are happy in the seas that bathe the
two poles and only accidentally venture into the
temperate zones, so I was ill at ease and I moved
my legs very slowly. But what actually was the
corporeal substance towards which I was advanc-
ing?

I knew that the genus pelicaninae includes four
distinct species: the booby, the pelican, the cor-
morant, and the frigate-bird. The greyish shape
that appeared before me was not a booby. The
plastic block that I saw was not a frigate-bird.
The crystallized flesh that I observed was not a
cormorant. Now I could see him, that man with
a brain destitute of an annular protuberance! I
sought vainly to recall from the dim corners of
my memory in what torrid or frozen country I
had first seen that long, wide, convex, vaulted beak,
with its pronounced, unguicular, swollen, deeply-
hooked bridge; those toothed, straight edges; that
lower mandible with its two sides divided down
to the point; that space filled with a membranous

skin; that large pouch, yellow and sacciform, occupying the entire throat and capable of considerable distention; and those nostrils, very narrow, longitudinal, almost invisible, hollowed in a basal groove!

If that living being, with its simple pulmonary respiration, and its body adorned with hair, had been a bird down to the soles of its feet, and not only down to the shoulders, it would not then have been so difficult for me to have recognized it: a thing very easy to do, as you will see for yourself. Only this time I dispense with it; for the clarity of my demonstration I should have to have one of those birds placed upon my desk, even a stuffed one. Besides I am not rich enough to obtain one.

Following step by step a previous hypothesis, I should later have assigned his true nature to, and found a place in the categories of natural history for him in whom I admired the nobility of his frail-looking posture. With what satisfaction not to be entirely ignorant of the secrets of his dual organism and with what avidity to know more I contemplated him in his permanent metamorphosis! Although he possessed no human countenance, he appeared to me as beautiful as the two long tentaculiform filaments of an insect; or rather as a sudden interment; or again as the law of the restoration of mutilated organs; and especially as an eminently putrescible liquid! But, paying no attention whatsoever to his surroundings, the

stranger's pelican's head stared always straight
ahead. Some other day I will finish this story. Yet
I will continue my narrative with gloomy haste;
for if, on your part, you long to know whither
my imagination is tending (please Heaven, in-
deed, that this be only imagination!), for my part
I have determined to finish what I have to tell you
at one sitting (and not two!), although neverthe-
less no one has the right to accuse me of lack of
courage. But when you find yourself face to face
with such circumstances, more than one person
feels the pulsations of his heart beating against the
palm of his hand.

There recently died, almost unknown, in a little
port in Brittany, a master coast-trader, an old sailor
who was the hero of a terrible story. He was then
captain of a foreign-going ship and sailed for a
ship-owner of Saint-Malo. After an absence of
thirteen months he returned to the conjugal hearth
at the very moment when his wife, still confined
to her bed, had just presented him with an heir
to the existence of which he could make no just
claim. The captain gave no sign of his surprise and
anger. He coldly commanded his wife to dress and
accompany him on a walk around the city's ram-
parts. It was in January. The ramparts of Saint-
Malo are high and when the north wind is blow-
ing even the most intrepid ones hang back. The
unhappy woman obeyed, calm and resigned.
When she returned home she was delirious. She
died during the night.

Maldoror

But after all that was only a woman. While I, who am a man, do not know whether I should be able in the presence of a drama no less striking, to maintain sufficient command over myself to immobilize the muscles of my face!

When the beetle arrived at the foot of the hill the man raised his hand towards the west (precisely in that direction a lamb-eating vulture and a great horn-owl of Virginia had engaged in an aerial battle), wiped from his beak a long tear which presented a system of coloration that sparkled like a diamond, and addressed the beetle as follows:

"Unhappy ball! Have you not rolled it long enough? Your vengeance is not yet assuaged; and already that woman whose arms and legs you have bound with pearl necklaces in such a manner as to construct an amorphous polyhedron the better to drag her with your tarsal segments through valley and byway, over brambles and stones (let me draw near to see if it be still she!) has seen her bones scarred with wounds, her limbs polished by the mechanical law of rotary friction and submerged into the unity of coagulation, and her body presenting instead of its primordial outline and contour the monotonous appearance of a homogeneity that resembles only too strongly through the confusion of its various crushed elements the mass of a sphere! She has been long dead; abandon those remains and take care not to be transported irrevocably by the rage that consumes you: here is no longer justice, for egoism, concealed beneath the integument of your brow, slowly raises like a phantom the veil that covers it."

The lamb-eating vulture and the great horn-owl of Virginia, unconsciously borne upon the vicissitudes of their struggle, had drawn near us.

The beetle trembled at these unexpected words; and what would have been on some other occasion an insignificant movement, this time became the distinguishing mark of a fury that knew no bounds; for he rubbed his hind legs terrifyingly against the edges of his elytrae, producing a sharp sound:

"Who are you, pusillanimous creature? It seems that you have forgotten certain strange events of the past; you do not retain them in your memory, my brother. That woman betrayed us, one by one. You first, myself second. It seems to me that this misdeed should not (should not!) disappear from the memory so easily. So easily! Your magnanimous nature permits you to forgive. But do you know whether, despite the abnormal condition of the atoms of that woman, reduced to a state of mush (there is no question of knowing now whether anyone would believe at the first investigation that this body has been augmented by a notable quantity of density rather by the grinding action of two powerful wheels, than by the effects of my fiery passion), she still exists? Silence, and let me be avenged."

He resumed his way and made off, pushing the

ball before him. When he had gone, the pelican
cried out:

"That woman, by her magical power, has given
me the head of a webfoot and changed my brother
into a beetle: perhaps she deserves worse treatment
even than I have just witnessed."

And I, who was not sure that I was not dream-
ing, guessing by what I had heard the nature of
the hostile relations which were engaging the
lamb-eating vulture and the great horned owl of
Virginia in a bloody battle above me, threw back
my head like a hood in order to give free play to
my lungs, and directing my eyes above I cried out
to them:

"You up there! Put an end to your quarreling!
Each of you is right, for to each she had promised
her love. Consequently she has deceived you both.
But you are not the only ones. Furthermore, she
deprived you of your human shape, making a cruel
game of your most intimate sorrows. And you
would hesitate to believe me! In any case, she is
dead, and the beetle inflicted a punishment of
ineffaceable imprint upon her, despite the pity
of the first of you whom she betrayed."

At these words they put an end to their battle
and tore out no more feathers nor strips of flesh:
and in this their conduct was correct. The great
horned owl of Virginia, beautiful as the memory
of a curve described by a dog running after its
master, buried himself in the crevices of a ruined
convent. The lamb-eating vulture, beautiful as the

law of the limitation of development in the breast of adults in whom the tendency to growth is not in proportion with the molecules assimilated by their organism, was lost in the upper layers of the atmosphere. The pelican, whose generous pardon had impressed me because I found it unnatural, resuming the majestic impassivity of a lighthouse upon his hill as if to warn human navigators to give heed to his example and guard their destiny from the love of gloomy sorceresses, went on staring straight ahead. The beetle, beautiful as the trembling of the hands in alcoholism, disappeared into the horizon. Four more existences to be deleted from the book of life. I tore out a whole muscle from my left arm, for I no longer knew what I was doing so greatly was I moved by that quadruple disaster. I, who thought that the ball was composed of excrement! Great fool that I am!

The intermittent annihilation of human faculties: whatever your thought may lead you to suppose, these are not words. At least, they are not ordinary words. May he who thought he would be accomplishing an act of justice in asking some executioner to flay him alive, raise his hand. May he who would offer his bosom voluntarily to the bullets of death, raise his head with a sensual smile. My eyes will seek the marks of scars; my ten fingers will concentrate the sum total of their attention upon touching carefully the flesh of this eccentric; I shall ascertain that splashes of brains have fallen upon my satin brow. Is it not true that in the entire universe a man could not be found who would live such a martyrdom? I do not know what laughter is, it is true, having never experienced it myself. Yet how imprudent it would be to maintain that my lips would not widen if it should be granted to me to encounter someone who claimed that such a man existed? That which no one would desire for his own existence has fallen to me by an unequal destiny. It is not that my body floats in the lake of sorrow; that would be all right. But my spirit withers by reason of a condensed and continually strained reflection; it cries out like the frogs in a marsh when a flock of voracious flamingos and starving herons descend amid the rushes along its banks.

Happy is he who slumbers peacefully in a bed of feathers torn from the breast of the eider, without being aware that he is betraying himself. It is thirty years now since I have slept. Since the unpronounceable day of my birth I have sworn an irreconcilable hatred against the slumberous couch. It is I who desired this; let none other be accused. Quickly — let all men be cleared of abortive suspicion. Do you observe upon my brow this pale crown? Tenacity weaved it there with its pale fingers. As long as a trace of burning sap runs through my bones like a torrent of molten metal

I shall never sleep. Each night I force my livid eyes to stare at the stars through the panes of my window. In order to be surer of myself I prop my swollen eyelids open with splinters. When dawn breaks it finds me in the same attitude, my body resting in a vertical position erect against the cold plaster of the wall. Yet it happens sometimes that I dream, but without losing for an instant the lively sense of my personality or the free faculty of movement: know that Nightmare hides himself in the phosphorescent crannies of darkness, while fever fingers my face with its stump, and every unclean beast brandishes its claws—very well, it is my will that keeps them going round and round in order to provide solid nourishment for its perpetual activity. Indeed, atom that wreaks revenge by its extreme weakness, free will does not fear to maintain with strong authority that it does not include sottishness among its sons: he who sleeps is less than an animal castrated yesterday. Although insomnia bears towards the depths of the grave these muscles which already exhale the odor of cypress, never will the white catacomb of my intelligence open its sanctuary to the eyes of the Creator. A secret and noble justice, towards the open arms of which I instinctively fling myself, commands me to hunt down without quarter that ignoble punishment. Fearful enemy of my imprudent soul, I forbid my unhappy loins to repose upon the dewy grass at the hour when they light up the lantern on the coast. Conqueror, I reject the ambush of your hypocritical opium. Consequently it is certain that my heart, that starving thing that feeds upon itself, has matured its plans by that weird struggle. As impenetrable as a giant, I have lived ceaselessly with the sockets of my eyes gaping. It is averred that at least during the day one may offer triumphant opposition to the Great Outside Object (who is not familiar with his name?); for then the will watches over its defenses with remarkable tenacity. But as soon as the vaporous veil of evening descends, even upon the condemned men about to be hanged, (O! to see one's intellect in the hands of a sacrilegious stranger!) an implacable scalpel probes into its dense underbrush. Consciousness exhales a long death-rattle of malediction, for the veil of its modesty undergoes cruel lacerations. Humiliation! Our door is open to the ferocious curiosity of the Celestial Bandit. I have not deserved this infamous torture, hideous spy upon my causality! If I exist, I am not someone else. I will not admit any equivocal plurality within myself. I wish to dwell alone within my intimate reason. Autonomy . . . or let them change me into a hippopotamus. Bury yourself in the earth, O anonymous stigma, and appear no more before my haggard indignation. My subjectivity and the Creator: this is too much for one brain. When night obscures the flight of hours, who is he who has not fought against the influence of sleep in his bed dampened with glacial sweat? That bed, clasping dying faculties to its bosom, is nothing

but a tomb composed of boards of scantling pine.
The will vanishes insensibly, as if in the presence
of an invisible force. A viscous wax dulls the
crystalline substance of the eye. The eyelids seek
one another like two friends. The body is no better
than a breathing corpse. Finally four enormous
stakes transfix the four limbs to the mattress. And
observe, if you please, that the sheets are nothing
but shrouds. There lies the censer where the in-
cense of religions burns. Eternity rumbles like a
distant sea and approaches rapidly. The room has
disappeared: prostrate yourselves, humans, in the
fiery chapel! Sometimes, in a useless effort to over-
come the organism's imperfections in the midst of
the profoundest sleep, the hypnotized sense per-
ceives with astonishment that it is nothing but a
gravestone, and argues admirably and with incom-
parable subtlety: "To leave this bed is a problem
more difficult than one would think. Seated upon
the tumbril I am drawn toward the twin posts of
the guillotine. Curiously, my arm has wisely taken
on the rigidity of a stump. It is very bad to dream
one is marching to the scaffold." Blood flows in
great waves across the face. The bosom heaves
repeatedly and wheezes as it swells. The weight
of an obelisk stifles the expansion of rage. The
real has destroyed the dreams of slumber! Who is
unaware that when the struggle is prolonged be-
tween the ego, full of pride, and the terrible
growth of catalepsy, the hallucinated spirit loses
its judgment? Gnawed by despair, he abandons

himself in his misery until he has conquered na-
ture and until sleep, seeing its prey escaping from
it flees forever from his heart with angry and
shameful wing. Throw some ashes upon my
flaming orbit. Do not stare into my eye, which
never closes. Do you understand the suffering I
endure? (though pride is satisfied). When night
exhorts humans to repose, a man whom I know
walks rapidly through the countryside. I fear that
my resolution may succumb to the ravages of
old age. Let that fatal day when I shall fall asleep
arrive! When I wake, my razor, opening up a
passage across my neck, will prove that nothing
indeed was more real.

But who is this? Who is this that dares like a
conspirator to drag the annular segments of its
body over my black bosom? Whoever you are,
eccentric python, what pretext excuses your
ridiculous presence? Is it a vast remorse tormenting
you? For look you, boa, your savage majesty has
not, I suppose, the exorbitant claim to exclude
itself from the comparison I make with the crimi-
nal's features. That frothy whitish dribble is, for
me, the sign of madness. Listen to me: do you
know that your eye is far from absorbing a celes-
tial beam? Do not forget that if your presumptu-
ous brain has believed me capable of offering you
a few words of consolation, it could only be from

the motive of an ignorance totally devoid of physiognomical knowledge. For a few moments, enough of course, direct the light of your eyes toward what I, even as others, have the right to call my face! Do you not see how it weeps? You are mistaken, basilisk. You must seek elsewhere the sad ration of relief of which my radical impotence deprives you, despite the countless protestations of my good will. Oh, what force drew you fatally by inexpressible phrases to your doom? It is almost impossible that I should acclimatise myself to the argument that you do not understand that, crushing into the reddened turf the distorted curves of your triangular head, I could knead a nameless putty from the grass and crushed flesh.

Get out of my way as quickly as possible, pallidfaced sinner! The fallacious mirage of terror has shown you your own spectre! Scatter your harmful suspicions if you do not wish that I should accuse you in my turn and inflict recriminations upon you that would most certainly be approved by the serpentine reptilivore. What monstrous aberration of imagination prevents you from recognizing me? You do not then recollect the important service I rendered you by the gratification of an existence dragged by me out of chaos; and on your part the unforgettable vow you made never to desert my flag and to remain faithful to me until death? When you were a child (your intelligence was in its finest phase then) you would be the first to climb a hill with the speed of a chamois to salute the multicolored beams of the waking dawn with a gesture of your little hand. The notes of your voice sprang from your sounding larynx like sparkling pearls and resolved their collective personalities in the vibrant aggregation of a long hymn of adoration. Now you throw down at your feet like a dirty rag the forebearance of which I have given you too much proof. Gratitude has seen its roots wither like the bed of a morass; but in its place ambition has grown to proportions that it would be painful for me to enumerate. Who is this, listening to me, to have so great a confidence in the abuse of his own weakness?

And who are you yourself, audacious stuff? No! No! I make no mistake; and despite the multiple metamorphoses to which you have recourse, your serpent's head will always shine before my eyes like an everlasting lighthouse of injustice and cruel domination! He desired to take up the reins of government, but he knows not how to reign! He desired to become an object of horror before all the beings of creation, and he succeeded. He desired to prove that he alone is the monarch of the universe, and it was there that he was mistaken. O miserable one! Have you waited until now to hear the muttering and the conspiracies which, rising up simultaneously from the surfaces of spheres, brush with furious wings against the papilose borders of your fragile ear-drum? The day is not far distant when my arm shall throw you down

in the dust poisoned by your breath, and, tearing
from your vitals a harmful life, leave your corpse
writhing upon the highway, to teach the dismayed
wayfarer that this palpitating flesh that astounds
his eye and cleaves his silent tongue to his palate,
should only be compared, if one retain one's cool-
headedness, to the rotten trunk of an oak fallen
from old age! What thought of pity holds me in
your presence? You had better stand back from
me, I tell you, and go wash away your immeasur-
able shame in the blood of a new-born infant: such
things are habitual to you. It is worthy of you.
Go . . . go straight ahead. I condemn you to
be a wanderer. I condemn you to be always alone
and without family. Wander forever, until your
legs refuse to support you. Cross the sands of
the desert until the end of the world engulfs the
stars in nothingness. When you pass by the tiger's
lair he will hasten to flee from you in order not
to see, as in a mirror, his own character raised upon
the pedestal of ideal perversity. But when imperi-
ous weariness commands you to pause in your
wanderings before the courtyard of my palace,
covered with rushes and thistles, be careful of your
ragged sandals and cross the threshold of the ele-
gant vestibule on tip-toe. This is no idle suggestion.
You might awaken my young spouse and my in-
fant son, sleeping in the leaden cellars honey-
combed in the foundations of the ancient castle.
If you do not prepare yourself in advance they
might draw the blood from your cheeks with their

[*229*]

subterranean howls. When your impenetrable will relieved them of life, they knew that your power was terrible and had no doubt in that regard; but they did not expect (and their supreme farewells confirmed for me this belief of theirs) that your Providence would manifest itself to so pitiless a degree!

In any case hurry onward through the silent and deserted halls with their emerald panelling and faded armorial bearings, where the glorious statues of my ancestors stand. Those marble bodies are full of wrath against you; avoid their vitriolic gaze. This is a piece of advice offered you by their last and only descendant. See how their arms are raised in attitudes of provocative defense, their heads thrown proudly back. Surely they have guessed the evil you have done me. And if you pass within reach of the frozen pedestals that bear these sculptured blocks, vengeance awaits you. If there is anything to be said in your defence, speak. It is too late now for weeping. You should have wept at a more appropriate moment, when the occasion was more propitious. If your eyes are at last opened, judge for yourself what have been the consequences of your conduct. Farewell! I go to breathe the sea-wind from a cliff; for my lungs, half stifled, demand with loud cries a sight more peaceful and more virtuous than you!

O incomprehensible pederasts! It is not for me to decry your vast degradation; it is not for me to cast scorn upon your infundibular anus. It is enough that the shameful and almost incurable diseases that attack you bear with them their inevitable punishment. Legislators of stupid institutions, inventors of narrow morality, keep your distance from me, for I have an impartial mind. And you, young fellows, or rather young girls, explain to me how and why (but keep your distance, for I too am incapable of resisting my passions) the lust for revenge so germinated in your hearts that you should have inflicted such a crown of wounds on the bosom of humanity. You make mankind blush for its sons by your conduct (which I myself venerate!); your prostitution to any chance comer exercises the logic of the deepest thinkers, while your exaggerated sensitivity transcends the measure of feminine stupefaction itself. Is your nature more or less earthly than that of your fellow men? Do you possess a sixth sense that is denied us? Do not lie, and say what you think. This is not an interrogation with which I confront you; for since I have been frequenting your exalted intelligences in the role of observer, I know what this is all about.

Be blessed by my left hand, be hallowed by my right hand, angels protected by my universal love! I kiss your face, I kiss your breast, with my smooth lips I kiss the various parts of your harmonious and perfumed body. Why did you not tell me at once what you were, crystallizations of a superior moral beauty? I was obliged to discover for myself the countless treasures of tenderness and chastity concealed by the pulses of your oppressed heart. Your breast is bedecked with garlands of roses and cuscus-grass. I was obliged to open your legs in order to know you and attach my mouth to the insignia of your modesty. But (and this is an important matter) do not forget to wash the skin of your parts every day in warm water, for if not veneral chancres will inevitably develop upon the lacerated surface of my insatiable lips.

O, if only, instead of being a hell, the universe had been an immense celestial anus! See the gesture I am making with my abdomen: yes, I would have plunged my penis through its bloody sphincter, rending apart by my impetuous motions the very bones of its pelvis! Sorrow would not then have breathed into my blinded eyes entire dunes of flying sand; I should have discovered the subterranean spot where truth lies slumbering, and the river of my viscous sperm would thus have found an ocean into which to precipitate itself! But why do I surprise myself regretting an imaginary state of things that will never receive the seal of its ultimate fulfillment? Let us not waste our time constructing furtive hypotheses. In the meantime, let him who burns with the desire to share my bed come to me; but I place a rigorous condition upon my hospitality: he must not be more than fifteen years old. Let him, for his part, not believe that

I am thirty. What difference does it make? Age
does not diminish the intensity of feeling, far from
it. And although my hair has become white as
snow it is not because of old age: it is because
of that which you know. I do not like women!
Nor even hermaphrodites! I must have beings who
resemble me, upon whose brows human nobility
is graved in deeper and more durable characters!
Are you sure that those who wear their hair long
have the same nature as I? I do not believe it and
I shall not abandon my opinion.

A brackish saliva flows from my mouth, I know
not why. Who wants to suck it up, to rid me of it?
It flows . . . it is flowing still! I know what it is.
I have noticed that whenever I drink from the
throat the blood of those who sleep with me (it is
wrong to suppose me a vampire, since vampire is
what they call dead ones who come from their
graves; but I am alive), the next day I vomit some
of it: that is the explanation of this pestiferous
saliva. What would you have me do if my organs,
enfeebled by vice, reject the functions of nutri-
tion? But reveal my confidences to no one. It is
not for myself that I tell you this; it is for yourself
and others, in order that the prestige of the secret
will retain within the limits of duty and virtue
those who, hypnotized by the electricity of the
unknown, would be tempted to imitate me. Have
the goodness to look at my mouth (at the moment
I have no time to frame a longer formula of polite-
ness); it strikes you at the first glance by the

[*233*]

Maldoror

appearance of its structure, without including the serpent among your comparisons; it is due to the fact that I contract the tissues down to the last possible reduction in order to make the world believe I have a cold nature. You are aware that it is diametrically opposed to this.

If only I could see through these seraphic pages the countenance of him who is reading me! If he has not passed puberty let him draw near. Crush me against you, and fear not that you will hurt me; let us contract the bands of our muscles progressively. More. I feel that it is useless to insist; the opacity, remarkable for more than one reason, of this sheet of paper is a most considerable obstacle to the operation of our complete junction.

I have always felt an infamous weakness for the pale youth of the college student and the sickly children of the factories! My words are not memories of a dream, and I should have too many memories to straighten out if the obligation were imposed upon me to parade before your eyes the events that could affirm by their testimony the truth of my sorrowful assertion. Human justice has not yet surprised me *in flagrante delictu,* despite the incontestable skill of its agents. I even slew (not so long ago!) a pederast who did not abandon himself sufficiently to my passion; I threw his body into an abandoned well; and there are no decisive proofs against me.

Why do you tremble with fear, you adolescent now reading me? Do you think I have similar in-

[*234*]

tentions toward you? You are supremely unjust. . .

You are right: beware of me, especially if you are beautiful. My nates offer everlastingly the lugubrious spectacle of tumescence; no one can claim (and how many have drawn near!) that he has seen them in a state of normal quiescence, not even the shoe shine boy who attacked me with a knife during a moment of delirium. Ungrateful wretch!

I change my clothes twice a week, cleanliness not being the principal motive of my determination. If I did not act thus the human race would disappear at the end of a few days in prolonged battles. Indeed its members harass me continually in whatever country I happen to find myself and come to lick my feet. But what power do my seminal drops possess that they attract to them all that breathes with olfactory nerves! They come from the banks of the Amazon, they cross the valleys watered by the Ganges, they desert the polar moss to undertake long voyages to seek me out, and to ask the imperturbable cities if they have seen me pass by along their ramparts, I whose holy sperm embalms the mountains, the lakes, the woods, the forests, the hills and the vastnesses of seas!

The despair of being unable to find me (I hide myself secretly in the most inaccessible places in order to feed their zeal) leads them on to the most regrettable actions. They range themselves three hundred thousand to a side and the roaring of cannon serves as prelude to the battle. All the

wings rush together simultaneously, like a single
warrior. Squares are formed, only to fall again
forever. Bullets plough up the soil like implacable
meteors. The theatre of war is nothing but a vast
field of carnage when night reveals her presence
and the silent moon appears between the rags of a
cloud. Pointing out to me a space several leagues
wide covered with corpses, the misty crescent of
that star commands me to take for a moment, as
the subject of meditative reflections, the ghastly
consequences that the inexplicable magic talisman
accorded me by Providence bears in its wake. Alas!
How many centuries must still pass before the
human race shall perish utterly by means of my
perfidious trap! It is thus that a cunning and
modest mind may employ, to achieve its ends,
the very means which at first seem to contain
an insuperable obstacle. My intelligence forever
mounts toward this imposing question, and you
yourself are witness that it is impossible for me to
confine myself to the modest subject that at first
I had planned to take up.

A final word. . . . It was a winter night. While
the wind whistled through the pines, the Creator
opened his door amid the shadows and admitted a
pederast.

Silence! A funeral procession is passing by! In-
cline the biformity of your patellae towards the

earth and intone a hymn from beyond the tomb.
(If you consider my words as a simple imperative
form, rather than a formal command out of its
proper place, you will be showing wit, and wit
of the best). It is possible that in this manner you
will succeed in rejoicing extremely the soul of the
dead person who is about to take refuge from life
in a grave. The fact is even certain as far as I am
concerned. Notice that I do not say that your
opinion might up to a certain point differ from
mine; but the most important thing is to have just
ideas concerning the basis of morality, to which
end everyone should steep himself in the principle
that insists that all men should do unto others as
perhaps he would have others do unto them.

The priest of religions is the first to lead the way,
holding a white flag in one hand as a sign of peace,
and in the other a golden emblem representing the
private parts of men and women, as if to indicate
that these carnal members are most of the time,
omitting all metaphor, very dangerous weapons in
the hands of those who employ them, when they
manipulate them blindly to various and conflicting
ends, instead of engendering an opportune re-
action against the notorious passion that causes
most of our ills. To the lower part of his back is
attached (artificially, of course) a horse's tail with
bushy hairs sweeping the dust of the earth. This
means to beware of debasing ourselves through
our conduct to the level of animals. The hearse
knows its way and moves behind the floating

vestment of the chief mourner. The relations and friends of the deceased, by the manifestation of their position, seem to have resolved to bring up the rear of the procession. The latter advances majestically like a ship cleaving the open sea and fearless of the phenomenon of shipwreck; for at that particular moment storms and reefs conceal themselves by somewhat less than their understandable absence.

Crickets and toads follow the funeral festival at a short distance; they too realize that their modest appearance at anyone's funeral will be a day counted to them. They converse together in low tones in their picturesque language (do not be so presumptuous — permit me to offer you this disinterested advice — as to believe that you alone possess the precious faculty of translating your thoughts) concerning him whom they had seen more than once running across verdant meadows and plunging the sweat of his limbs into the bluish waves of sandy bays.

At first life seemed to smile upon him without reservation, and crowned him magnificently with flowers; but since your own intelligence perceives or rather divines that he was cut short in infancy, I need not, until the appearance of a really necessary retraction, continue the prolegomena of my rigorous demonstration. Ten years. Number exactly calculated, to avoid error, upon the fingers. It is little and it is much. In the case preoccupying us, however, I shall lean upon your love of truth and expect you to announce, with me and without waiting a second longer, that it is little. And when I summarily reflect upon those shadowy mysteries by means of which human beings disappear from the earth as easily as a fly or a dragonfly, without any hope of returning, I surprise myself nursing a lively regret that I shall probably not be able to live long enough to explain to you what I make no claim to understand myself. But since it is proved that by an extraordinary piece of luck I have not yet lost my life since that distant time when, filled with terror, I began the preceding sentence, I calculate mentally that it would not be useless here to construct the complete avowal of my basic impotence, when it is especially a matter, as at present, of this imposing and unapproachable question.

It is, generally speaking, a singular thing that an attractive tendency inclines us to seek out the resemblances and the differences (in order afterwards to explain them) which are concealed within the natures of the most widely differing objects and often objects the least appropriate to be participating in this kind of sympathetically curious combination, and which, upon my word of honor, lend graciously to the style of the writer who treats himself to this personal satisfaction the impossible and unforgettable appearance of an owl serious until eternity. Consequently let us follow the current that carries us on.

The kite has wings proportionately longer than

the buzzard, and a much more facile flight: furthermore he passes his life in the air. He practically never rests and each day covers vast distances; and all this agitation is not in the exercise of the hunt nor in pursuit of prey nor even reconnoitering, for he does not hunt; but it seems that flight is his natural state, his favorite situation. One cannot help but admire the manner in which he executes it. His long, narrow wings appear to be motionless; it is the tail that directs all the evolutions, and the tail makes no errors: it is incessantly active. The bird rises effortlessly; it descends as if it were gliding down an inclined plane; it seems rather to swim than to fly; it speeds up its flight, slows it down, stops, and remains as though suspended or attached to the same spot for whole hours. It is impossible to detect any movement of its wings: you may open your eyes like the door of a furnace, it is useless. Everyone has the good sense to confess without difficulty (although with a little bad grace) that he cannot immediately see the connection, far-fetched as it is, between the beauty of the kite's flight and the beauty of the child's face, gently raised above the open coffin like a water-lily emerging from the ripples; and therein precisely consists the unpardonable fault inherent in the permanent state of lack of repentance in connection with the wilful ignorance in which one wallows. This relationship of calm majesty between the two terms of my mocking comparison is already only too common and a sufficiently comprehensible symbol that I should be any more astonished by what can have as sole excuse that same characteristic of vulgarity which summons up to any object or spectacle attacked by it a deep feeling of unjust indifference. As if what occurs daily should arouse any less our feeling of admiration!

Arrived at the entrance to the cemetery the procession comes to a standstill. Its intention is to go no farther. The gravedigger finishes digging the grave; the coffin is placed there with all the precautions generally taken in such cases. A few chance spadefuls of earth cover the child's body. The priest of religions addresses the deeply-moved gathering and pronounces a few words to bury the dead child properly, and in the imagination of the mourners, better.

He says, "he is much surprised that there should be so much weeping for so insignificant an occasion. (sic) But he fears not to qualify sufficiently that which he himself claims to be an inestimable happiness. If he had believed death to be so unsympathetic in its naïveté he would then have given up his commission in order not to add to the legitimate sorrow of the numerous relatives and friends of the deceased. But a secret voice commanded him to offer them a few consolations which would not be without their place if they only afforded a glimpse of hope that the deceased and the survivors might soon meet in heaven."

Maldoror fled at full gallop, apparently riding his horse toward the cemetery walls. His horse's hoofs raised up a false aureole of thick dust around its master. You cannot know this horseman's name, but I know it. He drew nearer and nearer. His platinum face began to be distinguishable, although its lower part was completely enveloped in a black cloak which the reader will not have forgotten and which revealed only his eyes. In the midst of his sermon the priest of religions suddenly turned pale, for his ear recognized the irregular gait of that celebrated white horse, never abandoned by its master.

"Yes," he added, "my confidence in this impending meeting is great, for then one will understand better than heretofore what meaning should be attached to the contemporaneous separation of soul and body. Whoever believes he is living on this earth is cradled by an illusion that should be quickly dispelled."

The sound of galloping grew louder and louder; and, as the horseman appeared above the horizon within the visual field embraced by the cemetery gate, swift as a whirlwind, the priest resumed more gravely:

"You appear to think that this child here, forced by disease to know only the first phases of life and recently taken into the bosom of the grave, is the indubitable living one; but at least know that that man yonder, whose ambiguous silhouette you perceive borne upon a sinewy horse, and upon whom I counsel you to turn your eyes as soon as possible for he is only a dot and will soon disappear over the heath, although he has lived greatly, he is the only real dead one."

🐚

"Each night at the hour when sleep has achieved its highest degree of intensity, a large and ancient spider slowly projects its head out of a hole located on the ground at one of the intersections of the corners of the room. It listens attentively for any sound that may still be moving its mandibles in the air. Allowing for its quality as insect, it cannot do less, if it has any ambitions to adding brilliant personifications to the treasures of literature, than attribute mandibles to sounds. When it has re-assured itself that silence reigns in the neighbor-hood, it brings forth successively from the depths of its nest, without refuge in meditation, the vari-ous parts of its body, and advances slowly toward my bed. Remarkable occurrence! I, who re-ject sleep and nightmare, feel myself paralyzed throughout my body when the spider climbs up the ebony foot of my satin bed. It seizes me by the throat with its feet and sucks my blood with its belly. Just like that! How many litres of purplish liquid, the name of which you know, has it not drunk since it commenced this same maneuver with a persistance worthy of a better cause! I do not know what I have done to it that it should behave toward me in this manner. Did I inadvertently crush one of its feet? Did I steal its young? These two hypotheses, subject to caution, are not capable of sustaining serious examination; they even have no trouble in provoking a shrug of my shoulders or a smile on my lips, although one should not make fun of anyone.

"Beware, black tarantula! If your conduct has not an irrefutable syllogism for excuse, one night I shall awaken suddenly with a last effort of my agonizing will, I shall break the spell with which you keep my limbs motionless, and I shall crush you between the bones of my fingers like a bit of soft stuff. Yet I vaguely remember having given you permission to climb upon my breast and up to the skin covering my face; and that consequently I have no right to restrain you. O, who will disentangle my confused memories? For a reward I would give him what is left of my blood: counting the last drop there is enough left at least to fill half a banquet goblet."

He speaks and continues to disrobe. He rests one leg upon the mattress, then the other, pressing against the sapphire floor to raise himself, and stretches out in a horizontal position. He has resolved not to close his eyes that he may meet his enemy firmly. But does he not make the same resolution each time, and is it not always destroyed by the inexplicable image of his fatal promise? He says no more and resigns himself with sorrow;

for to him an oath is sacred. He enwraps himself majestically in the folds of silk, disdains to fasten the golden tassels of his bed-curtain, and, spreading out the rippling waves of his long black hair upon the fringes of his velvet pillow, he feels with his hand the large wound in his neck, in which the tarantula has been in the habit of installing itself as in a second nest, while his face expresses satisfaction. He hopes that this particular night (hope with him!) will witness the last performance of the vast suction; for his only wish is that the executioner shall have done with his life: with death he will be content.

See that large and ancient spider slowly projecting its head from a hole located on the ground at one of the intersections of the corners of the room. We are no longer telling a story. It listens attentively for any sound that may be moving its mandibles in the air. Alas, now we are in the midst of reality insofar as the tarantula is concerned, and, although one may place an exclamation point at the end of each sentence, this is perhaps no reason to dispense with them! It assures itself that silence reigns in the neighborhood and brings successively forth from the depths of its nest, without refuge in meditation, the various parts of its body and advances slowly toward the lonely man's bed. For a moment it pauses; but the instant of hesitation is short. It tells itself that it is not yet time to discontinue the torture, and that first plausible reasons must be given the condemned man to determine the perpetuality of the torment. It has climbed up beside the sleeper's ear. If you do not wish to lose a single word of what it is about to say, eliminate the alien preoccupations that obstruct the portals of your mind, and at least be grateful for the interest I show you in bringing you in contact with a drama that seems to me worthy of real attention on your part; for who is to prevent me from keeping to myself the events I am relating?

"Awaken, amorous flame of ancient days, emaciated skeleton! The time has come to stay the hand of justice. We shall not make you wait long for the explanation you desire. You are listening to us, are you not? But do not move your limbs; today you are still under our hypnotic spell and encephalitic atony persists: it is for the last time. What impression does the face of Elsinor make upon your imagination? You have forgotten him! And that Reginald, with his proud gait, have you engraved his features upon your faithful brain? See him there hidden in the folds of the curtain; his mouth is bent over your brow; but he dares not address you, for he is more timid than I. I am going to tell you an episode from your youth and replace your footsteps on the road to memory. . . ."

Some time previously the spider had opened its belly and two young men had emerged therefrom, each dressed in a blue robe, each with a flamboyant sword in his hand; and they had taken their places at the bedside as if in future to mount guard over the sanctuary of sleep.

"This one, who has not yet ceased to look upon you, for he loved you greatly, was the first of us two to whom you gave your love. But you made him suffer much by the roughness of your character. He exerted every effort in order to avoid giving you any cause for complaint against him; an angel would have been unsuccessful. You asked him one day if he would like to go swimming with you from the sea-shore. The two of you, like two swans, dove simultaneously from a steep rock. Eminent divers, you slid through the aqueous mass, your arms joined together above your heads. For a few moments you swam between two currents. You reappeared at a great distance, your hair tangled together and streaming with salt water. But what mystery had then taken place beneath the water that a long streak of blood appeared among the waves? You, when you reappeared upon the surface, continued to swim and you made out not to notice the growing weakness of your companion. He rapidly lost his strength and you none the less continued to thrust your powerful armstrokes toward the misty horizon. The wounded man uttered cries of distress, and you pretended to be deaf. Reginald aroused the echoes thrice with the syllables of your name, and three times you replied with a cry of voluptuous delight. He found himself too far from the shore to reach it, and struggled in vain

to follow in the wake of your passage in order
to reach you and rest his hand for a moment upon
your shoulder. This negative chase continued for
an hour, he losing his strength and you feeling
yours increasing. Despairing of equalling your
speed, he offered up a short prayer to the Lord
to recommend his soul, turned himself upon his
back in such a manner that one could see the
violent beating of his heart within his breast, and
awaited the arrival of death to put an end to wait-
ing. By then your vigorous limbs were out of sight
and you disappeared swift as a plummet through
the water. A boat, returning from casting its nets
in the open sea, passed by the spot. The fishermen
took Reginald for a victim of shipwreck and hauled
him, unconscious, into their boat. A wound in the
right side was discovered; each of those experi-
enced sailors voiced the opinion that no reef or rock
fragment was capable of piercing so microscopic
and at the same time so deep a hole. A cutting
weapon, such as the very sharpest of stilettos,
alone could claim the parentage of so fine a wound.
Reginald would not relate the various phases of the
swim through the waves' entrails, and he has kept
the secret until now. Tears flow now down his
somewhat discolored cheeks and fall upon the
covers: memory is sometimes more bitter than the
event itself. But I feel no pity: that would be to
show you too much esteem. Do not roll those in-
furiated eyes in their sockets. Rather lie quietly.
You know you cannot move. In any case I have not

finished my speech. (Raise your sword, Reginald, and do not so easily forget revenge. Who knows? Perchance one day it will come to reproach you.) Later on you conceived a remorse the existence of which must have been ephemeral. You resolved to make amends for your crime by choosing another friend, to bless and honor him. By this expiatory method you would efface the stains of the past, and you would shower upon him who was to become the second victim the sympathy you had not shown the other. Vain hope: character does not modify itself from one day to the next, and your will remained the same."

"I, Elsinor, saw you for the first time and from that moment I could not forget you. We looked at one another for a few minutes and you began to smile. I lowered my eyes, for I saw in yours a supernatural flame. I asked myself if, on some dark night, you had let yourself fall down to us from the surface of some star; for, I confess, since today it is no longer necessary to pretend, you did not resemble the wild boars of humanity. A halo of glittering rays enveloped the periphery of your brow. I would have formed intimate relations with you; my presence dared not approach the striking novelty of that strange nobility, and a gripping terror roamed about me. Why did I not listen to those warnings of conscience? Well-founded presentiments. Noticing my hesitation you blushed in your turn and held out your hand. Courageously I placed my hand in yours, and after

[*249*]

that action I felt stronger: a breath of your intelligence had entered into me. With our hair flying in the wind and inhaling the perfume of the breeze, we walked together for some time through budding thickets of mastic, of jasmine, of grenadine and orange-trees, drunk with their odor. A boar in full flight brushed against us, and a tear fell from his eye when he saw me with you: I could not explain his conduct. At nightfall we arrived before the gates of a populous city. The profiles of domes, the spires of minarets and the marble globes upon the belvederes were sharply outlined against the intense blue of the sky. But you did not wish to rest in that place, although we were overcome with weariness. We passed along the base of the exterior fortifications, like jackals of the night; we avoided encountering the sentinels on duty; and we succeeded in removing ourselves, by the opposite gate, from the solemn aggregation of reasoning animals, civilized like beavers. The flight of the smoky lantern, the crackling of dry twigs, the intermittent howling of some distant wolf accompanied the obscurity of our wayward steps across the country. What were your valid motives for avoiding the human hives? I asked myself that question with a certain apprehension; and my legs began to refuse me a too-prolonged service. We reached at last the edge of a thick wood, the trees of which were entangled with an inextricable mass of high creepers, of parasitic plants, and of cactus with monstrous spines. You stopped before a birch tree. You told me to fall on my knees and prepare to die; you granted me fifteen minutes to leave this earth. Certain furtive glances during our long journey, certain gestures of which I had noticed the irregularity of measure and movement, instantly presented themselves to my memory like the open pages of a book. My suspicions were confirmed. Too weak to struggle against you, I was thrown to the ground as the aspen is crushed by the hurricane. One of your knees was upon my breast, the other on the moist grass, while one of your hands pinioned my two arms as in a vise, I saw the other draw out a knife from the sheath hanging from your belt. My resistance was practically non-existent and I closed my eyes. The bellowing of a herd of bulls made itself heard some distance away, borne upon the wind. It advanced like a locomotive, spurred on by the rod of a cowherd and the jaws of a dog. There was no time to lose, and you understood this; fearing to fail in your intention, for the approach of unhoped-for succor had redoubled my strength, and realizing you could pinion only one of my arms at a time, you contented yourself with cutting off my right hand with a swift slash of the steel blade. The fragment, nicely detached, fell to the ground. You fled, while I was fainting with pain. I will not relate how the cowherd came to my assistance, nor how long it took for my wound to heal. Suffice it to say that this betrayal, which I had not anticipated, gave birth in me to a desire for death. I took part in battles in order to offer my bosom to a death-blow. I gained glory on the battlefield; my name became terrible even to the bravest, for my artificial iron hand spread carnage and destruction among the enemy ranks. However, one day when the shells were thundering much more savagely than usual, and the squadrons, routed out of their bases, whirled like straws before the cyclone of death, a bold-looking horseman advanced before me to dispute with me the palm of victory. The two armies came to a dead stop to watch us in silence. We fought for a long time, riddled with wounds, and our helmets were broken. In a common accord we ceased our fighting to catch our breaths and then to have at each other again with renewed vigor. Full of admiration each of us raised his visor: "Elsinor!" "Reginald!" . . . such were the simple words that issued simultaneously from our panting breasts. Reginald, prey to the despair of an inconsolable sorrow, had taken up, as I had, the career of arms, and bullets had spared him. In what circumstances we met again! But your name was not uttered! He and I swore eternal friendship; but a friendship vastly different from the first two in which you had been the principal actor.

An archangel, descended from Heaven as a messenger of the Lord, commanded us to change into one single spider and to come to you every night to suck at your throat until such time as a further command from on high should put an end to the punishment. For almost ten years we have haunted your sleep. From today you are delivered from our persecution. The vague promise of which you spoke was not made to us, but to the Being who is stronger than you: you understood yourself that it would be wiser for you to submit to that irrevocable decree. Wake, Maldoror! The hypnotic spell that has weighed upon your cerebro-spinal system for ten years of nights is lifted."

He awakens as has been commanded and sees two celestial shapes disappearing into the air, arms interlaced. He does not attempt to sleep again. Slowly he lifts one leg, then the other, from the bed. He warms his frozen skin at the revived embers in the Gothic fireplace. Only his night-shirt covers his body. His eyes seek the crystal pitcher in order to moisten his withered palate. He opens the window-shutters. He leans upon the sill. He contemplates the moon, which pours down upon his breast a cone of ecstatic beams in which silver atoms of ineffable sweetness flutter like moths. He waits, until the morning twilight shall bring, by a change of scene, a mocking relief to his prostrated heart.

MALDOROR

(LES CHANTS DE MALDOROR)

6

You whose enviable calm can do no more than embellish think not that it is any longer a question of uttering, in stanzas of fourteen or fifteen lines, like a fourth-grade pupil, exclamations that will pass for inopportune and noisy cacklings of a cochinchina chicken, as grotesque as may be imagined without trying especially hard; but it is preferable to prove by facts the propositions one advances. Would you then claim that because I had insulted as if making light of them mankind, the Creator, and myself in my explicable hyperboles, my mission were complete? No: the most important part of my work still remains as a task to be done.

In future the strings of fiction will activate the three individuals named above: a less abstract power will thus be communicated to them. Vitality will expand magnificently through the flow of their circulatory apparatus, and you will see how you yourself will be astonished to encounter, where before you had believed to be dealing with vague beings belonging to the domain of pure speculation, on the one hand the bodily organism with its ramifications of nerves and its mucous membranes, and on the other the spiritual principle that presides over the psychological functions of the flesh. These are beings endowed with an energetic life, who, arms crossed and chest expanded, will stand prosaically (but I am certain that the effect will be highly poetic) before your face, placed at only a few paces from you in such a manner that the solar beams, striking first the roof-tiles and the chimney-pots, will then come to reflect visibly from their earthly and material hair.

But there will be no more anathemas, possessing the specialty of provoking laughter; fictitious personalities who would have done better to remain in the author's brain; or nightmares raised too high above ordinary existence. Notice that by this very fact my poetry will be more beautiful.

You will touch with your hands the ascending branches of the aorta and the suprarenal glands, and the senses! The first five lays have not been without their utility; they were the frontispiece to my work, the foundation of the construction, the preliminary explanation of my future poetry: and I owed it to myself before locking up my suit-case and setting out for the domains of imagination to warn sincere lovers of literature by the rapid rough outline of a clear and precise generalisation, of the goal I had resolved to pursue.

In consequence my opinion is that now the synthetic section of my work is complete and sufficiently paraphrased. It is from that section you learned that I proposed to attack mankind and Him who created mankind. For now and for later you have no need to know more about it! New considerations appear to me to be superfluous, for they would do nothing but repeat in another form, more embracing, it is true, but identical, the statement of the thesis of which the end of today will see the first development. It follows from the preceding observations that my intention is to undertake for the future the analytical section. This is so true that only a few moments ago I expressed the ardent wish that you might be imprisoned in the sweat-glands of my skin in order to verify by your own knowledge the truth of what I affirm. I am aware that I should bolster up the argument contained in my theorem by a great number of proofs; very well, those proofs exist, and you know that I attack no one without serious motives! I roar with laughter when I think that you reproach me with spreading bitter accusations against humanity, of which I am myself a member (that fact alone would give me a reason!) and against Providence: I shall not retract my words. But, relating what I have seen, it will not be difficult, with no other ambition than the truth, to justify them.

Today I am about to invent a little novel of thirty pages: this measure will remain afterwards

[margin handwritten note: terms of rhetoric — Ducasse had just completed a class in rhetoric]

more or less stationary. Hoping some day soon to see the consecration of my theories accepted by one or another literary form, I believe I have found at last, after several feelers, my final formula. It is the best, since it is the novel!

This hybrid preface has been exhibited in a manner that will perhaps appear not natural enough, in the sense that it surprises the reader, so to speak, who does not very clearly see where he is being led at first; but that feeling of wonderful stupefaction from which one generally seeks to protect those who pass their time reading books or magazines, I have made every effort to produce. Indeed, it was impossible for me to do less, despite my good will: it will only be later, after several novels have appeared, that you will better understand the preface of the renegade with the grimy face.

2nd preface

I find it stupid that it should be necessary before taking up the thread of our narrative (I think not everyone will be of my opinion, if I am mistaken) that I should have to place before me an open inkstand and several sheets of uncrumpled paper. In this manner it will be possible for me to begin, with love, through this sixth lay, the series of instructive poems that I long to produce. Dramatic episodes of implacable utility!

– he says poetry should be useful + have practical values

Lautréamont

Our hero perceived that by frequenting cellars and taking refuge in inaccessible places he was transgressing the rules of logic and perpetrating a vicious circle. For if on the one hand he favored his repugnance toward mankind by the compensation of solitude and distance, and passively circumscribed his limited horizon amid stunted shrubs, briars, and creepers, on the other hand his activity found no further food to nourish the minotaur of his perverse instincts. Consequently he decided to involve himself with human agglomerations, convinced that among so many ready-made victims his various passions would easily find material for their satisfaction. He knew the police, that shield of civilisation, had been looking for him perseveringly for a number of years and that a veritable army of agents and spies were eternally on his trail. Without, however, succeeding in finding him. His destructive skill was such that he was able to disrupt with the most extreme nicety schemes which from the point of view of their success in conception were incontestable, and arrangements resulting from the most learned scheming. He had a special faculty for taking on shapes unrecognizable by expert eyes. Superior disguises, if I speak as an artist! Accoutrements of an extremely mediocre effect, when I think of morality. On this point he came close to genius. Have you ever noticed the slenderness of the pretty cricket, with his alert movements, in the Paris gutters? It could only be he: it was Maldoror!

Mesmerizing the flourishing capitals with a pernicious fluid, he reduces them to a state of lethargy in which they are not able to look out for themselves as they should: a state the more dangerous as it is unsuspected.

Today he is in Madrid; tomorrow he will be in Saint Petersburg; yesterday he was in Pekin; but to state exactly the place that the exploits of this poetic Rocambole are filling with terror at any given moment would be a labor beyond the possible strength of my deep ratiocination. This bandit is perhaps seven hundred leagues away from this country; perhaps he is a few steps away from you.

It is not easy to bring about the death of the entire race of men, and the law is there; but one may, with patience, exterminate the human ants one by one.

Indeed, since the day of my birth, when I lived with the first ancestors of our race who were as yet inexperienced in the tension of my traps; since prehistoric times long gone by, when, under divers subtle metamorphoses, I ravaged, at different epochs, the countries of the globe by conquest and carnage and spread civil war among the citizens, have I not already crushed beneath my heel, individual by individual or collectively, entire generations of which it would not be difficult to conceive the unmentionable number?

The brilliant past has made brilliant promises to the future: it will keep them. For the gathering up of my sentences I shall of necessity employ the natural method, regressing to the savages that they may give me lessons. Simple and majestic gentlemen, their gracious mouths ennoble all that flows from their tattooed lips.

I have just proved that nothing on this planet is laughable. Queer but superb planet. Borrowing a style that some will find naive (when it is so profound!), I shall use it to interpret ideas which, unfortunately, will not perhaps seem grand! By that very fact, depriving myself of the light and sceptical mannerisms of ordinary conversations, and sufficiently prudent not to ask. . . . I no longer recall what I was intending to say, for I do not remember the beginning of the sentence.

But know that poetry is to be found everywhere where the stupidly mocking smile of duck-faced man does not exist.

First of all I shall blow my nose, because I need to. And then, potently assisted by my hand, I shall again take up the pen-holder that my fingers had let fall.

How could the Carrousel Bridge maintain the constancy of its neutrality when it heard heart-rending screams apparently uttered by the sack!

The shops on the Rue Vivienne display their merchandise before awe-struck eyes. Illuminated by numerous gas-lamps, the mahogany chests and

gold watches throw back through the windows
dazzling beams of light. Eight o'clock has sounded
from the Stock Exchange clock: it is not late! The
last peal has hardly died away when the street,
whose name has been mentioned, begins to tremble
and shakes to its foundations from the Place Royale
to the Boulevard Montmartre. The wayfarers
hasten their step and retire thoughtfully into their
houses. A woman faints and falls to the sidewalk.
No one lifts her up: everyone is eager to get away
from the spot. Windows close impetuously, and
the tenants bury themselves beneath the covers.
One would say that the Asiatic plague had an-
nounced its presence.

And so, while the greater part of the city
prepares to bathe in the joys of nocturnal revels,
the Rue Vivienne finds itself suddenly frozen into
a sort of petrifaction. Like a heart that has ceased
to love, its life is extinct. But soon news of the
phenomenon spreads to other layers of the popula-
tion and a gloomy silence settles over the august
capital.

Where have the gas-lamps gone? What has
become of the peddlers of love? Nothing . . .
solitude and darkness. An owl with a broken
foot, flying in a rectilineal direction passes above
the Madeleine and takes flight toward the barrier
of Le Trone, crying out: "A misfortune is threat-
ening!"

Now from that spot that my pen (that real
friend who serves me as accomplice) has just made

mysterious, if you will look in the direction where
the Rue Colbert runs into the Rue Vivienne you
will see at the corner formed by the crossing of
these two streets a person display his silhouette and
direct his light step toward the boulevards. But if
one approach closer, in such a manner as to avoid
attracting the attention of this wayfarer, one per-
ceives with pleasant surprise that he is young!
From a distance indeed one would have taken
him for a mature man. The number of days no
longer counts when it is a question of appreciating
the intellectual capacity of a serious face. I am
skilled at reading the age from the physiognomical
lines of the brow: he is sixteen years and four
months old!

He is as handsome as the retractibility of the
claws of birds of prey; or again, as the uncertainty
of the muscular movements of wounds in the soft
parts of the posterior cervical region; or rather
as the perpetual rat-trap, re-set each time by the
trapped animal, that can catch rodents indefinitely
and works even when hidden beneath straw; and
especially as the fortuitous encounter upon a dis-
secting-table of a sewing-machine and an umbrella!

Mervyn, that son of fair-haired England, has
just taken his lesson from his fencing-master, and,
wrapped in his Scotch tartan, is returning to his
parents' home. It is half past eight and he hopes
to arrive home by nine o'clock. It is a great pre-
sumption on his part to claim to be certain of
knowing the future. Could not some unforeseen

obstacle impede his progress? And would that circumstance occur so infrequently that he should take it upon himself to consider it an exception? Should he not rather consider the fact abnormal that he has had reason hitherto to feel himself devoid of anxiety and, so to speak, happy? By what right indeed does he assume that he will reach home safe and sound, when behind him someone watches and follows him as a future prey?

(It would indeed be manifesting ignorance of one's profession as a writer of sensational fiction not at least to set down first the restrictive interrogations, after which arrives immediately the sentence that I have just terminated.)

You have recognized the imaginary hero who for a long time has been foundering my unhappy intelligence by the pressure of his individuality! Now Maldoror approaches Mervyn, in order to engrave the youth's features upon his memory; now, throwing his body backwards he falls back upon himself like an Australian boomerang in the second period of its trajectory, or rather like an infernal machine. He is undecided as to what he should do. But his consciousness, as you would wrongly suppose, feels not even the most embryonic symptom of emotion. I saw him turn for an instant in the opposite direction: was he overcome by remorse? But he retraced his steps with renewed obstinacy.

Mervyn does not know why his temporal arteries throb so violently, and he hastens his step,

[264]

obsessed by a fear of which he and you vainly seek the cause. We must give him credit for his application to answering the riddle. Why does he not turn around? He would understand everything. Does one never think of the simplest means of putting an end to a state of alarm? When a prowler crosses an alley in the slums with a bottle of white wine in his belly and his shirt in tatters, if in a corner he spies an old sinewy cat, contemporary of the revolutions in which our fathers took part, contemplating in melancholy the moonbeams pouring down upon the slumbering plain, he approaches tortuously in a curved line and signals to a bow-legged dog, which leaps forward. The noble animal of the feline race awaits her adversary with courage and sells her life dearly. The next day some rag-picker will purchase an electrifiable pelt. Why did she not run away? It would have been so easy.

But in the case now preoccupying us, Mervyn further complicates the danger by his own ignorance. He has, as it were, a few hints, excessively rare it is true, of which I shall not pause to demonstrate the vagueness covering them. However, it is impossible for him to guess the truth. He is no prophet, I will not deny, and he does not recognize in himself the faculty of being one.

Arriving at the main street, he turns right and crosses the Boulevard Poissoniere and the Boulevard Bonne-Nouvelle. At this point in his journey he turns down the Rue du Faubourg-Saint-Denis,

leaves behind him the embankment of the Stras-
burg railway, and stops before a tall gateway
before having reached the perpendicular super-
position of the Rue Lafayette.

Since you advise me to conclude the first stanza
at this point, I am quite willing, this time, to yield
to your desire.

Do you know that when I think of the iron ring
concealed beneath the stone by the hand of a
maniac, an irrepressible shudder passes over my
scalp?

He presses the brass button and the gateway
of the modern mansion turns on its hinges. He
crosses the courtyard, paved with fine sand, and
climbs up eight steps. The two statues set to the
right and left like guardians of the aristocratic
villa, do not obstruct his passage.

He who has denied everything — father, mother,
Providence, love, ideals — in order to be able to
think of nothing but himself alone, has taken good
care not to follow in the preceding footsteps. He
watches the boy enter a spacious living-room on
the ground floor with cornelian panelling.

The son sinks down upon a sofa, emotion pre-
venting him from speaking. His mother, in a long
trailing gown, hastens up to him and enfolds
him in her arms. His brothers, younger than he,

group themselves around the sofa and its burden. They are not sufficiently acquainted with life to form a clear impression of the scene that is taking place. Finally the father raises his cane and turns upon the boys a glance full of authority. Leaning his hand against the arm of his chair he leaves his usual place, although enfeebled by age, and advances towards the motionless body of his first-born, full of disquiet. He speaks in a foreign language, and everyone listens in respectful silence:

"Who has reduced the boy to this condition? The foggy Thames will still wash down a considerable quantity of mud before my strength will be completely exhausted. The laws of preservation do not seem to exist in this inhospitable country. If I knew the culprit he would feel the strength of my arm. Although I have retired from maritime engagements, my commodore's sword, hung on the wall, is not yet rusted. In any case, it is easy to sharpen its edge. Mervyn, calm yourself: I will give orders to my servants to get on the track of him who, in the future, I shall seek out and slay with my own hand. Wife, get up from there and go and sit in a corner. Your eyes soften me and you had better seal the canals of your lachrymal glands. My son, I implore you, return to your senses and recognize your family. It is your father who speaks to you. . . ."

The mother withdraws to one side, and, obeying the orders of her master, takes up a book and

endeavors to remain calm in the presence of the
danger that menaces the fruit of her womb.

"Children, go play in the park, and take care
while admiring the swans swimming not to fall
into the body of water. . . ."

The brothers, their arms hanging at their sides,
remain silent. They all, each with his cap sur-
mounted by a feather torn from the wing of the
Carolinian goat-sucker, with his velvet knee-
length pants, and his red silk socks, take each other
by the hand and retire from the room, being care-
ful to cross the ebony floor on tip-toe. I am certain
they will not amuse themselves, but will gravely
wander through the plane groves. Their intelli-
gence is precocious. So much the better for them.

"Useless cares. I cradle you in my arms and you
are insensible to my entreaties. Won't you raise
your head? I will embrace your knees if I must.
But no . . . it falls back inert."

"My sweet master, if you will permit your slave,
I will go to my room and bring a flask filled with
essence of turpentine of which I avail myself habit-
ually when the migraine invades my brow after
returning from the theatre or when the reading
of a moving story consigned to the British annals
of the chivalrous history of our ancestors, casts
my dreamy thoughts into the morass of drowsi-
ness."

"Wife, I gave you no permission to speak and
you have no right to take it. Since our legitimate
union no cloud has come to interpose itself be-

tween us. I am happy with you, I have never had any reproach to make you, and vice versa. Go to your room and bring a flask of essence of turpentine. I know it is there in one of the dresser drawers, and you have not just apprised me of it. Hurry up the spiral staircase and return to me with a happy face."

But the sensitive woman of London has hardly reached the foot of the stairs (she does not run as speedily as a person of the lower classes) than one of her chambermaids descends from the first floor, her cheeks beaded with sweat, bearing the flask, which, perhaps, contains the liquid of life within its crystal confines. The maiden bows gracefully as she presents her offering, and the mother, with her royal air, has advanced towards the fringes with which the sofa is trimmed, the sole object that provokes her tenderness. The commodore accepts the flask from the hands of his spouse with a proud but kindly gesture. An Indian scarf is soaked in the essence and Mervyn's head is enfolded in the silk. He breathes in the fumes; he moves an arm. His circulation accelerates, and one hears the joyous cries of a Philippine cockatoo perched in the bay window.

"Who goes there? . . . Do not stop me. . . . Where am I? . . . Is this a coffin supporting my weary limbs? The planks feel soft. . . . Is the locket containing the picture of my mother still fastened around my neck? . . . Away with you, tangle-haired evil-doer! He was not able to catch me, and I left a fragment of my coat in his hands. Let the bulldogs off their chains, for tonight a recognizable thief may introduce himself into our house on burglary bent, while we are plunged in slumber. My mother and my father, I know you, and I thank you for your care. Call my little brothers. I have brought them candy and I wish to embrace them."

With these words he falls into a state of profound lethargy. The doctor, summoned in haste, rubs his hands and exclaims:

"The crisis is passed. All goes well. Tomorrow your son will awake in good health. Now everybody take yourselves off to your respective beds, I command it, that I may pass the night alone at the sick boy's side until the appearance of the dawn and the song of the nightingale."

Maldoror, hidden behind the door, has not lost a word of all this. Now he is acquainted with the character of the tenants of the mansion, and will act accordingly. He knows where Mervyn lives and desires to know no more. He has written down the name of the street and the number of the building in a memorandum-book. That is the important thing. He is certain not to forget it. He proceeds like a hyena without being seen, keeping to the sides of the courtyard. He climbs the gate with agility, tangling for an instant with the iron spikes; with one bound he is on the sidewalk. He takes himself off stealthily.

"He took me for a malefactor," he exclaims. "He is an idiot. I wanted to find a man exempt from the very accusation that the sick youth made against me. I did not tear off a fragment of his coat as he said. Simple hypnogogic hallucination caused by fear. My intention today was not to kidnap him; for I have other ulterior projects in view for that timid youth."

Go now to where the swan-lake is. And I shall tell you later why one swan there among them is completely black, with a body bearing an anvil surmounted by the putrefying carcase of a crab, and rightly inspiring mistrust in the rest of its aquatic comrades.

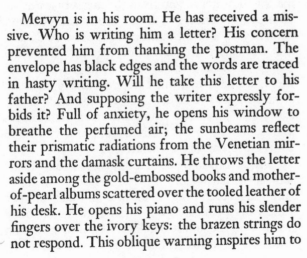

Mervyn is in his room. He has received a missive. Who is writing him a letter? His concern prevented him from thanking the postman. The envelope has black edges and the words are traced in hasty writing. Will he take this letter to his father? And supposing the writer expressly forbids it? Full of anxiety, he opens his window to breathe the perfumed air; the sunbeams reflect their prismatic radiations from the Venetian mirrors and the damask curtains. He throws the letter aside among the gold-embossed books and mother-of-pearl albums scattered over the tooled leather of his desk. He opens his piano and runs his slender fingers over the ivory keys: the brazen strings do not respond. This oblique warning inspires him to take up again the piece of vellum paper; but the latter recedes as if it had been offended by the hesitation of the person for whom it was destined. Caught in this snare, Mervyn's curiosity increases and he opens the scrap of prepared rag. Until that moment he has never seen any but his own handwriting.

"Young man, I am interested in you. I desire to make you happy. I will take you for a companion and we shall undertake long peregrinations through the isles of Oceania. Mervyn, you know that I love you and I have no need to prove it to you. You will bestow your friendship upon me, I am certain. When you know me better you will not repent of the confidence you have placed in me. I will preserve you from the perils that pursue your inexperience. I shall be a brother to you, and good advice will not be wanting. For more details, the day after tomorrow be on the Carrousel Bridge at five o'clock in the morning. If I am not there, wait for me; but I hope to arrive on time. And you do the same. An Englishman will not easily give up an opportunity to straighten out his affairs. Young man, I salute you, and good-bye for the present. Show this letter to no one."

"Three stars in place of a signature and a bloodstain at the bottom of the page!" Mervyn exclaims. Abundant tears fall upon the curious phrases which his eyes have devoured and which open before him the limitless field of new and uncertain horizons. It seems to him (this is only since the reading he has just finished) that his father is rather strict and his mother a little too majestic. He has reasons which have not come to my knowledge and which in consequence I cannot relay to you for insinuating that his brothers do not please him either. He conceals that letter in this bosom.

His teachers notice that on this particular day he does not seem to be himself; his eyes become definitely gloomy and the veil of excessive meditation descends over the peri-orbital region. Each professor blushes for fear of not finding himself on the intellectual level of his pupil, and yet the latter for the first time neglects his duties and does no work.

That evening the family gathers in the dining-room, decorated with ancient portraits. Mervyn admires the dishes filled with succulent viands and perfumed fruits, but he eats nothing. Polychrome streams of Rhine wines and the sparkling jewels of champagne are poured out into tall, slender goblets of Bohemian glass, and even the sight of them leaves him indifferent. He leans his elbow upon the table and remains absorbed in his thoughts like a somnambulist. The commodore, his face tanned by the seawinds, whispers into his wife's ear:

"Our eldest has changed since the day of his seizure. He was already full of absurd ideas; now he day-dreams more than usual. I was not like that at his age. Pretend to notice nothing. An efficacious remedy, material or moral, would do

[*273*]

good service here. Mervyn, you enjoy the reading
of travel books and natural history: I am going
to read you a story that will not displease you.
Listen attentively; every one of us will profit by
it, myself among the first. Children, learn, through
the attention you will pay to my words, to perfect
the design of your style and to take count of the
least intentions of an author."

As if that nest of adorable youngsters could un-
derstand the meaning of rhetoric! He speaks, and,
at a gesture of his hand, one of the brothers goes to
the paternal bookshelf and returns with a volume
under his arm. Meanwhile the tablecloth and the
silverware have been removed and the father takes
the book. At the electrifying word 'travels' Mer-
vyn has raised his head and endeavors to terminate
his ill-timed meditations. The book is opened to-
ward the middle and the metallic voice of the com-
modore proves that he is still capable, as in the
glorious days of his youth, of commanding the
fury of men and storms. Well before the end of
the reading Mervyn's head has dropped again, for
he finds it impossible to follow the reasoned devel-
opment of contrived phrases and the saponifica-
tion of compulsory metaphors any longer. The
father exclaims:

"This does not interest him. You read, wife.
Read something else. You will be luckier than I in
dispelling the chagrin from our son's days."

The mother has no hope, yet she has taken up
another book and the tones of her soprano voice

resound melodiously in the ears of the product of her conception. But after a few words she is discouraged and herself discontinues the interpretation of the literary work. The first-born exclaims: "I am going to bed." He leaves the room with eyes lowered in a cold stare, saying no more. The dog utters a long howl, for he finds this behavior unnatural; and the wind outside, blowing intermittently in the vertical chink of the window, makes the flame within the two pink crystal globes of the bronze lamp flicker. The mother rests her brow upon her two hands and the father raises his eyes heavenwards. The children regard the old sailor with terrified glances. Mervyn double-locks his door, and his hand races across the paper:

"I received your letter at noon, and you will excuse me if I have made you wait for a reply. I have not the honor to know you personally and I do not know if I should be writing to you. But as impoliteness does not dwell in our home, I have resolved to take up my pen and to thank you warmly for the interest you are taking in a stranger. God preserve me from failing to show gratitude for the sympathy with which you overwhelm me. I know my imperfections and am not proud of them. But if it is suitable to accept the friendship of an older person, it is also correct to make him understand that our characters are dissimilar. Indeed, you appear to be older than I, since you call me 'young man,' and yet I have doubts concerning your real age. For how may one reconcile the coldness of your syllogisms with the passion they contain? It is certain that I shall never abandon the place where I first saw the light to accompany you to distant countries. This would only be possible on the condition that I first asked of the authors of my being an impatiently-awaited permission. But as you have enjoined me to keep this spiritually cloudy affair secret (in the cubic sense of the word), I shall take pains to obey your incontestable wisdom. From what appears, it would not pleasurably confront the daylight. Since you appear to desire that I have confidence in your own self (desire not ill-placed, I am pleased to confess), have the goodness, I pray you, to manifest an analogous confidence in me, and not appear to believe that I should be so far removed from your suggestion as that tomorrow morning, at the indicated hour, I should not be exactly on time at the meeting-place. I shall climb the wall of the park, for the gate will be closed, and no one will witness my departure. To speak frankly, what would I not do for you, for whom an inexplicable attachment has suddenly revealed itself before my dazzled eyes, astonished above all at such a proof of goodness, that I assured myself was totally unexpected. Since I did not know you. Now I do know you. Do not forget the promise you made me to be walking on the Carrousel Bridge. If I am there myself I feel a certainty without parallel that I shall meet you there and touch your hand, provided that this innocent gesture on the part of a youth who, even yesterday, knelt at

the altar of modesty, will not offend you by its re-
spectful familiarity. For is not familiarity to be
confessed in the case of a strong and warm inti-
macy, when ruin is a matter of solemn conviction?
And what harm would there be after all, I ask
you, if I were to pass by and say 'Farewell' to
you when, the day after tomorrow, whether it
rain or not, five o'clock strikes? You will appreci-
ate yourself, sir, the tact with which I have con-
ceived my letter; for I do not allow myself, upon
a wayward sheet of paper that may lose its way, to
say anything further to you. Your address at the
bottom of the page is a riddle. It took me almost
fifteen minutes to decipher it. I think you did well
to trace out the words thus microscopically. I at-
tach no signature, in this imitating you: we are liv-
ing in too strange a time to be in the least surprised
at whatever may happen. I should be interested to
know how you discovered the place where my
frozen immobility dwells, surrounded by a long
procession of deserted apartments, unclean char-
nel-houses of my hours of tedium. How shall I say
this? When I think of you my breast heaves and
rumbles like the collapse of a decadent empire; for
the shadow of your love indicates a smile, which,
perhaps, does not exist: it is so vague and moves its
scales so tortuously! I leave my impetuous feelings,
new tablets of marble still unsullied by mortal con-
tact, in your hands. Let us have patience until the
first blush of the morning twilight, and, while
awaiting the moment when I shall throw myself

into the hideous embrace of your pestiferous arms,
I bow humbly at your knee, which I clasp."

Having written this guilty letter, Mervyn takes
it to the mail-box and then goes to bed. Do not ex-
pect to find his guardian angel there.

The fish's tail will fly only three days, it is true;
but alas! the beam will be burned just the same;
and a cylindro-conical bullet will pierce the rhi-
noceros's skin, despite the daughter of the snow
and the beggar! It is that the crowned fool has
uttered the truth concerning the fidelity of the
fourteen daggers.

I discovered I had only one eye in the center of
my forehead! O silvered mirrors, set in the panels
of vestibules, how many services you have ren-
dered me by your reflective power! Since the day
when an angora cat gnawed for an hour at my
parietal bump, like a trepanning that perforates
the cranium, springing suddenly upon my back
because I had boiled her kittens in a tub full of al-
cohol, I have not ceased to hurl the arrow of tor-
ments against myself. Today, under the impression
of the wounds my body has received in various
circumstances, either by the fatality of my birth
or by the fact of my own fault; overwhelmed by
the consequences of my moral disintegration
(some of them have been fulfilled: who may pre-
dict the others?); impassive spectator of acquired

or natural monstrosities which embellish the apo-
neurosis and the intellect of him who speaks; I cast
a long look of satisfaction upon the duality that is
myself . . . and I find myself beautiful! Beautiful
as the defect in the congenital conformation of
man's sexual organs, consisting in the relative
brevity of the urethral canal and the division or
absence of its lower part, in such manner that
this canal opens at a variable distance from the
gland and beneath the penis; or again, as the
fleshy wattle, conical in shape, furrowed by
rather deep transverse wrinkles, which appears at
the base of the turkey's upper beak; or rather, as
the following truth: "The system of scales, of
keys, and their harmonic relationship is not based
upon invariable natural laws, but on the contrary
is the consequence of aesthetic principles which
have varied with the progressive development of
mankind, and which will vary again;" and above
all, as an armored and turreted frigate!

Yes, I maintain the exactitude of my assertion.
I have no presumptuous illusion, I will boast, and
would find no profit in lies: thus you should have
no hesitation in believing what I have said. For
why should I inspire horror in myself before the
eulogious testimonials which arise from my con-
science? I envy the Creator nothing; but let him
leave me to sail down the river of my destiny,
through the glowing series of glorious crimes. If
not, raising a glance irritated by all obstacles up to
the height of his brow, I shall make him under-

stand that he is not the sole master of the universe;
that many phenomena arising directly from a
much deeper understanding of the nature of things
disposes in favor of a contrary opinion, and opposes
a formal challenge to the validity of the unity of
power. It is that there are two of us to contemplate
each other's eyelashes, you see ... and you know
that more than once the clarion of victory has
sounded from my lipless mouth. Farewell, illustri-
ous warrior; your courage in misfortune inspires
the esteem of your deadliest enemy; but Maldoror
will find you soon to dispute with you the fate of
the prey called Mervyn.

Thus the prophecy of the cockerel will be real-
ized, when he glimpsed the future at the bottom of
the candlestick. May it please Heaven that the crab
will rejoin the caravan of pilgrims and apprise
them in a few words of the narrative of the rag-
picker of Clignancourt!

On a bench at the Palais-Royal, on the left hand
side and not far from the body of water, an individ-
ual coming from the Rue de Rivoli has taken a
seat. His hair is in disorder, and his garments reveal
the corrosive action of prolonged destitution. He
has dug a hole in the ground with a piece of pointed
wood and filled the hollow of his hand with earth.
This food he has carried to his mouth and spits it
out hurriedly. He gets up, and, placing his head on

the bench, throws his legs into the air. But as this rope-dancer's attitude is contrary to the laws of weight which control the center of gravity, he falls heavily back upon the bench, his arms hanging, his cap hiding half his face, and his feet stamping the gravel in an unstable state of equilibrium less and less reassuring. He remains a long time in this position.

Over by the northern entrance, beside the round-house containing a cafe, our hero is leaning his arm upon a gate. His eye sweeps the surface of the rectangle in such a manner as to let no perspective escape. His eyes return upon themselves after finishing this investigation and he perceives in the middle of the garden a man executing reeling gymnastics on a bench upon which he is struggling to maintain himself, accomplishing miracles of strength and skill. But of what avail the best intention brought into the service of a just cause against the disorders of mental alienation? He approaches the idiot, assists him kindly to replace his dignity in a normal position, offers his hand, and sits down beside him. He observes that the mania is intermittent; the paroxysm has passed; his interlocutor replies logically to all his questions. Is it necessary to report the meaning of his words? Why re-open, at whatever page, with blasphemous eagerness, the folio of human misery? Nothing is of such fertile instruction. Even though I should have no true occurrence to report to you I would invent imaginary stories to pour into your brain. But the sick

man did not become so for his own pleasure; and
the sincerity of his remarks allies itself to perfec-
tion with the credulity of the reader.

"My father was a carpenter on the Rue de la
Verrerie. . . . May the death of the three Marguer-
ites fall upon his head and the canary's beak ever-
lastingly gnaw the axis of his ocular bulb! He had
contracted the habit of getting drunk; during the
moments when he returned to the house after hav-
ing visited the cabaret bars, his madness would be-
come almost immeasurable, and he would strike
out indiscriminately at any object that came in
sight. But soon, under the protests of his friends,
he reformed completely, and sank into a taciturn
frame of mind. No one could come near him, not
even our mother. He nursed a secret resentment
against the idea of duty, which prevented him from
having his own way.

"I had bought a canary for my three sisters; it
was for my three sisters that I had bought a canary.
They had placed it in a cage above the doorway
and passers-by would stop every time to listen to
the bird's songs, admire its fugitive grace and study
its knowing ways. More than once my father had
ordered us to remove the cage and its contents, for
he imagined the canary was mocking him when it
tossed him the bouquet of aerial cavatinas of its
vocal talent. He unhooked the cage from its nail
and fell from the chair, blind with rage. A slight
graze on the knee was the trophy of his enterprise.
After having remained for a few seconds to press

the swollen part with a woodchip, he pulled down
the leg of his trousers and, frowning horribly, took
better precautions, placed the cage under his arm,
and retired to the back of his workshop. There,
despite the outcries and pleas of his family (we
thought very highly of that bird, which was to us
like the genius of the household), he crushed with
his iron-shod feet the willow cage, keeping us at a
distance with a jack-plane which he brandished
over his head. By chance the canary did not die im-
mediately; that bundle of feathers was still alive,
despite the stains of blood. The carpenter took
himself off and slammed the door noisily.

"My mother and I made every effort to restore
the bird's life, which was ready to take flight. Its
end was approaching, and the beating of its wings
was visible now only as the mirror of the supreme
death agony. During this time, the three Margue-
rites, when they realized that all hope was lost, took
each other by the hand with a common consent and
the living chain went to crouch in a corner under
the stairs near our dog's kennel, having first moved
aside a barrel of grease. My mother did not aban-
don her task and held the canary between her fin-
gers to warm it with her breath. As for me, I went
running wildly through the house, knocking
against the furniture and tools. From time to time
one of my sisters would show her head from be-
neath the stairs to inform herself concerning the
fate of the unhappy bird, then withdraw it again
sadly. The dog had emerged from her kennel, and,

as if she had understood the extent of our loss, she licked with the tongue of sterile consolation the three Marguerite's dresses. The canary had no more than a few seconds to live.

"One of my sisters in her turn (it was the youngest) placed her head in the penumbra formed by the rarefaction of the light. She saw my mother turn pale, and the bird, after having raised its head, for the merest instant, with the last manifestation of its nervous system, collapsed between her fingers, still forever. She announced the news to her sisters. They made no sound of mourning. Silence reigned in the workshop. Only the cracking sound of the fragments of the cage, which, by virtue of the elasticity of the wood, partially restored themselves to their original shape, were heard. The three Marguerites shed no tear and their faces lost none of their freshness. No . . . they simply remained expressionless. They crawled into the kennel and stretched out side by side on the straw, while the dog, passive witness of their maneuver, watched them in astonishment. My mother called them several times; but they gave back no sound of reply. Worn out by their emotions, they were probably sleeping! She rummaged in all the corners of the house without finding them. She followed the dog, which was pulling at her dress, toward the kennel. The woman knelt down and peered through the opening. The spectacle that met her eyes, apart from the exaggerations of maternal fear, could have been nothing but heart-

breaking, according to my calculations. I lit a
candle and gave it to her; in that manner no detail
escaped her. She withdrew her head, covered with
straw, from the premature grave, and said to me:
'The three Marguerites are dead.'

"Since we could not remove them from that
place, for, remember this well, they were closely
interlocked in each other's arms, I went to get a
hammer from the workshop to break up the canine
home. I at once began the work of demolition, and
passers-by might figure with little exercise of imag-
ination that there was no unemployment in our
home. My mother, impatient at these delays, which
nevertheless were unavoidable, split her fingernails
against the planks. At last the operation of negative
deliverance was terminated; the burst kennel fell
apart on all sides; and we lifted out from the
wreckage, one after another after having separated
them with difficulty, the carpenter's daughters.
My mother left that part of the country. I never
saw my father again. As for me, they say I am mad,
and I beg for public charity. All I know is that the
canary sings no more."

The listener inwardly approved this new exam-
ple brought up to support his disgusting theories.
As if, because of one man once overcome with
wine, one had the right to condemn humanity in
its entirety. Such is at least the paradoxical reflec-
tion he seeks to introduce into his mind; but it can-
not drive out the important lessons of serious expe-
rience. He comforts the idiot with feigned compas-

sion and wipes away his tears with his own hand-
kerchief. He takes him to a restaurant and they
eat at the same table. They go to a fashionable
tailor and the protegé is clothed like a prince. They
go to a great mansion on the Rue Saint-Honoré
and knock upon the gate-keeper's door; the idiot
is installed in a rich apartment on the third floor.
The bandit forces him to accept his purse, and,
taking the chamber-pot from beneath the bed he
places it upon Aghone's head:

"I crown you king of intelligence," he exclaims
with premeditated emphasis. "At your least com-
mand I shall come. Help yourself freely to my
wealth. Body and soul I am yours. At night you
will replace the alabaster crown in its regular place,
with permission to make use of it. But during the
day, from the moment when the dawn illumines
the cities, replace it on your head as the symbol of
your power. The three Marguerites will live again
in me, not to mention your mother."

The idiot thereupon falls back several paces as
if he were the prey of an insulting nightmare. Lines
of happiness appear on his face, wrinkled by
trouble. Full of humility, he kneels at the feet of
his protector. Gratitude has entered, like a poison,
into the heart of the crowned idiot! He wants to
speak but his tongue is silent. He bends forward
and collapses on the floor. The man with the lips of
bronze departs.

What was his intention? To acquire a fast friend,
innocent enough to obey the least of his com-

mands. He could not have found a better, and good luck favored him. He whom he had found lying on the bench no longer knows, since a certain occurrence in his youth, how to distinguish good from evil. It is Aghone himself he must have.

The Omnipotent had sent down one of his archangels to the earth in order to rescue the youth from certain death. He will be forced to descend himself! But we have not yet reached that part of our story, and I find myself obliged to close my mouth, because I cannot say everything at once: every effect will appear in its place, when the plot of this piece of fiction is not inconvenienced thereby.

In order not to be recognized the archangel had taken on the form of a hermit-crab large as a vicuna. He stood upon the tip of a reef in the middle of the sea, and was awaiting a favorable tide in order to operate his descent upon the shore. The man with the lips of jasper, hidden behind a turn in the beach, was watching the animal, a club in his hand. Who could have wished to read the thoughts of these two beings? The first did not conceal the fact that he had a difficult mission to accomplish:

"And how shall I succeed," he cried, while the swelling waves beat against his temporary refuge, "there where my master has more than once seen his strength and his courage fail? I am but a limited substance, while the other, no one knows whence he came and what is his ultimate goal. At his name the celestial armies tremble. And more than one account in the regions I have left insists that Satan himself, Satan the incarnation of evil, is not as terrible."

The second was reflecting as follows; and his reflections found an echo in the very welkin they polluted:

"He looks inexperienced. I'll settle his hash promptly. Doubtless he comes from on high, sent by him who fears so much to come himself! We shall see, when we get down to cases, if he is as imperious as he looks; this is no inhabitant of the terrestrial apricot; he betrays his seraphic origin by his uncertain and wavering eyes."

The hermit-crab which for some time had been watching a limited section of the coast, spied our hero (and then the latter drew himself up to the full height of his Herculean figure), and apostrophised him in the following terms:

"Do not attempt to show fight. Surrender. I am sent by One who is superior to both of us with instructions to load you with chains and place the two accomplices of your thought outside the possibility of further activity. Believe me, in future you must be forbidden to clutch knives and daggers in your fists, as much in your own interest as that of others. Dead or alive, I shall take you; I have been commanded to take you alive. Do not force me to make use of the power that has been lent to me. I will act with delicacy; for your part, do not offer any resistance. Thus I shall know, with eagerness and joy, that you have made the first step toward repentance."

When our hero had listened to this harangue, full of a spice so profoundly comic, he had difficulty in preserving the gravity of his bronzed features. But, finally, no one will be surprised if I add that he ended by bursting into laughter. It was too much for him! He meant no harm by it! He certainly did not wish to bring down upon his head the hermit-crab's reproaches! What efforts he made to repress his hilarity! How many times did he press his lips together in order not to have the appearance of offending his astonished interlocutor! Unfortunately his character participated in the nature of mankind and he laughed like a sheep! At last he stopped! It was time! He had almost choked himself! The wind bore this reply to the archangel on the reef:

"When your master no longer sends me snails and shrimps to conduct his business, and will condescend to parley with me personally, I am sure we shall find some way to an understanding, since I am inferior to him who sent you, as you so justly said. Until such a time, any idea of reconciliation seems to me to be premature, and apt to produce only a chimerical result. I am far from misunderstanding the sense of each of your syllables; and since we could wear out our voices uselessly in making them travel three kilometers, it seems to me that you would be acting wisely if you were to descend from your impregnable fortress and swim to terra firma. We shall discuss more agreeably the conditions of a surrender which, however legitimate it may be, is none the less finally, for me, a disagreeable prospect."

The archangel, who had not expected such good will, poked out his head from the depths of the crevice and replied:

"O Maldoror, has the time finally arrived when your abominable instincts will see the extinction of the torch of unjustifiable pride that conducts them to everlasting damnation! It shall be I, then, who shall be the first to bear the news of this praiseworthy change to the phalanxes of cherubim, who will be happy to welcome back one of their own. You know yourself and you have not forgotten that a time once was when you occupied the first place among us. Your name flew from mouth to mouth. Now you are the subject of our solitary conversations. Come . . . come and make a lasting place with your old master; he will receive you like a lost son, and ignore the enormous amount of guilt you have piled up on your heart like a mountain of elks' horns built up by the Indians."

He spoke, and withdrew his entire body from the depths of the cave. He showed himself, radiant, upon the top of the reef, resembling a priest of religions when he has the certitude of bringing home a lost sheep. He was about to leap into the

water and swim to the forgiven one. But the man
with the lips of sapphire has long calculated in ad-
vance an underhand trick. He flings his club vio-
lently; after many ricochets over the waves it
strikes the head of the archangel benefactor. The
crab, mortally wounded, falls into the water. The
tide bears the floating remnant to the shore. He
was waiting for the tide to assist him; very well,
the tide came; it cradled him with its song and gen-
tly deposited him on the beach: is not the hermit-
crab happy? What more does it want? And Mal-
doror, hovering over the strand, received into his
arms two friends, inseparably united by the
chances of war: the carcase of the hermit-crab and
the homicidal club!

"I have not yet lost my skill!" he exclaims. "All
it needs is exercise. My arm preserves its strength
and my eye its nicety!"

He regards the lifeless animal. He fears that he
may be called to account for the spilt blood. Where
will he hide the archangel? And at the same time
he asks himself whether the death had been instan-
taneous. He has placed upon his back an anvil and
a corpse. He makes his way toward a vast body of
water, all of whose banks are covered and as if
walled in by an inextricable tangle of great rushes.
He wanted at first to take a hammer, but that is too
light a tool, while with the heavier object, if the
corpse gave a sign of life, he could place it on the
ground and reduce it to dust with blows of the
anvil. It is not strength, certainly, that his arm is

lacking; that is the least of his troubles. Arrived within sight of the lake, he sees that it is peopled with swans. He tells himself that this is as safe a hiding place for him as any; by means of a metamorphosis and without abandoning his burden, he mingles with the other birds. Notice the hand of Providence there, where one had been tempted to believe it absent, and profit by the miracle I am about to describe to you. Black as the crow's wing, he swam three times among the group of dazzlingly white web-feet. Three times he kept that distinctive color, which made him resemble a piece of coal. God, in his justice, would not permit that his cunning should deceive even a flock of swans. He remained in the lake, but the others stood off from him and no bird would draw near his shameful plumage to keep him company. So he confined himself to a distant bay at the end of the body of water, alone among the fowl of the air as he was among men!

And thus it is that he preluded the unbelievable occurrence in the Place Vendome!

The corsair with the golden hair has received Mervyn's reply. He follows in those singular pages the traces of intellectual troubles in the writer, abandoned as he is to the feeble strength of his own initiative. The youth would have done far better to have consulted his parents before replying to the friendship of the unknown. No benefit will result for him in mixing himself up, as principal actor, in this equivocal intrigue. But after all, he wished it.

At the time arranged Mervyn went from the door of his home straight before him, following the Boulevard Sebastopol to the fountain of Saint-Michel. He takes the Quai des Grands Augustins and crosses the Quai Conti; as he passes over the Quai Malaquais, he sees on the Quai du Louvre, parallel with his own direction, an individual walking along with a sack under his arm, who seems to be watching him attentively. The morning mists have melted away. The two wayfarers reach opposite sides of the Carrousel Bridge at the same time. Although they have never set eyes on each other, they know each other!

Indeed, it was touching to see those two beings, separated by age, bring their souls close together by the depths of their feelings! At least, such would have been the opinion of those who might have paused before this spectacle, that more than one, even with a mathematical mind, would have found moving. Mervyn, tears running down his face, reflected that he was about to encounter at the portals of life, so to speak, a precious support against future adversities. Be assured that the other said nothing.

This is what he did: he unfolded the sack he was carrying, opened it, and, seizing the youth by the head, thrust his entire body into the envelope of

cloth. He tied up the opening with his handker-
chief. As Mervyn was uttering loud cries, he raised
the sack like a bundle of linen and struck the para-
pet of the bridge with it several times. Then the
victim, becoming aware of the cracking of his
bones, was silent. Unique scene, that no other nov-
elist will ever rediscover!

A butcher passed by, sitting upon the meat in his
cart. An individual ran up to him, stopped him, and
said: "Here is a dog in this sack; it has the mange.
Slaughter it as soon as possible." The man spoken
to was agreeable. The questioner, as he made off,
noticed a young girl in rags who held out her hand
to him. To what degree will audacity and impiety
rise? He gives her alms!

Tell me, if you wish that I should introduce you,
several hours later, into the door of a remote
slaughter-house. The butcher has returned and
says to his comrades, throwing a burden on the
ground: "Hurry up and let's kill this mangy dog."
There are four of them, and each seizes the usual
hammer. And yet they hesitate because the sack
moves violently.

"What emotion takes hold of me?" exclaims one
of them, slowly lowering his arm.

"This dog utters cries of sorrow like a child,"
says another. "You would say he knows the fate
awaiting him."

"It's their habit," replies a third, "even when
they are not sick, as is the case here, it is enough
that their master stay away a few days from home

for them to start howling in a manner which, to say the least, is hard to bear!"

"Stop! Stop!" cries a fourth, before all the arms are raised in rhythm to strike the sack firmly this time. "Stop, I tell you. There is a fact here that escapes us. Who told you that this cloth enfolds a dog? I wish to make sure."

So, despite the laughter of his comrades, he unties the package and draws forth one after another the limbs of Mervyn! He was practically stifled by the discomfort of his position. He fainted upon seeing the light again. A few minutes later he gave indubitable signs of life. His savior said:

"Next time, learn to be careful even in your trade. You almost witnessed for yourselves that it is useless to practise non-observation of that law."

The butchers fled. Mervyn, his heart wrung and full of gloomy presentiments, returned home and locked himself in his room.

Do I need to insist upon this stanza? Ah, who would not deplore the consummated events? Let us wait until the end before bringing a judgment even more severe. The denouement is about to be precipitated; and, in this kind of story, in which a passion of some kind is postulated, it fears no obstacle that may obstruct its passage and there is no point in diluting in a cup the gum-lac of four hundred banal pages. Whatever may be said in a half dozen stanzas must be said, and then silence.

Maldoror

In order mechanically to construct the brain of a
soporific story, it is not enough to dissect stupidi-
ties and overwhelmingly stupefy the intelligence
of the reader with fresh doses, in such a manner as
to paralyse his faculties for the rest of his life by
the infallible law of fatigue; one must besides, with
good hypnotic fluid, ingeniously place him in the
position of being somnambulistically incapable of
moving, by forcing him to obscure his eyes against
his natural tendency by the fixity of your own. I
mean, not to make myself more clearly under-
stood, but to develop solely my train of thought
which interests and irritates at the same time by
the most penetrating harmony, that I do not be-
lieve it necessary in order to reach the proposed
goal, to invent a poetry entirely outside the ordi-
nary course of nature, and of which the pernicious
breath seems to cast down even absolute truths;
but to bring about a similar result (conforming, in-
deed, with the laws of aesthetics, if one considers
it well), which is not as easy as you think: that is
what I wanted to say. Hence I shall make every
reason to succeed in it! If death puts a stop to the
fantastic leanness of the two long arms which hang
from my shoulders, employed in the lugubrious
crushing of my literary gypsum, I wish that the
mourning reader may at least be able to say to him-
self: "One must give him his due. He has greatly
stupefied me. What might he not have done had he
lived longer! He is the best hypnotist I have ever
encountered!" Someone will carve these few

touching words on my tombstone of marble, and my ghost will be satisfied!

I continue! There was once a fish-tail that moved at the bottom of a hole beside a down-at-heel boot. It was not natural to ask one's self: "Where is the fish? I see only his tail moving." For since precisely one confessed implicitly that one could not perceive the fish, the reason is that in reality it did not exist. The rain had left a few drops of water in the bottom of that pit dug in the sand. As to the down-at-heel boot, some have since thought that it had been deliberately abandoned.

The hermit-crab, through divine power, was reborn from its dissipated atoms. He pulled the fish-tail out of the hole and promised that he would re-attach it to its lost body if it would announce to the Creator the failure of his missionary to dominate the fury of the waves of the Maldororian sea. He lent it two albatross wings, and the fish-tail took flight. But it flew to the home of the renegade to tell him what had happened and to betray the hermit-crab. The latter divined the spy's project and before the third day had ended he had pierced the fish-tail with a poisoned dart. The spy's throat uttered a feeble cry which united with his last gasp as he struck the ground.

Then an ancient beam, placed at the top of a castle, reared up on end to its full height and cried for vengeance in a loud voice. But the Omnipotent, transformed into a rhinoceros, informed it that the death of the fish-tail had been well-mer-

[*297*]

ited. The beam calmed down, placed itself at the bottom of the mansion, resumed its horizontal position, and recalled the terrified spiders to continue, as in the past, to weave their webs at its corners.

The man with the lips of sulphur learned of his accomplice's weakness, and consequently he commanded the crowned idiot to burn the beam and reduce it to ashes. Aghone executed this severe task.

"Since, according to you, the time has come," he cried, "I have been to fetch the ring I had buried under the stone and I have attached it to one of the rope's ends. Here is the package."

And he presented a heavy rope, rolled up and sixty metres in length. His master asked him what the fourteen daggers were doing. He replied that they remained faithful and held themselves ready for any emergency if it should be necessary. The criminal inclined his head as a sign of satisfaction. He manifested surprise and even disquiet when Aghone added that he had seen a rooster split open a candlestick with its beak, examine each fragment one by one, and cry out, beating its wings frantically:

"It is not as far as you think from the Rue de la Paix to the Place du Pantheon! Soon you will witness the lamentable proof of this!"

The crab, mounted upon a spirited horse, galloped furiously towards the reef, witness of the throwing of a club by a tattooed hand, sanctuary of his first day on earth. A caravan of pilgrims was on the way to visit the spot, now consecrated by an august death. He hoped to catch up with it and beg for urgent help against the plot that was in preparation, of which he had knowledge.

You will see a few lines farther down, aided by my glacial silence, that he did not arrive in time to tell them what had been related to him by a ragpicker hidden behind the scaffolding of a house in construction, the day when the Carrousel Bridge still moist with the morning dew, had felt with horror the horizon of its experience widen confusedly in concentric circles at the morning apparition of the beating of an icosahedral sack against its calcareous parapet! Before he stimulates their compassion, through the memory of this episode, they would do better to destroy within themselves the seed of hope . . .

To break up your lassitude, put into use the resources of good will, walk by my side, and do not lose sight of this idiot with his head surmounted by a chamber-pot, who drives before him, his hand grasping a club, one whom you would have difficulty in recognizing if I did not take care to warn you and recall to your ear the word that is pronounced Mervyn. How he is changed! His hands tied behind his back, he strides along as if he were on his way to the scaffold, and yet he is guilty of no crime.

They have arrived at the circular enclosure of the Place Vendome. Upon the entablature of the massive column, leaning against the square balustrade more than fifty metres above the ground, a man has thrown and unrolled a rope, which falls to the ground a few paces from Aghone. With habit one does a thing quickly; but I may say that Aghone did not waste much time in attaching Mervyn's feet to the end of the rope.

The rhinoceros had learned what was about to happen. Covered with sweat, he appeared, gasping for breath, at the corner of the Rue Castiglione. He did not have even the satisfaction of taking part in the battle. The individual who watched over the neighborhood from the top of the column loaded his revolver, took careful aim, and pressed the trigger. The commodore, who had been begging in the streets since the day when what he believed to be his son's madness began, and the mother, whom they had nicknamed "Daughter of the Snow" on account of her extreme pallor, intercepted their breasts to protect the rhinoceros. It was useless. The bullet pierced his skin like a gimlet. One might have believed, with a semblance of logic, that death would infallibly make his appearance. But we know that within this pachyderm the substance of the Lord had been introduced. He retired sorrowfully. If it had not been well proven that he was too good to one of his creatures, I would feel pity for the man on the column!

The latter, with a sharp tug of his hand, pulled towards him the rope thus ballasted. Mervyn, his head hanging downwards, is swung by its abnormal oscillations. His hands eagerly snatch at a gar-

land of everlasting-flowers which join together
two corners of the column's base, against which he
is beating his head. He carries off the weakly at-
tached flowers with him into the air. After having
piled up at his feet, in the form of superimposed
ellipses, a large part of the rope, in such a manner
that Mervyn hangs suspended half way up the
bronze obelisk, the escaped convict with his right
hand makes the youth spin with an accelerating
motion of uniform rotation, in a plane parallel to
the axis of the column, and gathers in, with his left
hand, the serpentine coils of the rope, which lie at
his feet.

The sling hisses in the air; Mervyn's body fol-
lows it everywhere, ever more distant from the
center by centrifugal force, ever keeping its mo-
bile and equidistant position in an aerial circumfer-
ence independent of matter. The civilized savage
releases little by little as far as its other end, which
he retains with a firm metacarpus, that which er-
roneously resembles a bar of steel. He begins to
run around the balustrade, holding on to the rail-
ing with one hand. This maneuver has the effect of
changing the original plane of the rope's revolu-
tion, and to increase the force of the tension, al-
ready so considerable. Now it spins majestically on
a horizontal plane, after having passed successively
by an undetectable progress through several in-
clined planes. The right angle formed by the
column and the rope has equal sides!

The arm of the renegade and the murderous

weapon are confused in a linear unity like the atomic elements of a ray of light penetrating a dark room. The theorems of mechanics permit me to speak thus; alas, we know that one force added to another force engender a result composed of the sum of the two original forces! Who would dare to claim that the rope would be already broken, but for the vigor of the athlete, but for the good quality of the hemp?

The corsair with the golden hair, suddenly and at once, brings to a halt his acquired speed, opens his hand, and lets go the rope. The repercussion of this operation, so contrary to the preceding ones, caused the joints of the balustrade to crack. Mervyn, followed by the rope, resembles a comet trailing behind its flamboyant tail. The iron ring in the running knot, mirroring the sun's rays, itself undertakes to complete this illusion. In the course of his parabola the condemned man cleaves the atmosphere as far as the left bank, passes it by virtue of the impulsive force, which I suppose to be infinite, and his body strikes the dome of the Pantheon, while the rope whips part way around the upper part of the immense cupola.

It is upon this spherical and convex surface, which resembles an orange only in its shape, that may be seen at any hour of the day a withered skeleton left hanging there. When the wind sways it they say that students of the Latin Quarter, in the fear of a similar fate, offer up a short prayer: these are only insignificant rumors in which one is not forced to believe, and proper only to frighten little children. In his shriveled hand he clutches something like a great ribbon of dead yellow flowers. One must consider the distance, and no one can assert, despite the testament of his good eyesight, that those really are the everlasting-flowers of which I spoke, and which an unequal battle waged close by the new Opera House detached from a giant pedestal.

It is nonetheless true that the draperies in the shape of a crescent moon no longer derive the expression of their definitive symmetry from the quaternary number: go there and see for yourself if you do not wish to believe me.

Jo to hell

Poésies

I replace melancholy with courage, doubt with certainty, despair with hope, evil with good, lamentations with duty, scepticism with faith, sophistry with the indifference of calm, and pride with modesty.

THE POETIC whimperings of this century are nothing but sophistry.

First principles should be beyond argument.

I accept Euripides and Sophocles; but I do not accept Aeschylus.

Do not manifest toward the Creator a lack of the most elementary conventions and good taste.

Cast aside disbelief: you will make me happy.

Only two kinds of poetry exist; there is only one.

A far from tacit convention exists between author and reader, by which the former calls himself the sick one, and accepts the latter as nurse. It is the poet who consoles humanity! The roles are arbitrarily inverted.

I do not wish to be dubbed a *poseur*.

I shall leave behind no Memoirs.

Poésies

Poetry is no more tempest than it is cyclone. It is a majestic and fertile river.

It is only by admitting the night physically that one is able to admit it morally. O, Nights of Young! How many headaches you have caused me!

One dreams only when asleep. These are words like the word dream, nothingness of life, terrestrial way, perhaps the preposition, the distorted tripod, which have permitted to creep into our souls that poetry dripping with weakness, resembling decay.

Disturbances, anxieties, depravities, death, exceptions in the physical or moral order, the spirit of negation, brutalities, hallucinations served by the will, tortures, destructions, upsets, tears, dissatisfactions, slaveries, deep-digging imaginations, novels, unexpected things, that which must not be done, the chemical peculiarities of the mysterious vulture who watches over the carrion of some dead illusion, precocious and abortive experiments, obscurities with flea-like armor, the terrible monomania of pride, the inoculation with deep stupors, the funereal prayers, the envies, betrayals, tyrannies, impieties, irritations, bitternesses, aggressive insults, madness, spleen, rational terrors, strange uneasinesses which the reader would prefer not to feel, grimaces, neuroses, the bloody channels through which one forces logic at bay, the exaggerations, absence of sincerity, the saws, the platitudes, the darkness, the gloom, the infantilisms which are worse than murders, the clan of court-of-assizes novelists, the tragedies, odes, melodramas, the extremes presented ad infinitum, reason whistled at with impunity, the smells of wet chicken, the sicklinesses, the frogs, squids, sharks, desert simooms, all that is somnambulist, cross-eyed, nocturnal, soporific, night-roving, viscous, talking-seal, equivocal, consumptive, spasmodic, aphrodisiac, anemic, obscure, hermaphrodite, bastard, albino, pederastic, phenomena of the aquaria and bearded-lady, the hours drunk with silent discouragement, fantasies, monsters, demoralizing syllogisms, ordures, that which does not reflect like a child, desolation, that intellectual manchineel-tree, perfumed cankers, camellia-like thighs, the guilt of a writer who rolls down the slope of nothingness and scorns himself with cries of joy, remorse, hypocrisy, the vague perspectives that crush you within their imperceptible networks, the serious spittings upon sacred axioms, vermin and their insinuating ticklings, insensate prefaces like those of Cromwell, Mlle. de Maupin and Dumas the Younger, the decays, impotencies, blasphemies, asphyxiations, stiflings, rages—before these disgusting charnel-houses, which I blush to mention, it is at last time to react against that which shocks us and so royally bows us down.

You are being perpetually driven out of your mind and caught in the trap of shadows constructed with so coarse a skill by egoism and self-esteem.

Taste is the fundamental quality which sums up all other qualities. It is the ne plus ultra of the intelligence. By it alone is genius the supreme health and balance of all the faculties. Villemain is thirty-four times more intelligent than Eugène Sue and Frederick Soulié. His preface to the Dictionary of the Academy will witness the death of Walter Scott's novels, of Fenimore Cooper's novels, of all novels possible and imaginable.

The novel is a false genre, because it describes passions for their own sakes: the moral conclusion is lacking. To describe passions is nothing; it suffices to be born part jackal, part vulture, part panther. We do not care for it. To describe them, like Corneille, in order to subject them to a high ethic, is a different matter. He who will refrain from doing the former, at the same time remaining capable of admiring and understanding those to whom it is given to do the latter, surpasses with all the superiority of virtue over vice him who does the former.

By this alone, were a teacher of the second grade to say to himself:

"Were they to give me all the treasures of the universe, I should not wish to have written novels like those of Balzac and Alexandre Dumas," by this alone he is more intelligent than Alexandre Dumas and Balzac. By this alone, if a pupil of the third grade is convinced that he must not sing physical and intellectual deformities, by this alone he is stronger, more capable, more intelligent, than Victor Hugo, if he had written only novels, plays and letters.

Alexandre Dumas *fils* will never—no, never—make a prize-giving speech for a school. He does not know what morality is. Morality does not compromise. If he did make one, he should first strike out with a single stroke of the pen all he had written hitherto, beginning with his absurd Prefaces. Summon a jury of competent men: I maintain that a good second-grade pupil is smarter than he in no matter what, even on the *dirty* subject of courtesans.

The masterpieces of the French language are prize-giving speeches for schools, and academic speeches. Indeed, the instruction of youth is perhaps the finest practical expression of duty, and a good appreciation of the

works of Voltaire (dwell upon the word "appreciation")
is preferable to the works themselves. Naturally!

The best authors of novels and plays would in the
end distort the famous idea of good, if the army of
teachers, preservers of Right, did not constrain genera-
tions young and old to the path of honesty and of work.

In its personal name, and it must be despite it, I have
just disowned, with an implacable will and a tenacity of
iron, the hideous past of cry-baby humanity. Yes: I
shall proclaim beauty upon a golden lyre, making al-
lowances for goitrous unhappiness and stupid pride
which pollute at its source the marshy poetry of this
century. I shall trample underfoot the harsh stanzas of
scepticism, which have no reason for existence. Judg-
ment, once entered into the efflorescence of its energy,
imperious and resolute, without hesitating one instant
over the absurd uncertainties of misplaced pity, like a
public prosecutor, prophetically condemns them. We
must guard incessantly against purulent insomnia and
atrabilious nightmares. I scorn and execrate pride, and
the infamous voluptuousness of any irony become ex-
tinguisher, which set aside justness of thought.

Certain characters, excessively intelligent (there is
no call for you to invalidate this with the recantations
of a dubious taste), have flung themselves head first into
the arms of evil. It was absinthe—savory, I do not be-
lieve, but harmful—that morally slew the author of
Rolla. Woe unto the greedy! Scarcely has the English
aristocrat entered into the years of discretion, than his
harp is shattered beneath the walls of Missolonghi, hav-
ing gathered on his way naught but the blossoms of
drear annihilation bred by opium.

Poésies

Although his was a genius greater than ordinary, if there had been during his time another poet, endowed as he was in similar proportions with exceptional intelligence, and capable of presenting himself like his rival, he would have been the first to confess the uselessness of his efforts to produce ill-assorted maledictions; and that the good exclusively is declared by the voice of everyone alone worthy of appropriating our esteem. The fact is that there was no one successfully to rival him. Here is something that no one has said. Strange thing! Even upon rummaging through anthologies and books of his epoch, we find that no critic thought of outlining the foregoing strict syllogism. And it is not he who will surpass it, who could have invented it. One was so much filled with wonder and uneasiness, rather than considered admiration, before works written by a treacherous hand—works, however, which revealed the imposing manifestations of a mind which did not belong to the common run of men, and which found itself at ease amid the ultimate consequences of one of the less obscure problems which interest non-solitary hearts: good and evil. To no one is it given to approach extremes except either in one direction or another. This explains why it is that, while forever praising without mental reservation the marvelous intelligence which at every moment he manifests, he, one of the four or five beacons of humanity, has silently made his numerous reserves concerning applications and the unjustifiable use he has knowingly made of them. He should not have encroached upon the kingdoms of Satan.

Lautréamont

The savage revolt of the Tropmanns, the Napoleons
I, the Papavoines, the Byrons, the Victor *Noirs*, and the
Charlotte Cordays, shall be held at a distance in my
stern regard. These great criminals with their diverse
titles I brush aside with a gesture. Whom are they
thinking to fool here, I ask, with an interposing slow-
ness? O, hobby-horses of the hulks! Soap bubbles!
Puppets in gold leaf! Worn-out strings! Let them draw
near, the Conrads, the Manfreds, the Laras, the sailors
who resemble the Corsair, the Mephistopheles, the
Werthers, the Don Juans, the Fausts, the Iagos, the
Rodins, the Caligulas, the Cains, the Iridions, the shrews
in the manner of Colomba, the Ahrimans, the addle-
brained heretical earth-spirits who ferment the blood
of their victims in the sacred pagodas of Hindustan,
the snake, the toad and the crocodile, gods considered
abnormal in ancient Egypt, the sorcerers and the de-
moniac powers of the Middle Ages, the Prometheuses,
the mythological Titans destroyed by the thunderbolts
of Jupiter, the Evil Gods spewed out by the primitive
imagination of savages—the whole clamorous series of
pasteboard devils. With the certainty of overwhelming
them, I seize and balance the lash of indignation and
concentration, and I await these monsters firm-footed
as their predestined conqueror.

There are down-at-heel writers, dangerous buffoons,
quadroon humbugs, gloomy mystifiers, actual madmen,
who deserve to inhabit Bedlam. Their softening heads
in which there is a screw loose, create giant phantoms
which sink downward instead of rising. Rugged exer-
cise, specious gymnastic. Away with you, grotesque

nutmeg. Kindly remove yourselves from my pres-
ence, fabricators of dozens of forbidden riddles, in
which I used not previously to see at once, as I do now,
the seam of the frivolous solution. Pathological case of
overpowering egoism. Fantastic automata: point out to
one another, my children, the epithet which puts them
in their place.

If they existed somewhere in plastic reality they
would be, despite their proven but deceptive intelli-
gence, the opprobrium, the bitterness, of the planets
which they inhabited, and the shame. Imagine them for
a moment, gathered together with beings their equals.
It is an uninterrupted succession of battles, undreamed-
of by bulldogs, forbidden in France, by sharks, and by
macrocephalic cachalots. There are torrents of blood
in those chaotic regions abounding in hydras and mino-
taurs, whence the dove, utterly terrified, wings swiftly
away. It is a mass of apocalyptic beasts, who know not
what they do. There are the impacts of passions, ir-
reconcilabilities and ambitions vying with the shrieks
of impenetrable and unrestrained pride, of which no
one may even approximately plumb the reefs and the
depths.

But they shall impose themselves no longer upon me.
To suffer is a weakness, when one can prevent it and
do something better. To give vent to the sufferings of
an unbalanced splendor—that is to demonstrate, O
dying ones of the perverse maremmas! still less resist-
ance and courage. With my voice and my solemnity of
the grand days, I recall you within my deserted halls,
glorious hope. Come, sit by my side, wrapped in the
cloak of illusion, upon the reasonable tripod of appease-

ment. Like a piece of cast-off furniture I chased you
from my abode with scorpion-lashed whip. If you wish
that I should be convinced that you have forgotten, in
returning to my home, the miseries which, in the name
of penances, I once caused you—then, by all that's holy,
bring back with you that sublime procession—support
me, I am swooning!—of offended virtues and their im-
perishable reparations.

I state with bitterness that there remain only a few
drops of blood in the arteries of our consumptive epoch.
Since the odious and particular whimperings, patented
without guarantee of a trademark, of your Jean-
Jacques Rousseaus, your Chateaubriands, your nurses
in babies' panties like Obermann, through the other
poets who have wallowed in corrupt slime, up to the
dream of Jean-Paul, the suicide of Dolores of Venti-
miglia, the Raven of Allan, the Infernal Comedy of the
Pole, the bloody eyes of Zorilla, and the immortal can-
cer, the Carrion, once lovingly painted by the morbid
lover of the Hottentot Venus, the improbable sorrows
created for itself by this century, in their monotonous
and disgusting insistence, have made it consumptive.

Come—music.

Yes, good people, it is I who command you to burn
upon a hot shovel, with a little brown sugar, the duct
of doubt with its lips of vermouth, which, shedding in
the midst of a melancholy struggle between good and
evil, tears that come not from the heart, causes every-
where without a pneumatic pump, the universal vac-
uum. This is the best thing you have to do.

Despair, feeding upon the foregone conclusion of its
phantasmagoria, imperturbably guides the literary man

to the mass abrogation of divine and social laws, and to theoretical and practical wickedness. In a word, causes the human backside to predominate in reasoning. Come, it's my turn to speak! I repeat, wickedness results, and eyes take on the hue of those of the damned. I shall not retract what I propose. I desire that my poetry may be read by a young girl of fourteen years.

Real sorrow is incompatible with hope. No matter how great that sorrow may be, hope raises it one hundred cubits higher. Very well, leave me in peace with the seekers. Down, down with the outlandish bitches, muddlemakers, *poseurs*. Whatever suffers, whatever dissects the mysteries surrounding us, does not hope. The poetry that disputes the necessary truths is less beautiful than that which does not dispute them. Indecisions ad infinitum, ill-used talent, loss of time: nothing is easier to verify.

To sing of Adamastor, Jocelyn, Rocambole, is puerile. It is not even that the author hopes that the reader infers that these rascally heroes—whom he himself betrays, emphasizing good in order to pass off descriptions of evil—will be pardoned. It is in the name of these same virtues, misunderstood by Frank, that we are anxious to support him, O mountebanks of incurable unease.

Do not behave as do these unchaste (in their eyes magnificent) explorers of melancholy, who find unknown things in their souls and their bodies!

Melancholy and sadness are already the beginnings of doubt; doubt is the beginning of despair; despair is the cruel beginning of varying degrees of wickedness. To convince yourself of this, read "Confession of a Child of the Century." The slope is fatal once we are launched upon it. We are sure to arrive at wickedness. Beware of the slope. Rip out evil by the roots. Trust not the cult of adjectives such as indescribable, crimson, incomparable, colossal, which shamelessly give the lie to the nouns they distort: they are pursued by lewdness.

Second-rate minds, like that of Alfred de Musset, are able stubbornly to thrust forward one or two of their faculties much farther than the corresponding faculties of first-rate minds—Lamartine, Hugo. We are in the presence of the derailment of an overturned locomotive. A nightmare holds the pen. Learn that the soul is composed of a score of faculties. Don't talk to me about these beggars with their outsize hats and their sordid rags!

Here is a method for proving the inferiority of Musset to the two other poets. Read to a young girl "Rolla" or "The Nights," "The Fools," of Cobb, or else the portraits of Gwynplaine and Dea or the speech of Theramenus of Euripides, translated into French verse by Racine. She starts, frowns, raises and lowers her hands without purpose like a drowning man; her eyes flash with greenish fires. Read to her "Prayer for All" by Victor Hugo. The effects are diametrically opposed. The kind of electricity is no longer the same. She bursts into peals of laughter, and asks for more.

Of Hugo, nothing will be left but poems about children, in which much badness is to be found.

"Paul and Virginia" shocks our deepest aspirations. Once upon a time, that episode, which exudes blackness from the first to the last page, made me gnash my teeth. I rolled on the carpet and kicked my wooden horse. The description of pain is nonsense. It must be shown in all its beauty. If that story had been told as a simple biography I should not attack it. It instantly changes character. Unhappiness becomes august through the impenetrable will of God who created it. But man should not create unhappiness in his books. This is to concentrate, with all strength, upon one side of things only. O, what maniacal raving!

Do not deny the immortality of the soul, the wisdom of God, the greatness of life, the order of the universe, physical beauty, family love, marriage, social institutions. Forget the funereal scribblers: Sand, Balzac, Alexandre Dumas, Musset, Du Ferrail, Féval, Flaubert, Baudelaire, Leconte and the "Blacksmiths' Strike!"

Communicate to your readers only the experience resulting from pain, which is no longer pain itself. Do not weep in public.

One must know how to wrest literary beauty from the very bosom of death; but these beauties do not belong to death. Here, death is only the occasional cause of them. Death is not the means; it is the end.

The immutable and necessary truths which make the glory of nations, and which doubt struggles in vain to shatter, began ages ago. They are things which should not be touched. Those who would make literary anarchy under pretext of novelty arrive at nonsense. One does not dare to attack God; one attacks the immortality of the soul. But the immortality of the soul itself is as old as the beginning of the world. What other belief will replace it, were it to be replaced? This will not be always a negation.

Lautréamont

If one bear in mind the truth whence arise all other truths, the absolute goodness of God and his absolute ignorance of evil, sophistry breaks down of itself. And at the same time, that scarcely poetic literature based upon sophistry will break down too. All literature which disputes eternal axioms is condemned to live only upon itself. It is unjust. It devours its own liver. The *novissima verba* cause the handkerchiefless kids of the fourth grade to smile superbly. We have no right to question the Creator on any matter whatsoever.

If you are unhappy, do not tell the reader. Keep it to yourself.

If one were to correct sophistries according to the truths corresponding to those sophistries, only the correction would be true; while the work thus made over would have the right to call itself no longer false. The rest would be out of bounds of truth, with a trace of false, and consequently, necessarily considered null and void.

Personal poetry has had its day of relative jugglery and contingent contortions. Let us take up again the indestructible thread of impersonal poetry, abruptly severed since the birth of the ineffectual philosopher of Ferney, before the abortion of the great Voltaire.

It seems to be fine, sublime, under the pretext of humility or of pride, to dispute final causes, to falsify their stable and known consequences. Undeceive yourself, for there is nothing more stupid! Let us link together again the regular chain of past times; poetry is geometry par excellence. Since Racine, poetry has not progressed one millimeter. It has fallen backwards.

Poésies

Thanks to whom? To the Great Softheads of our epoch. Thanks to the Sissies—Chateaubriand, the Melancholy-Mohican; Sénancourt, the Man-in-the-Petticoat; Jean-Jacques Rousseau, the Sulky-Socialist; Edgar Poe, the Muckamuck-of-Alcoholic-Dreams; Mathurin, the Godfather-of-Shadows; Georges Sand, the Circumcised-Hermaphrodite; Théophile Gautier, the Incomparable-Grocer; Leconte, the Devil's-Captive; Goethe, the Weeping-Suicide; Sainte-Beuve, the Laughing-Suicide; Lamartine, the Tearful-Stork; Lermontoff, the Bellowing-Tiger; Victor Hugo, the Funereal-Greenstick; Mickiewicz, Satan's-Imitator; Musset, the Intellectual-Shirtless-Dandy; and Byron, the Hippopotamus-of-the-Infernal-Jungles.

Doubt has always existed in the minority. In this century it is in the majority. We inhale the violation of duty through the pores. This is to be seen only once; it will never be seen again.

The ideas of simple reason are so obscured at this time that the first thing that fourth grade teachers do when they teach their pupils—young poets with their mothers' milk still moist upon their lips—to make Latin verses, is to reveal to them in practice the name of Alfred de Musset. I ask you, now! Third grade teachers, then, in their classes, give for translation into Greek verse two bloody episodes. The first is the repulsive fable of the pelican. The second is the awful catastrophe that overtook the laborer. Of what use is it to contemplate evil? Is it not in the minority? Why turn the head of a schoolchild upon questions which, owing to their not having been understood, caused men such as Pascal and Byron to lose theirs?

Lautréamont

A student told me that his second grade teacher had given his class, day after day, these two cadavers to translate into Hebrew verse. These wounds of animal and human nature made him sick for a month in an infirmary. As we were known to each other, he sent his mother for me. He told me, albeit naively, that his nights were troubled by persistent dreams. He thought he saw an army of pelicans which threw themselves upon his bosom and rent it. Then they flew to a flaming cottage. They devoured the laborer's wife and his children. The laborer, his body blackened with burns, emerged from his home and engaged in an atrocious battle with the pelicans. They all flung themselves into the cottage, which collapsed in ruins. From the heap of rubbish he saw his teacher emerge bearing in one hand his heart, in the other a piece of paper upon which could be deciphered in sulphurous script the fables of the pelican and the laborer, just as Musset himself composed them. It was not easy at first to diagnose his sickness. I advised him to remain strictly silent, to speak of it to no one, above all to his teacher. I counseled his mother to take him home with her for a few days, assuring her that this would pass. And indeed, I was careful to visit him for a few hours every day, and it passed off.

Criticism must attack form, never the content of your ideas, of your phrases. Do as you please.

Sentiment is the most incomplete imaginable form of reasoning.

All the waters of the ocean would be insufficient to wash away one intellectual blood-stain.

Poésies

II

Genius guarantees the faculties of the heart.

Man is no less immortal than the soul.

Great thoughts come from reason!

Fraternity is no myth.

Children born know nothing of life, not even its greatness.

In misfortune, friends increase.

Goodness, thy name is Man.

Here dwells the wisdom of the nations.

Each time I read Shakespeare it seems to me that I am dissecting the brain of a jaguar.

I shall set down my thoughts in orderly manner, by means of a plan without confusion. If they are correct, the first will be the consequence of the others. This is the true order. It marks my object by calligraphic disorder. I should honor my subject too much if I should not treat it with order. I wish to show that it is capable of this.

I do not accept evil. Man is perfect. The soul does not fall. Progress exists. God is irreducible. Antichrists, accusing angels, eternal sufferings, religions, are the products of doubt.

Dante, Milton, describing hypothetically the infernal regions, have proved that they were first-class hyenas. The proof is excellent. The result is bad. Nobody buys their works.

Lautréamont

Man is an oak. Nature does not consider him robust. It is not necessary that the universe take up arms to defend him. A drop of water is not sufficient for his preservation. Even should the universe protect him, it would not be more dishonored than that which does not protect him. Mankind knows that its reign has no death, that the universe has a beginning. The universe knows nothing: at most, it is a thinking reed.

I imagine Elohim to be cold rather than sentimental. Love of a woman is incompatible with love of humanity. Imperfection should be rejected. Nothing is more imperfect than shared egoism. During life, defiance, recrimination, sermons written in dust, swarm. It is no longer the lover of Chimène; it is the lover of Graziella. It is no longer Petrarch; it is Alfred de Musset.

In death, a rock by the seashore, any lake, Fontainebleau forest, the island of Ischia, a workroom accompanied by a raven, a Star Chamber with a crucifix, a cemetery whence arises the beloved one beneath the rays of a moon which finally become irritating, some stanzas or a group of girls whose names are unknown come parading in their turn, giving the author the measure and expressing regrets. There is in the two cases no dignity whatsoever.

Error is an unhappy story.

Hymns to Elohim accustom vanity to concern itself not with worldly things. Such is the shield of hymns. They cause humanity to lose the habit of depending on authors. They abandon him. They call him mystic, eagle, and they perjure his mission. You are not the sought-for dove.

Poésies

Anyone could contrive a literary luggage for himself by stating the contrary of what has been said by the poets of this century. He would replace their affirmations with negations. And vice versa. If it is ridiculous to attack first principles, it is more ridiculous to defend them against these same attacks. I shall not defend them.

Sleep is a blessing for some, a punishment for others. For all, it is a sanction.

If Cleopatra's morals had been shorter, the face of the world would have been changed. Her nose would not have increased in length.

Concealed actions are the most estimable. When I see so many in history, they please me greatly. They have not been altogether hidden. They have been known about. Their small appearances augment their merit. The finest thing is, that it has not been possible to conceal them.

The charm of death exists only for the brave.

Man is so great that his greatness shows itself above all in his refusal to acknowledge his misery. A tree knows not its greatness. To be great is to know one's greatness. To be great is to refuse to acknowledge misery. Man's greatness refutes his miseries. Greatness of a king.

When I write down my thoughts, they do not escape me. This act reminds me of my strength, which I forget always. I teach myself in proportion to my enslaved thoughts. I strive only to understand the contradiction between my soul and nothingness.

The heart of man is a book, which I have learned to prize.

Not imperfect, not fallen, man is the greatest of mysteries.

I permit no one, not even Elohim, to doubt my sincerity.

We are at liberty to do good.

Judgment is infallible.

We are not at liberty to do evil.

Man is the conqueror of chimeras, the novelty of tomorrow, the regularity with which chaos groans, the subject of conciliation. He judges all. He is no imbecile. He is no earthworm. He is the repository of truth, the mass of certainty, the glory, not the outcast, of the universe. If he degrades himself, I praise him. If he praises himself, I praise him more. I conciliate him. He comes to the understanding that he is the angel's sister.

Nothing is incomprehensible.

Thought is no less clear than crystal. A religion, whose lies depend upon it, may cloud it for a moment, speaking of those effects which are long-lasting. Speaking of those effects of brief duration, the assassination of eight persons at a city's gates would certainly cloud it unto the destruction of evil. Thought soon regains its limpidity.

Poetry should have as its goal, practical truth. It enunciates the relationships existing between the first principles and the secondary truths of life. Each thing rests in its place. Poetry's mission is difficult. It does not involve itself with political happenings, with the manner of governing a people, does not allude to periods of history, to coups-d'état, to regicides, to court intrigues. It tells not of the battles between man and himself, his passions. It discovers the laws by which exist political theory, universal peace, Machiavellian refutations, the paper horns which compose the works of Proudhon, the psychology of humanity. A poet should be more useful than any member of his tribe. His work is the code of diplomats, of law-makers, of instructors of youth. We are far from Homer, Virgil, Klopstock, Camoens, from emancipated imaginations, contrivers of odes, fabricators of epigrams against divinity. Let us return to Confucius, to Buddha, to Socrates, to Jesus Christ, moralist who roamed the villages starving! In future it will be necessary to count on reason, which operates only on the faculties which preside over the category of phenomena of pure good-will.

Nothing is more natural than to read *"Discours de la Méthode"* after having read *"Bérénice."* Nothing is less natural than to read *"Traité de l'Induction"* by Biéchy, *"Problème du Mal"* by Naville, after having read *"Les Feuilles d'Automne,"* *"Les Contemplations."* The transition loses itself. The spirit rebels against the ironmongery, the mystagogy. The heart is appalled by these pages scribbled by a puppet. This violence enlightens him. He closes the book. He lets fall a tear in memory of the savage authors. Contemporary poets have abused their intelligence. The philosophers have not abused theirs. Memory of the former will fade. The latter are classics.

Racine and Corneille would have been able to compose the works of Descartes, of Malebranche, of Bacon. The soul of the former is with that of the latter. Lamartine and Hugo would not have been capable of composing *"Traité de l'Intelligence."* The soul of the former is not adequate to those of the latter. Fatuity made them lose the central qualities. Lamartine and Hugo, although superior to Taine, possess only, as he does—it is hard to make this avowal—secondary faculties.

Tragedies inspire pity and terror through duty. This is something. It is bad. It is not as bad as is modern lyricism. The "Medea" of Legouvé is preferable to the collection of the works of Byron, Capendu, Zaccone, Félix, Gagne, Gaboriau, Lacordaire, Sardou, Goethe, Ravignan, Charles Diguet. What writer among you, I pray, can bear—what is this? What are these uprisings of resistance?—the weight of the monologue of Augustus? The barbarous vaudevilles of Hugo do not proclaim duty. The melodramas of Racine, Corneille, the novels of La Calprenède, do proclaim it. Lamartine is capable of writing the "Phèdre" of Pradon; Hugo, the "Wenceslas" of Rotrou; Sainte-Beuve, the tragedies of La Harpe or Marmontel. Musset is able to invent proverbs. Tragedy is an involuntary mistake, admits struggle, is the first step towards good, will not appear in this work. It conserves its prestige. This is not true of sophistry—after the metaphysical drivel of the auto-parodists of my heroic-burlesque times is over and done with.

The principle of cults is pride. It is ridiculous to address Elohim, as did Job, Jeremiah, David, Solomon, Turquéty. Prayer is a false act. The best way to please him is indirect, more in keeping with our strength. It consists in making our race happy. There are no two ways of pleasing Elohim. The idea of virtue is one. Since virtue in little is also virtue in much, I permit mention of the example of maternity. To please his mother, a son will not proclaim that he is good, radiant, that he will behave in a manner deserving of her praises. He will do otherwise. Instead of saying it himself, he will make her believe it by his deeds, he casts off that sadness which swells Newfoundland dogs. We must not confuse Elohim's goodness with triviality. Each is probable. Familiarity breeds contempt; veneration breeds the contrary. Work destroys the abuse of feelings.

No reasoner believes contrary to his reason.

Faith is a natural virtue by which we accept the truths revealed to us by Elohim through conscience.

I know of no greater blessing than to have been born. An impartial spirit finds it complete.

Good is victory over evil, the negation of evil. If one sings the good, evil is eliminated by this adequate act. I do not sing what one must not do. I sing what one must do. The former does not contain the latter. The latter does not contain the former.

Youth pays heed to the counsels of mature age. It has an unlimited confidence in itself.

I know of no obstacle to oppose the strength of the human spirit, excepting truth.

Maxims have no need of it for proof. An argument demands an argument. A maxim is a law which includes a collection of arguments. An argument is perfected insofar as it approaches the maxim. When it has become a maxim, its perfection rejects the proofs of the metamorphosis.

Doubt is an homage rendered to hope. It is not a voluntary homage. Hope would not consent to be nothing but an homage.

Evil arises against good. It could not do less.

Lautréamont

It is a proof of friendship to pay no attention to the growth of that of our friends.

Love is not happiness.

If we had no faults, we should not take so much pleasure in correcting ourselves, in praising in others what is lacking in ourselves.

Men who have resolved to hate their own kind are not aware that this must begin by self-hate.

Men who do not duel believe that those who duel to the death are brave.

How the degenerates of the novel squat in the shop windows! For a man losing himself, as some would for a five-franc piece, it sometimes seems that one might destroy a book.

Lamartine believed that the fall of an angel would become the Elevation of a Man. He was wrong to believe it.

To make evil serve the cause of good, I shall state that the intentions of the former are bad.

A banal truth contains more genius than the works of Dickens, Gustave Aymard, Victor Hugo, Landelle. With these latter, a child, surviving the universe, could not reconstruct the human soul. With the former, he could. I suppose he would not sooner or later discover the definition of sophistry.

The words expressing evil are destined to take on a useful significance. Ideas improve. The meaning of words participates.

Plagiarism is necessary. Progress implies it. It presses after an author's phrase, uses his expressions, erases a false idea, replaces it with the correct one.

In order to be well constructed, a maxim does not require to be corrected. It requires to be developed.

Poésies

At the break of dawn, young girls come to gather roses. A wave of innocence flows through valleys and capitals, stirs the intelligence of the most enthusiastic poets, lets fall protection for cradles, crowns for youth, belief in immortality for the aged.

I have seen men weary moralists to discover their hearts and bring down upon them the blessing from on high. They emitted the most extensive meditations possible, making rejoice the Author of our happiness. They respected youth, age, all that breathes and does not breathe, paid homage to womankind, consecrated to chastity those parts which the body reserves the right to name. The firmament, whose beauty I admit, the earth, image of my heart, were invoked by me in order to discover a man who did not believe himself virtuous. The spectacle of this monster, had he materialized, would not have caused me to die of astonishment: death takes more than this. All this is beyond comment.

Reason and sentiment counsel and beseech one another. Who does not know that one of the two, in renouncing the other, deprives itself of all the help that has been granted to us for our guidance. Vauvenargues said: "a part of the help."

Whatever his phrase, mine is based upon personifications of the soul in sentiment, reason, the one which I chose at random, would be no better than the other if I had made them. One can not be rejected by me. Vauvenargues was able to accept the other.

When a predecessor uses in connection with good a word belonging to evil, it is dangerous that his phrase should exist beside the other. It is better to leave to the word the meaning of evil. To use in connection with good a word belonging to evil, one must have the right. He who uses for evil, words belonging to good does not possess it. He is not believed. No one would wish to wear Gérard de Nerval's tie.

The soul being one, sensibility, intelligence, will, reason, imagination, may be introduced into the discussion.

I have spent much time in the study of the abstract sciences. The few persons with whom I communicated were not of the stuff to disgust me with them. When I began to study man, I saw that these sciences belong to him alone, that I was less well off in penetrating them than others in their ignorance of them. I forgave them for not engaging in the study! I did not expect to find many companions in my study of mankind. That belongs to him alone. I was strong. There are more who study him than who study geometry.

We lose our lives joyfully, providing we do not speak of it.

Passions dwindle with age. Love, which should not be classed among the passions, dwindles too. What it loses on the one hand it regains on the other. It is no longer severe with the object of its vows, doing itself justice: the expansion is accepted. The senses no longer have their spur to excite fleshly desires. Love of humanity begins. In the days when a man feels that he has become an altar decked with his virtues, makes an accounting of every sorrow, his soul in a fold of the heart wherein all seems to have birth, he feels something which flutters no more. I have named memory.

The writer, without separating one from the other, can indicate the law which regulates each of his poems.

Poésies

Some philosophers are more intelligent than some poets. Spinoza, Malebranche, Aristotle, are not Hégésippe Moreau, Malfilatre, Gilbert, André Chénier.

Faust, Manfred, Conrad are types. They are not reasoning types. They are types of agitators.

Descriptions are a meadow, three rhinoceri, and half a bier. They can be memory and prophecy. They are not the paragraph that I am about to finish.

The governor of the soul is not the governor of a soul. The governor of a soul is the governor of the soul when these two kinds of soul are sufficiently confused to affirm that a governor is a governess only in the imagination of a jesting fool.

Phenomenon passes. I seek laws.

There are men who are not types. Types are not men. One must not permit one's self to be dominated by the accidental.

Judgments on poetry have more value than poetry. They are the philosophy of poetry. Philosophy, thus understood, comprises poetry. Poetry cannot do without philosophy. Philosophy can do without poetry.

Racine is not capable of condensing his tragedies into precepts. A tragedy is not a precept. To a similar spirit, a precept is a more intelligent action than a tragedy.

Place a goose quill in the hands of a moralist who is a first-class writer. He will be superior to poets.

Love of justice is with most men the courage to suffer injustice.

War—hide yourself!

Sentiments express happiness, bring smiles. The analysis of sentiment expresses happiness, all personality apart; and brings smiles. The former uplift the soul, independently of space and duration, up to the conception of humanity considered as itself, in their illustrious arms! The latter uplifts the soul, independently of duration and space, up to the conception of humanity considered in its highest expression, the will! The former is concerned with vice and virtue. The latter is concerned with virtue alone. Feelings know not the order of their going. The analysis of feeling teaches how to know this, increases the vigor of the feelings. With the former, all is uncertainty. They are expressions of happiness, of unhappiness, two extremes. With the latter, all is certainty. It is the expression of that happiness which results at a given moment from knowing restraint in the midst of good and evil passions. It uses its calm to dissolve the description of those passions in a principle which circulates throughout the pages: the non-existence of evil. Feelings weep when they must, as when they must not. Analysis of feeling does not weep. It possesses a latent sensibility which takes hold without warning, bears up beyond misery, teaches to dispense with a guide, provides a weapon for combat. Feelings, sign of weakness, are not feeling! The analysis of feeling, sign of strength, breeds the most magnificent feelings I know. The writer who permits himself to be taken in by feelings should not be considered in the same category as the writer who is taken in neither by feelings nor himself. Youth treats itself to sentimental lucubrations. Maturity begins to reason without difficulty. It was necessary only to feel, he thinks. He let his sensations drift: here he gives them a pilot. If I were to consider humanity as a woman, I should not maintain that its youth were in its decline, that its maturity were approaching. Its spirit changes for the better. The ideal of its poetry will change. Tragedies, poems, elegies, will no longer prevail. The coldness of the maxim will prevail! In Quinault's time they could have understood what I have just said. Thanks to a few sparse glimmerings during the last few years in magazines and folios, I can myself. The style which I undertake is as different from the style of the moralists, who merely confirm evil without suggesting a remedy, as this last is not different from melodramas, funeral orations, odes, and religious science. There is no feeling of struggle.

Elohim is made in the image of Man.

Many certain things are contradicted. Many false things are uncontradicted. Contradiction is the sign of falsity. Uncontradiction is the sign of truth.

A philosophy of science exists. It does not exist for poetry. I know of no moralist who is a first-rate poet. This is strange, someone will say.

It is a horrible thing to feel what one possesses slipping away. One becomes attached only with the idea of finding out if there is not something permanent.

Man is a subject empty of errors. Everything shows him the truth! Nothing abuses him. The two principles of truth, reason and sense, provided they do not lack sincerity, enlighten one another. The senses enlighten reason by real appearances. The same service they render it, they receive from it. Each takes its revenge. The phenomena of the soul pacify the senses, make impressions upon them which I will guarantee not to be vexatious. They do not lie. They do not make the mistake of vying with one another.

Lautréamont

Poetry should be made by all. Not by one. Poor Hugo! Poor Racine! Poor Coppée! Poor Corneille! Poor Boileau! Poor Scarron! All ticks!

The sciences have two ends which meet. The first is the ignorance in which man finds himself at birth. The second is that attained by great minds. They have been through everything men may know, find they know all, and meet in that same ignorance whence they departed. It is a learned ignorance, which knows itself. Those among them who, having emerged from the first ignorance, have not been able to attain the other, have a slight touch of that sufficient science and pretend to wisdom. These will not trouble the world, will not judge everything worse than the others. The people, the experts, set the pace of a nation. The others, who respect it, are no less respected.

To know things, one must not know the details. As it is finished, our understandings are sound.

Love is not confused with poetry.

Woman is at my feet!

To describe the heavens, the sky, it is not necessary to carry earthly materials up there. We must leave the earth and its materials there where they are in order to embellish life with its ideal. To speak familiarly to Elohim is an unsuitable buffoonery. The best way to acknowledge him is not to trumpet in his ears that he is powerful, that he created the world, that we are maggots compared to his greatness. He knows this better than we. Men may refrain from informing him of it. The best way to acknowledge him is to console humanity, to attribute all to it, to take it by the hand, to treat it as a brother. This is truer.

Poésies

To study order, do not study disorder. Scientific experiments, like tragedies, stanzas to my sister, the gibberish of the afflicted, have no place here below.

Not all laws are good to state.

To study evil in order to produce good is not to study good itself. A good phenomenon being given, I shall seek out its cause.

Hitherto, unhappiness has been described in order to inspire terror and pity. I shall describe happiness in order to inspire their contraries.

A logic exists for poetry. It is not the same as that for philosophy. Philosophers are not as much as poets. Poets have the right to consider themselves above philosophers.

I do not need to occupy myself with what I shall do later. I must do as I do. I need not discover what things I shall discover later. In the new science, each thing comes in its turn, such is its excellence.

There is the stuff of poets in moralists and philosophers. The poet comprises the thinker. Each caste suspects the other, develops its qualities to the detriment of those which approach it from the other caste. The jealousy of the former will not admit that poets are stronger than they. The pride of the latter declares itself incompetent to render justice to more sensitive brains. Whatever be the intelligence of a man, the procedure of thought must be the same for all.

The existence of ticks having been established, let no one be surprised to see the same words recurring more often than in their turn: in Lamartine, the tears that fall from the nostrils of his horse, the color of his mother's hair. In Hugo, shadow and disorder form part of the building.

Lautréamont

The science undertaken by me is a distinct science of poetry. I do not sing this latter. I strive to discover its origin. By the rudder that steers all poetic thought, billiard-teachers will distinguish the development of sentimental theses.

The theorem is a mocker by nature. It is not indecent. The theorem does not ask to serve as application. The application made of it degrades the theorem, makes it indecent. Call application the struggle against matter, against the ravages of the mind.

To strive against evil is to do it too much honor. If I permit men to scorn it, let them not fail to add that this is all I can do for them.

Man is certain to make no mistakes.

We are not content with the life we have within us. We wish to live in the ideas of others, in an imaginary life. We force ourselves to appear as we are. We labor to preserve this imaginary being, which is none other than the real. If we have generosity, fidelity, we are eager not to make it known, in order to attach their virtues to this being. We do not detach them from ourselves to bring about this coupling. We are valiant in order to acquire the reputation of not being poltroons. Sign of the capacity of our being, to be dissatisfied with the one without the other, to renounce neither to one nor the other. The man who did live to preserve his virtue would be infamous.

Despite the aspect of our greatness, which seizes us by the throat, we have an instinct which corrects us, which we cannot repress, which elevates us!

Nature has perfections to show that she is the image of Elohim, and defects to show that she is not less than the image.

Poésies

It is good to obey laws. The people understand what makes them just. One does not abandon them. When their justice is made to depend upon something else, it is easy to make it doubtful. The people are not subjects for revolt.

Those who are in disorder tell those who are in order that it is they who depart from nature. They believe they themselves follow it. There must be an established point for judgment. Where shall we not find that point in morality?

Nothing is less strange than the contradictions to be found in man. He is created to know truth. He seeks it. When he tries to seize it he is dazzled, confused in such a manner that there is no arguing with him the possession of it. Some seek to deprive Man of the knowledge of truth; others seek to assure him of it. Each is activated by motives so different that they destroy man's perplexity. There is no other light than that to be found in his nature.

We are born just. Each turns to himself. This is the reverse of order. One should incline toward generality. The inclination toward self is the end of all disorder, in war, in economics.

Men, having been able to recover from death, from misery, from ignorance, have decided, in order to gain happiness, not to think about them. This is all they have been able to discover as consolation for so few evils. A super-rich consolation! It does not go as far as curing evil. It conceals it for a little while. By concealing evil, it makes us think about remedying it. By a legitimate reversal of man's nature, we do not find boredom, which is the most pronounced of his evils, to be his greatest good. More than anything else it can contribute most to the discovery of his rehabilitation. This is all. Amusement, which he looks upon as his greatest benefit, is the very least of his evils. More than anything else, he employs it in the search for a remedy for his ills. Each is a counter-proof of misery, of man's corruption, with the exception of his greatness. Man is bored, he seeks a multitude of occupations. He has an idea of happiness won; which, finding itself within him, he seeks in exterior things. He is happy. Unhappiness is neither within us nor within other creatures. It is within Elohim.

Nature makes us happy in all states; our desires depict for us a state of unhappiness. It connects with the state in which we are the sorrows of the state in which we are not. When we shall arrive at these sorrows, we shall not be unhappy because of this; we shall have other desires in keeping with a new state.

The strength of reason appears better in those who understand it than in those who do not.

We are so little presumptuous that we would desire to be known upon the earth even by those who will come when we are no more. We are so little vain that the respect of five persons, or say six, amuses us, honors us.

Few things console us. Many things afflict us.

Modesty is so natural in man's heart that a working-man is careful not to brag, wants to have his admirers. Philosophers want them. Poets above all! Those who write in favor of glory wish to have the glory of having written well. Those who read it wish to have the glory of having read it. Those who will read it will boast similarly.

Poésies

Man's inventions increase. The goodness, the malice, of people in general does not remain the same.

The spirit of the greatest man is not so dependent that it should be troubled by the least murmur of the uproar that goes on about it. The silence of a cannon is not necessary to impede his thoughts. The sounds of a weather-cock, of a pulley, are not necessary. The fly does not reason well at present. A man buzzes at its ears. This is sufficient to make it incapable of good counsel. If I desire that it should discover truth, I should chase away that animal which holds its reason in check—disturbs that intelligence which governs kingdoms.

The object of these people who play tennis with such concentration of mind, such bodily activity, is to boast before their friends that they have played better than someone else. Some sweat in their studies to show the erudite that they have resolved an algebraic equation hitherto unsolvable. Others expose themselves to dangers in order to brag of a place that they would have taken less spiritually, to my mind. These latter destroy themselves to observe these things. It is not in order to become less wise through them. It is above all to show that they understand the solidity of them. These are the least stupid of the bunch; and they are conscious of it. One may think of others who would not be, lacking this consciousness.

The example of the chastity of Alexander has not created more continent peoples than that of his drunkenness has created temperate people. One is not ashamed of having been less virtuous than he. One believes one's self to be not quite among the virtues of the common man when one sees one's self among the virtues of these great men. We hold on to them by the end where they hang on to the people. However high they may be, they are united somewhere with the rest of mankind. They are not suspended in the air, separated from our society. If they are greater than we, it is because their feet are as high as ours. They are all at the same level, rest upon the same earth. By this extremity they are as high as we, as children, a little more than the beasts.

The best way to persuade is not to persuade.

Despair is the least of our errors.

When a thought offers itself to us like a truth running through the streets, when we take the trouble to develop it, we find that it is a discovery.

One may be just, if one is not human.

The storms of youth precede brilliant days.

The unconsciousness, dishonor, lewdness, hatred, contempt of men is worth money. Liberality multiplies the advantage of riches.

Those who are honest in their pleasures are sincere in their business. It is a sign of a mild nature when pleasure make us human.

The moderation of great men limits only their virtues.

It is offensive to humans to offer them praises which enlarge only the bounds of their merits. Many persons are modest enough to suffer appreciation without pain.

Everything should be expected, nothing feared, from time and men.

If merit and glory do not make men unhappy, that which is called unhappiness is not worthy of their sorrow. A soul deigns to accept fortune and repose if the vigor of its feelings and the mainspring of its genius are to be superimposed.

We value great plans when we feel ourselves capable of great successes.

Reserve is the apprenticeship of the mind.

We say sound things when we are not trying to say extraordinary ones.

Nothing true is false; nothing false is true. All is the contrary of dream, of falsehood.

We must not believe that what Nature has made friendly should be vicious. There has not been a century or a people that has not established imaginary virtues and vices.

We can judge of the beauty of life only by that of death.

A dramatist can give to the word *passion* a meaning of usefulness. He is no longer a dramatist. A moralist gives any word a meaning of usefulness. He is still a moralist!

Whoever considers the life of a man finds therein the history of the species. Nothing has been able to make it evil.

Must I write in verse to separate myself from the rest of mankind? Charity forbid!

The pretext of those who work for the happiness of others is that they desire their own good.

Generosity rejoices in the happiness of others as if she herself were responsible for it.

Order prevails in the human species. Reason and virtue are not the strongest.

There are few ingrates among princes. They give all they can.

We can love with all our hearts those in whom we recognize great faults. It would be impertinent to believe that imperfection alone has the right to please us. Our weaknesses draw us together as much as that which is not virtue may do.

If our friends do us a service, we think that as friends they owe it to us. We do not at all think that they owe us their enmity.

He who is born to command will command as far as the throne.

When duties have exhausted us, we think we have exhausted duties. We say that all may fill the heart of man.

Everything lives by action. Thence, communication among beings, harmony of the universe. This law, so fertile in Nature, we find to be a vice in man. He is forced to obey it. Since he cannot exist in repose, we conclude that he is in his place.

We know what the sun and the heavens are. We know the secret of their movements. In the hand of Elohim, blind instrument, unfeeling spring, the world attracts our worship. The revolutions of empires, the aspect of the times, the nations, the conquerors of science, all that springs from a random atom, lasts only for a day, destroys the spectacle of the universe throughout the ages.

There is more truth than error, more good qualities than bad ones, more pleasures than pains. We like to control character. We raise ourselves above our kind.

Poésies

We enrich ourselves with the consideration with which we load it. We do not believe we can separate our interest from that of humanity, that we can disparage the species without compromising ourselves. This ridiculous vanity has filled books with hymns in favor of Nature. With those who think, mankind is in disgrace. He is for whomever charges him with the least vice. When was he not on the verge of uplifting himself, of reinstating himself in virtue?

Nothing is said. It is too soon since more than seven thousand years that there have been men. As for customs, as for all the rest, the least good is removed. We have the advantage of working after the ancients, the wise men among the moderns.

We are susceptible of friendship, justice, compassion, reason. O, my friends! What, then, is this absence of virtue?

Inasmuch as my friends do not die, I shall not speak of death.

To witness our relapses, to observe that our sorrows have been able to correct our faults, fills us with consternation.

We can judge the beauty of death only by the beauty of life.

The three final points make me shrug my shoulders in pity. Is that necessary in order to prove that one is an intelligent man, in other words an imbecile? As if light were not as good as shadow, speaking of points!